Also by Liza Wieland

THE NAMES OF THE LOST

DISCOVERING
AMERICA

DISCOVERING AMERICA

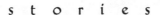

stories

Liza Wieland

RANDOM HOUSE NEW YORK

Library of Congress Cataloging-in-Publication Data

Wieland, Liza.
Discovering America: stories / Liza Wieland.
p. cm.
ISBN 0-679-42459-8
I. Title.
PS3573.I344D57   1993
813'.54—dc20   93-25411

Book Design by Anne Scatto

Manufactured in the United States of America on acid-free
paper

2   4   6   8   9   7   5   3

First Edition

For my mother and father

For my mother and father

and then a sudden golden silence
in which the traveller takes a notebook, writes:

"Is it lack of imagination that makes us come
to imagined places, not just stay at home?
Or could Pascal have been not entirely right
about just sitting quietly in one's room?

Continent, city, country, society:
the choice is never wide and never free.
And here, or there . . . No. Should we have stayed at home,
wherever that may be?

—ELIZABETH BISHOP

The Eagle of his Nest
No easier divest—
And gain the sky
Than mayest Thou—

Except Thyself may be
Thine Enemy—
Captivity is Consciousness—
So's Liberty.

—EMILY DICKINSON

Acknowledgments

I would like to thank Dona Chernoff and David Rosenthal for their generosity, and Connie Hales for permission to quote her poem "Rabbit Hunting," from *Underground* (Ahsahta Press, 1986), and for her friendship.

Thanks also to Nancy and Carl Wenske for peace and quiet, space and time.

And to Eric Rystrom, *in memoriam*.

Contents

Tommy Wadell   1

Lessons and Carols   21

The Columbus School for Girls   39

Aisle Help   57

Who It Really Was   77

Called By Name   97

Faye Gold's Story   123

Close to Falling   143

The True Story   163

Discovering America   183

TOMMY WADELL

My first boyfriend has a shirt with NORTON COMMANDO stitched over his heart. When I first see him, I wonder if that's his name, but he tells me it's the name of the motorcycle he'll have this time next year, when he turns sixteen. He says he wants the kind you have to jump-start. Norton Commando. I say the words over to myself. I like the sound of that name, the way the words lick around inside and outside your mouth, like the first time you French-kiss, and for a second you don't know if you're doing it right, but then you don't care and you only want to keep doing it forever.

When I picture him now, I'm looking over one of his shoulders, and I see his hands, brown and always warm, like he'd just been holding them over a fire. I see him leaning against a wall with his arms crossed high over his chest, four fingers tucked inside his armpits and the thumbs hooked around, pointing straight up. He's wearing a cap that says WADELL CHEVROLET. He's Tommy Wadell.

Myself, I'm thirteen, nearly out of the seventh grade and already a bit of a genius. It's the year I keep forgetting my math homework; it just slips my mind, and then we'll be trading papers to check answers, and I'll look across the aisle at Robert Kelly, whisper to him I don't have it again. I do a report on earthworms, and for the whole first page I write *mouse* instead of *worm*. Geniuses are like that. They can only do one thing at a time, and they get distracted easily. I read all their biographies—Einstein, Newton, Shakespeare, Marie Curie, Thomas Edison—and they all talk about getting lost in their own hometowns, about wherever they are seeming like foreign territory. I know what they mean.

When I get home from school every day, the first thing I have to do is lie down, my heart hurts so bad, or else I have to walk around Lake Brookhaven taking deep breaths, telling myself this is supposed to happen. I say the word *heart,* but I know it's growing pains. No one told me they would hurt this much, not even Noreen and Robbie Lynn, who've been having theirs for a year. At night in the dark I touch my chest, and it feels like two bags of marbles, heavy and hard. I dream that a boy cuts me open, and all the marbles come spilling out, green and blue and yellow, cat's eyes, tiger's eyes, and they swirl over the floor like pebbles at the end of a kaleidoscope while the boy chases them and laughs. I'm so light I float above him, watching it all, feeling the breezes blow through the cuts in my chest.

One Saturday in February my mother and I go to the movies, and in the ladies' room I see I've started to bleed. It doesn't hurt, and even though I've read all the books and seen all the movies in health class, I still think it should feel like being pierced, like Saint Sebastian, who had a hundred arrows in his body and a trickle of blood from every wound, or like a hand pulling at my insides, stripping off old layers of wallpaper in heaves and sighs.

When I go back into the theater the movie has already started, and I don't say anything to my mother. I watch the screen, but the images stop before they get into my eyes. My body's closed itself off, it's full, a hotel with no vacancies, only wanting more of itself. I'm too young to know these things, but I know them anyway. I know inside I'm a lush red garden tangled in vines, and all around me my own smell, the smell of that blood, is sweet, cloudy-sweet in the air, like it might have come out of a flower.

—

When I first see Tommy Wadell, he's down behind the boat-house at Lake Brookhaven, flat on his belly with one arm in the water, flush against the lake's bank. It's the end of March and warm, so he's taken his shirt off, and the skin on his back is the pearly white of places that have never been in the sun. He's tall and skinny, and I can see the backs of his ribs where they curve around him, his spine snaking roughly down his back and disappearing under the waistband of his jeans. He has an india-ink tattoo on his far arm. I know it's not real because my brother has one too, a star on his right shoulder. That first day, I don't get a good look at Tommy Wadell's tattoo because we don't know each other yet, but later I see it's a cutlass with an irregular curve to the blade. I like to run my finger along its edge and pretend that his skin could cut mine.

His hair is blond and straight, the kind that turns yellowy green in the summertime. It's hanging to his shoulders, falling forward almost into the water. He keeps trying to tuck it behind his ears. I see him before he sees me, and I know he isn't one of the neighborhood kids. I don't want to talk anyway, and I start to walk back up the hill.

"Hey!" His voice is the kind you turn around for. "Do you fish here?"

"Sometimes."

We have bamboo poles hanging in the garage. In the summer my brother goes fishing and then leaves the guts out in the sun. Every time he does it we talk about how fish don't bleed.

"Bass or bream?"

"Both. More bass, though. They're dumb, easier to catch."

"You can tickle up the bream," he says. "That's what I'm doing. Watch."

He starts to turn back toward the water, then waves me over with his free hand, without turning around, like he knows I'll come.

"You reach your arm down the bank, and you can get them right under the chin."

He looks up at me.

"Fish have chins," he says.

I sit down on the heels of my sneakers, and he stretches out again on his belly. His left shoulder blade shudders when all his weight shifts over to that arm. I can see how all the pieces of him are connected.

"Have you caught any yet?"

"No, I just got here." He turns his head like he's listening, but then he speaks instead. "Do you live around here?"

"Up by the eleventh green. Do you?"

I say this, but I'm pretty sure he doesn't. If he did, I would have run into him before now. There's also something about him I never see in the boys who live around here. He's a redneck, and the way I can tell is by his manners. Redneck boys treat girls in a way that's different from regular boys. They don't act like they're scared when they get around girls, and they don't act like God's gift either. I've seen them in Florida and at Northlake Mall. They act like a girl is this neat creature they've just discovered and want to keep around forever.

"I live over off Buford Highway, but I ride my bike here sometimes. I can make it in twenty minutes. On a motorcycle it would take ten."

"Do you have a motorcycle?"

"No, but I will this time next year."

"How do you get the fish home?"

"After I grab them, I put them in here."

He pulls a basket out of the water. It's attached to the bank by a leather thong and a nail. I want to sit here all day and watch a boy pull fish out of the water with his bare hands. There's something about it that gets down inside me. Without thinking, I rock forward and reach my arm into the water, just to see how cold it is, just to get the feel of it.

"Want to try?" he asks.

"There are water moccasins down there," I tell him. "I've seen them."

I say this because it's true.

"They're deeper and they feel different in the water. You get to know how the water moves. Don't stick your hand into any mud, just thrill it along the bank."

I try it for a couple of minutes, but my arm aches with the cold and then starts to go numb, so I sit up again. It's nice here by the lake, cooling off a little in the late afternoon. I pull my knees up to my chest and watch.

"It's not going so good today," he says. "Too cold. It works best with catfish anyways. I'm just branching out."

Still he lies there with his arm in the water.

"Maybe it's me," I say. "Maybe I'm a jinx. I should be going."

"You? You're not a jinx."

He sits up and reaches down into his boot.

"See this? It's a fillet knife. It's from Finland."

I take it from him. Inside the leather sheath is what looks like the steak knives we have at home, only more dangerous, more like something a pirate would have. The blade is thin, curved up at the end, the way you think ice-skate blades must look when you're up on them. A blade like that could slip right into your heart.

The sheath is soft, light cowhide, probably worn smooth from being carried, with tooled arrows and triangles along its slim sides. On one end there's a whale smoking a pipe. I laugh out loud when I see it.

"What's the matter?" he asks me.

"The whale, look at its mouth."

He puts his head over my shoulder and laughs too.

"Did you know that thousands of years ago whales left the water, came to land, and then went back into the water again?"

I shake my head no.

"It's true," Tommy says. "Some of them still have tiny feet buried inside their bodies. My daddy told me. He's been to Boston once and seen the Aquarium."

"I like this," I say, trailing my fingers along the thinnest edge of the sheath.

"I have to go now, but I'm coming back on Saturday morning. You can keep it and bring it to me then."

"What if I don't come back?"

"I'll hunt you up and I'll find you."

From the beginning Tommy Wadell spoke to me this way, like I was the girl who went everywhere with him, like he always knew where I was going to be next.

⸻

I take the knife back to the lake on Saturday, and Tommy Wadell is down by the dock. He smiles when he sees me, his white teeth bright in the sun. He's already caught one bream, but with a regular fishing pole, bamboo, like the ones in our garage. He holds up the fish to show me. I unsheathe the knife, and I keep walking toward him like that. While he's threading a piece of rope through the fish's gills and out the mouth, he tells me his name, tells me that he lives in Doraville, is fifteen, Wadell Chevrolet is his uncle Simmons Wadell, who just bought the business from Tommy's father but is keeping him on as a salesman. He doesn't ask who I am, but I tell him anyways.

"Gus for Augusta," he says. "It's nice. It suits you. People's names have a way of doing that. Simmons is a good name for my uncle. My momma says it's the face you make when you suck on a lemon, and that's just what my uncle is, that face."

He takes the knife and flicks the point at the bream's eye. Then he hands the knife back, along with the fish, and I do the other eye.

"My uncle lives with us, and my daddy hates him, even though he'd never say it. He says we're going to South Carolina when it gets too bad. Now it's just them all yelling. I sleep out on the roof most nights, but I don't mind. I've got candles and a mattress. It's pretty with all the stars and people's windows to look into. A couple months back I woke up covered with snow, and I laughed so loud the neighbors got scared."

By noon, we've caught four more fish, Tommy's three to my one. We're hungry, so we hide the catch and walk up to Peachtree, to where it becomes Peachtree Industrial Boulevard. There's a Burger King where a friend of Tommy's works, and he gives us our Cokes for free. We carry our hamburgers over to Brookhaven Supply and cut behind the main building to the woodlot.

"Listen to that," he yells over the noise of the saw. "It makes your teeth rattle in your head."

I want to put my hands over my ears, but I close my eyes instead, and I can feel my whole body shaking, just a bag of timber, ready to be sized and bundled into matchsticks, red-hot at the ends. When I open my eyes again, Tommy's looking at me with his head dipped to one side, and he's smiling. We go sit by the curb and eat where the traffic's coming right at us.

"Did you ever notice," Tommy asks me, "how the men always drive and the women always show them where to go? My daddy told me that's the way it is."

The rest of the afternoon we walk, for miles, I tell myself later, through the neighborhoods near my house, then deeper into the woods that run thick along Peachtree Dunwoody and north to Sandy Springs. Tommy has a pocketknife with two blades, a bottle opener, and a can opener, and he has a skinning knife. He tells me that if anything happens to us, we could cut our way out of it. Every so often we stop to rest, and Tommy whittles some. He talks about how he wants to go to Florida, get a job as a shark walker.

"If sharks don't keep moving, they'll die. They need people to hold leashes and keep them going."

Tommy Wadell wants to be near water more than anything else in this world, except having a motorcycle. He wants to be hot all the time, to never wear shirts. Or he wants to be in planes on dangerous missions. He talks about panzers, the blitzkriegs. He wants to know what it would be like to see the earth catch fire right under you, or to fly across the Atlantic Ocean at night when there isn't anything to see but stars and planets. That's when I first think Tommy Wadell must hate gravity.

When I get home it's after seven, and I've missed supper. I say I lost track of time, and I go into the bathroom, lock the door, and stare at myself in the mirror to see if I look any different. An hour earlier, when we were coming out of a creek bed, I let Tommy Wadell take my hand and keep it for a while. Next week I'll let him kiss me. I'll want him to, and when I think about that kiss, something flutters deep in my belly, a tiny hand tickling along the walls of what I think must be my womb.

That spring girls in the seventh grade are invited to sign up for Ballroom Dancing with the DiStefanos. I get one of the invitations in the mail, explaining how this is the first important step to Junior Cotillion, then the debutante societies, then Cotillion. I go off by myself and look up the word *cotillion* in the dictionary. Then I write a nice note thanking the DiStefanos for thinking of me, but saying I did not now intend to join them.

At school my friends Noreen and Robbie Lynn can't understand why I don't want to ballroom-dance.

"Everybody's doing it," Noreen says.

"Not everybody," I tell her.

"We're all clumsy, Gus," Robbie Lynn says. "We could use a little help, learn some manners. We're all clumsy larvae, and they want to make us into social butterflies. That's all."

I get this picture in my head of butterflies becoming moths, flying into lit candles and coming out with their wings singed, then sending themselves straight back into the flames.

We go into the cafeteria and sit down together, at the last table by the door, like always. None of us gets a tray. Robbie Lynn takes an apple out of her coat pocket and starts to eat it. She stops when she gets to the seeds and puts it down on the table between us.

"Gus," Noreen starts up again.

"I know, I know. Whatever it is, I know already."

We sit there, the three of us, for the rest of the lunch period.

Nobody gets up and walks off. We don't hang up the phone on each other either. That's the manners we already know.

That night I dream I've swallowed the seeds out of everything in the refrigerator: oranges, apples, cucumbers, black olives, the sesame seeds on rolls, and they all sprout inside me and send dark shoots out through my pores.

—

A week later I wake up telling myself that I'm in love with Tommy Wadell. The afternoon before, we rode our bikes to the Dekalb Peachtree Airport, almost halfway between our houses. My father's travel agency is right next door, so we had to be careful, but we hid our bikes in the bushes, sat on the bank near the end of the runway, and watched the planes come in and go out. They're mostly private planes, and Tommy knew all their names: Cessna, Beechcraft, Piper Aztec, all sounding like words in another language. I reached up under his shirt to work out a kink in his back, and then he did the same for me.

"Open your eyes," he said when he kissed me.

We looked at each other, and there was that tiny hand again, thrilling inside me, twinging on and off, the way heat lightning looks at night—light, dark, light, dark, no sound at all.

Nobody knows about Tommy Wadell. If they did, I have a feeling they wouldn't understand, so I keep quiet. My mother thinks I'm going around with one of the Clifton boys, the one who keeps calling. She likes it that I have secrets, as long as she knows what they are. Tommy and I don't go anyplace we can't get out of fast, and he doesn't call me very often. When he does, anybody who answers thinks it's just a boy from school. One night, though, the phone rings during supper. My father answers it, then hands the receiver across the table to me.

"It's Tommy," the voice says. "I have to know something. I have to know if you'll die for me. I just now decided that I'd die for you, and then I started thinking, and I wondered if you would too."

There's a noise like his teeth are chattering. Everyone at the table is looking at me.

"Yes. Yes, I would. Are you at home?"

"No, this is a pay phone, so I have to go. I'll be at the lake tomorrow." Then he hangs up.

"Goodbye," I say to thin air.

All that night I lie in bed seeing policemen and security guards with guns trying to shoot Tommy Wadell, and always I step into the path of the bullet, take the blast with my eyes wide open.

—

Tommy Wadell tells me he loves his mother almost as much as he loves me, that she's the only other woman he'd die for. Her name is Jan Wadell, and she works for UPS. Tommy is her only child.

"One night I heard her tell my daddy that she wanted me to learn to drive trucks. You know they make you go to school for that, to drive trucks and make boxes. My momma can make a box out of anything. You say 'box,' and she takes out her pocketknife, zip, zip, there it is."

I lie there under the pine trees by the lake thinking I want to be like Tommy's mother. He pulls a billfold from his back pocket and takes out a picture, a snapshot of a woman at the beach, right at the edge of the water, her dress blowing out in front of her. She's looking at the camera, one hand up to shield her eyes from the sun, so her face is mostly in shadow. Her hair is blond, curling at the chin, and she's got Tommy's same nose, jutting away from her face like half of a perfect triangle.

"That's at Myrtle Beach. You can tell she's about to have a baby. She had two babies that died before I was born, not even old enough to name or get baptized. She says they're in heaven watching out for me."

I know these babies aren't in heaven, they're in Limbo, where babies go if they're not baptized. I don't say anything about it because it would be mean, and I have better manners than that. Manners makes me think of Noreen and Robbie Lynn ballroom-dancing their way in slow circles around the clubhouse at Bagley Park, right this very minute. I want to say something nice to Tommy, something to cancel out my thoughts. "I'd want us to have three kids at least."

Tommy tries to keep from smiling, but he doesn't do a very good job of it. He pulls a vine off the trunk of the tree we're sitting under and opens his pocketknife with one hand.

"And I'd stand right there, every time, and when they said it's okay, I'd cut the cord."

He slices into the vine, and then I can't help myself.

"Do you know what Limbo is?"

He puts his arm around me and pulls me back against his chest.

"Sure. It's that dance they do where you have to get from one side to the other under this stick that they keep moving closer to the ground."

I can see it all in my head like a movie, the barre going lower and lower, Noreen and Robbie Lynn in their church dresses arching to shimmy their hips, then finally slithering under on their backs.

In May Noreen's mother and father give her a new record player for her fourteenth birthday. The next Saturday afternoon, Robbie Lynn and I come over to her house, to see the record player where it sits on its little altar of milk crates in Noreen's bedroom. The first thing she does is show us how it works, how the arm slides over automatically after it feels a record's been put down on the turnta-ble. We help her set up the speakers so that the sound will seem to come from nowhere, like there's a ghost in the room playing both treble and bass parts. Noreen's father stands in the doorway watching us, drinking a beer. When Robbie Lynn and I walked up the driveway half an hour ago, he was outside cutting the grass, and now he presses the beer can to his forehead and tells himself how good that feels.

"I don't suppose you want any help there," he says.

"No, thanks," Noreen tells him.

Just then, I back out of the closet where I've been stacking empty stereo boxes.

"Hey there, Gus." He salutes me with the beer. "Long time no see. How's your dad?"

"Fine."

"Me and him got to have lunch one of these days. I'm thinking about a trip to Australia."

"You are?" Noreen says. "When?"

"Does he handle Australia, Gus?"

"I think so," I say, "but you'd have to check."

"When are you going?" Noreen asks again.

"Oh, I don't know. Soon. Later. Sometime."

"Why do you want to go to Australia, Dad?"

"I don't really know, except I think it would be like China without the Chinese. You know how people want to go to China because they want to see how the other half lives? Going to Australia would be like that too."

"What's wrong with the Chinese?"

"Probably nothing, but ever since I saw that movie *The Sand Pebbles,* they scare me."

Noreen's father talks like this; everything he says makes you have to ask him another question.

"What happens in *The Sand Pebbles* that's so scary?"

"They cut out a guy's guts while he's still alive."

It's Ray's voice. Ray is Noreen's younger brother. He's standing behind his father where we can't see him.

"That's right," Noreen's father says. "They do everything with knives over there. You can't hear a knife. It makes me nervous. Anyway, Gus, tell your dad I'll be in touch."

I say I will, and he turns around, takes Ray by the shoulders, and propels him down the hall. Noreen watches them go, looks at us and starts to say something, but changes her mind. She closes the bedroom door, then kneels down in front of a stack of record albums. I know what she'll play, and I think if I have to hear "American Pie" all the way through one more time, I'm going to go crazy.

"How about Roberta Flack?" Robbie Lynn says. She's sitting at the foot of the bed reading the stereo warranty. "Get this: 'Manufacturer not responsible for damage to parts due to assembly, processing, shipping, handling or user carelessness.' Jesus. They should just write 'So long, sucker.' That's probably what the Japanese below it says. And the French too. *'Au revoir, lacan.'* "

Noreen and I laugh out loud. Our French teacher, who worked for the Resistance, is teaching us some great slang.

"Robbie, you know I don't have any Roberta Flack," Noreen says.

"Just testing. Play anything, then. I don't care."

"How's ballroom?" I ask.

Noreen and Robbie Lynn look at each other.

" 'Love Lies Bleeding,' " Noreen reads. "It's fine. We're learning the box step. We've been learning the box step for three weeks. The second class they told us everything is really just the box step."

"The best part is pressing up against the boys," Robbie Lynn says. "It drives them crazy. Their hands get sweaty, then their foreheads get sweaty. One kid from Sandy Springs sweats under his eyes so it looks like he's crying. God. I just thought of it. Maybe he is crying."

There's a single knock on the door, then it opens, and Ray's standing there. He's talking to Noreen, but he's looking at Robbie Lynn and me.

"Want to play my record?"

"What's your record?" Noreen asks.

He glances down at the 45 he's holding like he's forgotten what it is.

" 'The Night the Lights Went Out in Georgia.' "

"Come on, Ray," Noreen says. "You don't really like that, do you? It's redneck music."

"I do like it. It's a theme song."

"No, it's not," Noreen says. "You don't even know what a theme song is."

"Yes I do. It's a song that tells you everything that's going to happen."

"I don't care. It's still a hick redneck song. Get it out of here."

"Noreen," Robbie Lynn says, "it won't hurt you to play it once."

"Let's hear it," I say.

Ray's walking out the door, but when he hears our voices, he turns around again. His face has turned red, and he's shaking his head like a horse trying to get loose from its bridle.

"I don't need your sympathy vote," he says.

Then he's looking at me.

"Gus probably likes this song too," he says. "She goes around with rednecks, her and her redneck boyfriend riding around on their bikes."

Then he slams the door shut. Noreen and Robbie Lynn are staring at me now, now that they've finished looking at the door where one of the hinges has broken.

"What's he talking about?" Noreen asks.

"I have no idea," I say, looking her right in the eye.

In early June the night air isn't so filled up with crickets and bats and starlings crying in their sleep, so you notice sounds, where they come from and how long they last. You notice how the calliope music of the Good Humor truck doesn't ever seem to get farther away, until all at once it's just gone. You hear the differences in kids' mothers' voices calling them home.

Tonight I can hear that Skiff Wager and his sister Ellie are still outside in the street after I've gone to bed, and I know they're doing wheelies on their Spyder bikes. I hear their voices catch in their throats as they pull up on the handlebars and then the plomp of the front tire as it touches down. It's the same noise all my muscles make when they finally ease down and let me sleep. It sounds like a body falling overboard.

Then I'm awake again, sure I hear him coming when he's still in the next yard. Something makes me sit up in bed and hold myself perfectly still. In a few minutes I see a shadow outside the window, and he whispers my name. I go to the screen and Tommy Wadell's voice blows in at me, along with the smell of gardenias, like both are billowing out of his mouth at the same time.

"Can you come out?" he says. "I have to tell you something."

I unhook the screen and sit with my legs hanging outside the window. Tommy's standing in front of me with his hands on my knees. Even this close, he's just a shadow with skin. I ask him what's wrong.

"They decided tonight," he says. "We're moving to Spartanburg at the end of the month. Me and my momma are supposed to go earlier."

I don't want him to say anything else, and he doesn't. He turns and leans his back into my chest, and I wrap my arms around his bony shoulders.

We stay that way for a long time. I think I've fallen asleep, and then I'm not sure because I look around and nothing's changed. The same stars twitch over us, only Tommy's turned around again, and he's looking at my face. I don't know how much of it he can see. Twice he turns toward the neighbor's yard to listen for a dog's bark or a voice, and I see his profile, his hard jaw, his hair like straw, lifting off his head in the breeze and settling down again. I tell him he has to go, and in my head the words sound like tiny switches being flipped off.

When I see Tommy Wadell the next day, I can tell he hasn't been to sleep. We're down by the lake, and I let him lie with his head in my lap.

"Alls I can think of," he tells me, "is this thing that happened to me in third grade. One day the teacher comes in for our Georgia history lesson, and she's telling us about names. The one thing I remember is that all the Peachtree streets weren't Peachtree at first, they were Pitchtree because of all the pitch pines around here. After that I felt like I didn't know where I was. All us kids felt that way. I was just learning names of streets and getting my bearings and whoosh, it's all different. I know it doesn't matter, I know they're all Peachtree now, but I had to think about everything all over again, make a whole new map in my head."

Tommy has his eyes closed, so he can't see me nodding my head, but I'm sure he feels my body moving, the muscles in my belly going up and down.

School lets out, and then for two weeks after that Tommy and I are quiet together, sitting down by the lake every day we can. We talk about what we'll give each other before he goes, and we decide to trade clothes. I'm going to give him everything that might fit, and he's going to do the same for me. Every day around noon we talk about hiking out to Burger King again, but then I get to feel that standing up would put us too far apart, so we never go. In the evening I eat three helpings of supper and then sit outside, leaning up against the fence between our property and the golf course.

I wait for him to come back at night and tell me that he isn't really going, that he'll stay here, move into one of the half-built houses down the street. I'll take care of him, bring him the food my mother makes. We'll find some way to keep him warm in the winter. I've seen a movie about a boy who lives in the crawl space of a house owned by people he doesn't know, and when they discover him, they're good and kind. My thoughts go on like this until it gets dark, and then I realize he isn't coming back tonight, but I stay out a little longer, just in case.

When I go in to kiss my parents good night, my father's suitcase is lying open on their bed. In it are shoes and shirts a color blue I have never seen anywhere else in the world. There's a bottle of gin and his shaving kit that opens like an old woman's change purse, the kind you have to squeeze like you're crumpling up paper.

"Where are you going?" I ask him.

"Oh, Gus, there you are. Baltimore, just for two days, back before you know I'm gone."

That was what he always said, and sometimes it was true.

In the morning my mother kisses him goodbye and then circles the day on the calendar, the day he'll be back. She goes in to make the bed, and I think she must be putting her hands in the sheets to try to find where he's been.

—

The day before he's supposed to leave with his mother, Tommy Wadell meets me by the lake. I feel almost like I don't want to touch him, but then I do. He's holding a knife his father's just given him, one for dressing deer.

"It's only a loan. He wants it back when he gets to Spartanburg, but I'll tell him I lost it in the move. I think you should keep it."

It's a Buck knife, says so on the sheath. It's a name I'll remember years later because I'll still have it.

"I'll never not know where this is," I tell him. I can't talk right.

"I want to show you how sharp it is," Tommy says.

He lays me down next to him. I want him to tell me not to worry, it isn't going to hurt, but he doesn't say these things. He unzips my jeans, and I think that whatever he's going to do, it's something I want. He leaves the jeans open on my hips and pulls down the elastic of my underpants, just a little, just below the line where the dark hairs start. With the knife's edge, he shaves away a few of these hairs, leaving a small stroke of white skin that waits, then blossoms red.

"You might have a scar there," he says, "and you might not. I'll be back to check."

Tommy Wadell didn't come back, not once. And though it's years later, I still think about him and how maybe he was the only true one. Even today, talking to Noreen and Robbie Lynn, I said, There was a boy once, but I didn't finish, and they didn't ask.

LESSONS AND
CAROLS

I was once the kind of girl who built treehouses and then lived in them. I did this for the entire year after my father died in Oneonta, New York, and we moved to Atlanta, Georgia. I was fourteen, building one treehouse and then another and then another because I had to learn to be alone off the ground. In those twelve months the weather went crazy all over the Deep South—snow, ice storms, and in the spring the rains were the heaviest in years. I needed a place to be out of the house but not get soaked, so I rigged up a lean-to, from plywood and black tarp, facing into the woods, into forsythia and spikes of pine. After school I'd hide out, smoke cigarettes, and watch the sky for signs of clearing. Sometimes I'd thumb through my mother's copy of *Complete Herbal* by Nicholas Culpeper, a good book to have around if you think you could be sitting on top of something poisonous.

When it got dark I'd light candles and wait to be called inside for supper, then wait again for Mother to say the two things she always said: no wonder there were never candles around when she needed them, and someday I'd cause a forest fire if I wasn't careful. I trusted my mother in this, even if I didn't act like it. I believed her because candles were her claim to fame. At my new school in Atlanta she played Lucia, the queen of the Festival of Lessons and Carols. She wore her wedding dress and a wreath of battery-powered candles in her white-blond hair, and she led the choir into the auditorium and up onto the stage. The older students read lessons from the gospels of Luke and John, and the choir followed each reading with a carol. My mother stood at stage right, radiant and doing absolutely nothing for the entire hour and fifteen minutes, but even so, I was proud of her, the kind of pride that brings you to tears. And I was also afraid, afraid that surrounded by all those children, she would forget me. She would fall in love with the other girls' beautiful washed faces and their neatly ironed choir robes, their high, clear singing. She would beg me to give up my treehouses and learn to be more like them.

That year the boy standing beside my mother set her hair on fire with his candle. I was in the audience, because I couldn't carry a tune, and looked up from the third verse of "Hark the Herald Angels Sing" to see her face surrounded by a blazing halo. For maybe three seconds I thought it was a sign from heaven, though of what, I couldn't have said. The choir director slapped out the flames, and she left the stage unhurt. Later, out on the playground, I punched the boy, who was much younger than I, and knocked him unconscious. My mother said to the school principal, fire will make a child do such things, crazy things. He said, well, Lucy, if that's so, you better teach her what a young lady is supposed to do in case of a fire emergency, and make it so she'll never forget. He said it like he thought my mother was already making terrible mistakes in my upbringing and would surely make more.

The next week, I built my first real treehouse, in a crab apple. It was a platform around the main trunk, five feet up, more like a deer hunter's tree stand set a little too low. When the crab apple bloomed, so would the dogwoods beside it, and then I would be lost inside a snowstorm of flowers, drifting in the very white of its eye where nothing moves. The boys in the neighborhood came by to view my handiwork, and they were quiet and respectful. The incident in the playground was burned into their minds, just where I hoped it would be.

All spring I sat inside the crab-apple blossoms and thought about what had happened two Decembers before: My father told us he was catching a cold, got into bed, and stayed there for two days, until Christmas Eve, when he decided to take a walk. He lay down in the snow, and his heart stopped, and he never woke up. When I went out to look for him, it was dark, but I had a flashlight, and I saw him lying on his back, staring up at the stars. I watched him for a minute, then knelt down and held the flashlight over his head. I couldn't think of anything, except that his eyes were open and he knew I was there. His face was perfect, his skin transparent, like a sheet of ice over all the veins and bones, so that it might freeze my hand to touch him.

I heard Mother come to stand behind me, and I switched off the light. I told her to stay where she was, but she kept coming. I don't know why I didn't want her to see him, but it seemed the most important thing in the world. I threw the flashlight into the woods, as hard as I could, so it would break and stay out for good. I remember her crying got louder and louder until it became a high wailing. She kept it up all Christmas morning, standing at the dining room window with her forehead pressed against the cold glass. For a while I held her by the shoulders, whispering *there, there.* I remember that my own voice rose in a strange way, like I was giving a direction, the way you tell someone when you see an animal break cover or a lightning flash at night. You say *over there,* but it's always too late.

When I couldn't think about my father anymore, I was off to build something new, staking a claim farther back in the woods. I got up high enough in a Japanese elm to see my mother standing at the kitchen window, talking to our neighbor from next door, who I knew wanted to marry her. I was worried that she would say yes, worried sick. I wanted her to be talking to me, not to him, or listening for the *thrung* of my ax as I marked out a new site. We had all the same aches then, I believed, identical hatchet marks on our two hearts that burned and burned and could never be consumed.

Every week Mother and I made the trip to the local lumberyard, the Brookhaven Supply Company, looking for plywood sheathing, two-by-fours, stiles and rails for wainscotting, which was forever going to be my next improvement. I also sometimes wanted green wood, maple or white ash, to make us snowshoes. You never know when you might need them, I told her, and my father had all the instructions, copied out of *Fine Woodworking*. On Saturday mornings we'd leave for Brookhaven Supply by ten. In the car I'd explain how builders calculate board measurements, the kerf that's lost in sawdust, how carpenters say five and a half is six, wrong and right at the same time.

We bought wood for the treehouses from two black men out behind the main building. We were there so often it turned into a game they played with us, mostly with Mother, because she was young and pretty and she used to blush when men teased her. They would whisper a price in her ear and put their fingers to their lips, like they were secret lumber agents, but we knew their names were Elbert Jenkins and Ross Rice. Elbert was missing his right arm at the shoulder. The rest of his body, at least what parts of it could be seen, was covered with warts the size of peas, marbles, and birds' eggs. When we were alone, Mother wondered if his missing arm had warts on it too, or if it was the only clean part of him, and that was why he had to lose it.

"Don't stare," she would whisper to me. She would keep her own eyes locked with Elbert's, and she'd listen to him like his was the last voice on earth. It made me fidgety to watch her, so that I would have to get up and do something dangerous to attract her attention, climb on a pile of loose boards or trail my fingers over the edge of the circular saw. Once when I looked back at her, she'd taken Elbert's hand, and she held on to it a long time.

"That nigger's hand is the one you should be holding," Elbert told her, pointing to Ross. "He saved my life. Would have lost both my arms, cutting bad wood on this very saw, but he pulled me out just in time. Thanks to that nigger, I can still dance with a pretty woman like you."

"You name the day," my mother said. "You name the day, and we'll have that dance."

"Mother," I said to her when Elbert went out to get our lumber, "how do you think you're going to go dancing with a black man?"

When Elbert came back and turned on the saw, Mother stood right beside him, just in case. Elbert and I took turns running the boards through, and when he cut the motor, Mother trailed her own fingers over the blade to see how sharp it was. Elbert watched her, lovingly, was the word I thought at the time. Then we sat in the coolest corner of the shed, to rest our hearts, Ross said. Even before noon the mercury got sucked into the nineties, and my clothes stuck to my skin. Elbert took a kerchief out of his pocket and wiped his face.

"A real scorcher," he said.

Up and down Peachtree Street the buildings shimmered like Atlanta was a town made of mirages. The cars alone could dazzle you with their power to appear and disappear. I was mesmerized by the Brookhaven Pharmacy, the cleaner's, the new diner named Handy B-B-Q, all their windows gone silver from the light. Humidity made the air look greenish, like it was coughed out from the bottom of somebody's lungs. If you wanted to breathe, you had to work for it.

"Your girl ain't afraid of much, far as I can tell."

Elbert said this to my mother out of the blue. I wanted to think about whether it was true or not, try to remember what I might be afraid of.

"I used to be afraid of you," I said, "but not anymore."

"He ain't nothing," Ross said.

"Naw, you is fearless, I knows it," Elbert said, and then he looked at my mother for a long time before telling her he could see it's fearlessness in the blood.

A car pulled into the Brookhaven Supply driveway and honked its horn. Elbert looked over his shoulder, then walked out to the parking lot and leaned in on the passenger side. Mother followed him over to the car, but a minute later I felt her hand on my back, pushing me out the door. I tried to turn around, but she wouldn't let me. Outside, in the daylight, I could see tears in her eyes. She could barely talk.

"The lady he's speaking to, she's just like him," Mother says. "She has warts too. He was holding her hand."

I looked hard at my mother. I could see that she envied the woman in the car, envied the face and arms and hands that boiled and bubbled up, as if there was something in the woman's heart that couldn't be kept secret. I saw in my mother's wide eyes that her jealousy was blade-sharp and unexpected. She hated to be on the outside. She was always furious to find she'd been left behind.

—

When I finished the last treehouse, I knew there wouldn't be any others. I had this thought: I have to go back to learning how to be a girl, or I'll never get it right, and I have to learn from my mother. I knew this the whole time I worked on that last treehouse. I listened to the scroll saw I borrowed from our neighbor, the sound of it like an impossible lesson, asking and telling, asking and telling.

The last treehouse was my best ever, a triangle set between three pines, eight feet by nine feet by nine feet, twelve feet off the ground. It had four windows facing exactly north, south, east, and west, built-in seats below them, shelves and two bunks, the floor covered with strips of blue and sea-green carpet we found in the attic. Our neighbor came over for a look, hiking in the back way, up through the golf course. He didn't say a word until Mother joined us, then he put his arm around her shoulders and told her she ought to be proud. He said this was probably the last house of its kind to come out of Brookhaven Supply.

"Transit Authority bought them out," he explained, "or they will in a week or so. They're sending track for the rapid transit right through the front door, parking lot for about a million vehicles, the works."

He told me to take pictures of the treehouse for Elbert and Ross. They wouldn't be coming out to see it.

"They've got no business traipsing through this neighborhood," he said.

"Why not?" Mother said.

Our neighbor looked at me for a second, then shook his head.

"It's an ill wind blowing, Lucy," he said, and I saw my mother try to hold back a smile. "I predict it'll be coloreds living in this neighborhood in less than five years."

"We can only hope," my mother said, and our neighbor paused to catch his breath before he told her she certainly was a caution.

It was September then, and Indian summer, the skies blue like they were in picture books, a color you couldn't believe, couldn't remember until you saw it again in June. All that fall I sat in my last treehouse, above the line of dogwood and honeysuckle, watching over the neighborhood like a forest ranger in his fire tower. I saw our neighbor run over his own dog. Later I believed I saw the dusty head and whipping tail of a tornado over the northwest side of town, but Mother said it was the wrong season, there weren't ever tornadoes in November. I saw couples by the lake, tangled in blankets, swimming over each other, trying to reach land they were already on. I saw Elbert walking home the long way —at least I thought it was him, moving so slowly, his face turned away from me even when I called out his name.

—

The Saturday before Christmas we heard the demolition of Brookhaven Supply had already started, much earlier than anybody thought.

"The whole place looks sad," Mother said. "What's this town need to go fooling with mass transit for, anyhow? Nobody will take it except damn northerners. These people can get around by themselves good enough."

"And who's going to give Elbert a job?" I said. "People will take one look and close the door in his warty old face."

"Elbert believes Jesus will take care of him and Ross," my mother said.

"Sure thing," I said, but she acted like she hadn't heard.

There was going to be a big farewell party at Brookhaven Supply. When our neighbor asked to take us, Mother said yes, and she whispered to me that going would make us both feel better. On the way over, though, she wanted to stop by Patterson's Funeral Home to see the Nativity scene, a big affair every year, with different high school choirs for five nights in a row and live organ music. That year, when it came time to sing "Silent Night," everybody in the audience got a candle to hold, and when we all reached for the high note at the word *peace,* I felt that note, it was so pure-sounding, and my skin prickled and ached like it was shrinking around my bones. I walked away from the rest of the audience to stand by myself. Mother stared at me and raised her eyebrows to ask was something the matter. I shook my head no and looked past her face.

"He's a little premature, isn't he?" Mother said when she saw that the porcelain baby Jesus was already in his crib. Her voice was louder than it had to be. "Preemie Jesus. Do you think he'll make it?"

"Lucy," our neighbor said. He told her she was talking blasphemy, but she said no, it was an honest question.

Jesus stared at the stable roof with his arms out like he wanted to be picked up. A little girl leaned over the manger to look at him, and she told her parents his eyes were green, like it was the most shocking thing in the world. Then she reached down to gather him into her arms, but she couldn't because he was attached to the manger by copper wire. She held herself bent over, frozen, and her parents didn't seem to know what to do, whether to pull her away and get back in the car or untie the baby Jesus and let her hold him the way she wanted to.

"Jesus," she said, "get up now."

"Sweetheart," my mother said, reaching to take her hand. "Come look at the lambs."

The girl went away with my mother to see the cardboard flock, and the two of them stood together with our neighbor, like they were the holy family. I was suddenly sure that this was my mother's true daughter, somebody who could be distracted from hurt and want and need, somebody who could still be as a little child. I tried to recall Elbert's words about my being fearless, but it didn't help.

A block down Peachtree, at Brookhaven Supply, there was a huge bonfire in the parking lot, with twenty or thirty cars and pickup trucks parked in close enough to shine with the reflected flames. Floodlights hung all along the gutters of both warehouses. People moved out of the shadows and back into them again, men and women, their arms around each other, holding beer cans or paper cups. We could hear more Christmas carols, a choir singing "O Little Town of Bethlehem," and a man's voice, loud, dropping in and out of the melody.

We pulled up next to a station wagon full of kids—three in the backseat eating hamburgers and a fourth asleep on the seat behind them. The front passenger door was open so everybody outside might listen to the radio, tuned to a station playing carols twenty-four hours without commercial interruption. The kids couldn't hear a thing with the music turned up so loud, so they were talking in sign language, pointing, grinning, and stopping to sing along when they knew some of the words.

"Once in poor old David's city," they sang, "oh tanning bomb, oh tanning bomb."

Elbert stood close to the bonfire, holding out his one hand toward its heat. The temperature had dropped all through the day, to just above freezing. There was talk of snow, maybe a white Christmas if the weather held, the first in more years than anyone could remember.

"My sister sure would get a charge out of that," I heard Elbert say. "She ain't never seen snow at Christmas. Me, I've been up north some, but Sister's never traveled seventy-five miles from La Grange in any direction."

Elbert's sister came to stand beside him, and I knew right away she was the same woman in the car Mother got so worked up over last summer. The firelight made their skin look to be boiling, or maybe newly washed. For all the warts on their faces, there weren't any shadows, no place the light couldn't find them.

From inside the front warehouse there was a burst of laughter. Other people turned in that direction, and their movements made Elbert look away from the fire, directly into my eyes.

"Well, look who's here," he said, coming over to put his hand on my shoulder and then pull it away to hold Mother's hand. He introduced us to his sister. "A pleasure to have you at the party. Kind of sad, but then again, we all got to move on."

"Yes, we do," Mother said, circling her arm around Sister's waist and saying how glad she was to make her acquaintance.

Inside, the warehouse was lit by candles in tin lanterns. It looked like an airplane hangar, huge and empty, except for stacked cases of beer, plates of barbecue, and cookies in the shapes of stars and bells and angels. All the lumber and hardware had been sold off to outfits in Chamblee and Doraville, leaving only a few tall tiers of metal shelving and aisle bins that held the smaller bulk items. Stray nails, links of chain, splinters, and piles of sawdust skittered and eddied underfoot. There were stacked boxes of lantern candles that said, "Free for our faithful patrons, oh come all ye," and I stopped to slip a handful into my pocket, and then another handful for Mother. I walked the entire length of the building, taking in all that empty space, letting it fill me up and shift things around somewhere in the vicinity of my heart.

Elbert was leaning on his broom against the far wall, talking to our neighbor, who was sitting beside him on a concrete block. They were both holding cans of beer, and they handed one to me. Mother saw the beer and frowned, then shook the look off her face like it was something else to be lost in the air.

Our neighbor was doing all the talking, saying it was like a wake, the way people just kept showing up to say goodbye. Mother nodded, but she wasn't really listening. I could tell by the way her eyes went shooting up the sides of the warehouse, then dropped down slowly, like she was looking for moulding but not finding any.

"You have people around here?" Mother said to Elbert. "My daughter wants to know. People to look after you?"

She glanced down to Elbert's missing arm, then shifted her gaze over to me.

"Me and Ross gots people in Lynwood Park going to see about getting us jobs."

"That's good," Mother said.

There was a portable radio playing at the other end of the warehouse, Robert Shaw directing the Atlanta Symphony's Festival of Lessons and Carols. My mother had not been the Atlanta Symphony's Lucia, but I knew she had wanted to be. The governor's daughter was Lucia on opening night, and after that the part went to local businesswomen, realtors mostly. My mother got the drift. She was a good loser, though; she wrote sweet notes to the whole audition committee, thanking them for their time.

Robert Shaw began to read from Luke's gospel, and everybody went quiet, listening to words they could say in their sleep. His voice over the airwaves was strong and gravelly, a little breathless from conducting the orchestra, but it came out sounding like wonder, a kind of spoken carol throwing itself into the high corners of the warehouse, knowing full well its place. Fear not, he read, for behold, I bring you good tidings of great joy, which shall be to all people.

I watched my mother carefully to see if she was thinking about those old auditions, to see if this broadcast was going to be one more thing in the world to make her sad. Even now, years later, I almost can't explain what I saw in her face that night. Something in my mother was crossing over, her face bloomed with light and color and hardened at the same time. It's what you see happen to the winners of beauty contests when they're hugging the first runner-up—sympathy and a kind of cold distance. She was lost to me in that moment, and I didn't know if I'd ever get her back.

When the choir started "The First Noel," the radio got tuned to the all-carols station again, and men and women moved into each other's arms. "O Tannenbaum" turned into a polka, and Mother asked Elbert to join her. She said a fast polka is the only way to dance, and they began to circle the long cement floor. Every other couple stopped dancing to watch them. When the song was over, Mother moved out of Elbert's arm and looked at me. She picked up a handful of the free candles and told me to say my thank-yous because it was time to go. I tried to read the expressions on the faces that surrounded us, but there was nothing to see, and for that I loved every single man, woman, and child in the room.

In the middle of the night there was a sharp knocking on my bedroom window.

"Merry Christmas in there," Mother said through the glass, even though she was three days early, "merry, merry Christmas. It's snowing, do you believe it? Snowing. It's going to be a white Christmas, and you're not dreaming."

She stepped back away from the window, knocking into the camellia bush and sending a flash of snow across her face. She started to laugh and, with her head back, turned slow circles in the middle of the yard, catching flakes of snow on her tongue. Her arms went up as she turned, like wings unfolding, until they were level with her shoulders, and it was then I saw Elbert on the back-porch steps, watching her. Mother sat down on Elbert's right, close, so that her arm lay where Elbert's would be if he'd still had it. They were like shadows, broken only by the whites of their eyes and snow in the creases of their coats. The night was perfectly quiet, muffled by the surprise of snow in Atlanta, waiting breathlessly for even stranger weather. Then I heard the low growl of our neighbor's new dog on its side of the fence. Mother dropped her cheek onto Elbert's shoulder, and he kissed the top of her head.

—

The next day, Mother and I went to watch the demolition. We had to stand a good ways off from the buildings, almost into the post office parking lot, outside the cyclone fence. Only Elbert was there in the morning, and we heard him try to give the wrecking crew a few last-minute instructions before he left. On his way out he came to stand beside us. He said not to worry, he'd be seeing us around, and then he walked off toward Lynwood Park.

The crew used sledgehammers and pneumatic drills to take off the roof, cutting beams and girders into sections, then lowering them to the ground with a crane. Every so often trucks hauled away the fallen debris, dumped it up north, probably in some industrial trash heap in Cobb County. They came back empty and pulled in to receive another load.

We watched for an hour, and I told my mother the names of structures as they fell out of the crane's maw.

"Don't use that word," she said.

"Crane?"

"No, maw. It doesn't sound like you."

"There goes the siding," I said. "That's a whole mess of insulation."

"Don't say 'whole mess,' " she told me next.

"The proper name for that piece is flange," I said as precisely as I could.

She curled her fingers through the chain links of the fence.

"The proper name for this is waste," she said, more to herself than to me, and I knew it was time to go home.

—

A week after Christmas and the night before my fifteenth birthday an ice storm knocked the stuffing out of the whole city. Fifty-foot pine trees sagged under the weight of the ice and crushed people's houses. Some of our neighbors moved out to motels in Gwinnett County, where there was still electricity. Mrs. Early down the street was watching out her picture window when she saw the hemlock in her front yard falling toward her. In that instant her heart stopped. The tree missed her house by six inches, but she was just as dead.

My treehouse was another casualty. We knew it was gone for sure at five in the morning, right when it happened. We'd been sitting up since the electric furnace quit at eleven-thirty, tending the fire and drifting along the crackly edge of sleep, the way small children can walk on ice-crusted snow without falling through. We knew the treehouse was gone because the sound of dead wood cracking apart is different from the sound of branches breaking off trees. Dead wood creaks and groans, the way trucks' gears sound like they're breaking their own hearts going uphill, and the sound lasts longer, dragging itself out to the last splinter. Tree branches go off like gunshots and land like bodies falling. When we heard it, we looked at each other but didn't say anything. In the firelight my mother's eyes were enormous.

Outside just before dawn the world was bigger, enchanted, like someone had shaken the whole planet loose. Branches and slabs of bark covered the ground, so thick in places that we couldn't see the snow underneath, couldn't walk except by kicking through the debris. We didn't need to go far, though, to see one of the pines leaning in through the middle of the treehouse, which was held up only by its far wall, the guts of the place dropping out through the bottom.

"You can build another one," Mother said.

"No, I can't," I told her. "We'll have to take out that tree. I don't use it all that much anyways. I'm getting too old."

I turned to look at her, and in the light reflected off the snow, I saw her face was hard, her jaw set against the cold. My being too old made her remember my birthday.

"I won't be able to bake you a cake," she said. "There's no electricity."

Right then a branch snapped off one of the pine trees and fell close behind us. We started to run toward the golf course, toward open ground. When I got clear of the rough and the pines, I stopped and waited in the middle of the fairway, but Mother kept going past me, down the hill to the creek. Everything around us was white, a white tunnel veined on either side by black tree branches. I could see her far ahead, the dark green parka, still running. I didn't know if it was momentum carrying her downhill or if she was that scared. Maybe she thought no place was safe.

Maybe she was thinking how not so long ago, the whole world and everyone in it seemed built to last. Maybe it was the ice, and she saw how it smashes things, breaks them, all the while making you want to believe your eyes, believe nothing could be prettier than this destruction.

At the bottom of the hill a figure walked out from among the trees. I knew it was Elbert, even before I saw the sleeve of his jacket fluttering in the wind. He and my mother stood facing one another, and then my mother took hold of Elbert's empty sleeve and brought it to her face. She bowed her head into the dark material.

All at once, I felt very tired, more exhausted than I had ever been in my whole life. I lay down in the snow in the middle of the fairway and closed my eyes, even though my mother had taught me that this was not a smart thing to do. She said the moisture in my body, the sweat on my skin, under my clothes, would turn to ice. I would be encased in a smooth sheet of ice that would fit me like a glove, and I would freeze to death. She had taught me this, and yet as I lay there in the snow, the lesson was fading from my memory, lost from the inside out, moving to the surface of my skin to become as dead and cold as ice. As if in a dream, I heard "O Tannenbaum" and saw Mother and Elbert dancing across the warehouse floor at Brookwood Supply. I did not want to know about them, about my mother and Elbert. I did not want it explained to me, what they meant to each other, the way I should behave toward them. I did not want to learn one single thing more than I already had. Learning how to act was like freezing: it happened to you against your will, and you could never get over it, never stop it. You learned a small truth, and then it became big and powerful and solid, and then it left you behind.

THE COLUMBUS
SCHOOL FOR
GIRLS

"It's the oldest story in America," Mr. Jerman says, "only no one seems to know it. When Christopher Columbus went to ask Queen Isabella to bankroll his voyage to the East, she just laughed at him, and she told him it was about as likely he could make that trip as it was that he could make an egg stand on its end. But that Columbus, he said, okay, Isabella, watch closely. And he took out an egg—the one he always carried for state occasions just like this—and tapped it ever so gently on one end, not enough to shatter it, but enough to flatten that end just slightly, and there the egg stood, and Isabella gave Columbus the dough, and the rest is history."

We love this story, and we love the teacher who tells it to us and girls like us, year after year at The Columbus School for Girls. We love the way he stands over the lectern at Chapel, right in front of the red-and-white banner that says EXPLORE THYSELF!, below the headmaster's favorite words of wisdom, copied from money, IN GOD WE TRUST. We like to sit left of center and close one eye. Half-blind, we see Mr. Jerman's face like a hieroglyph in the midst of wisdom, a blessed interruption, and the words say IN GOD WE RUST.

We don't care much for the other teachers, the ones who tell us to spit out our chewing gum, pull up our knee socks, and button our blouses all the way up, the ones who warn us we'll never amount to anything. We know how they fear us, we're walking danger to them, the way we whoop in the halls, the way we dance in slow circles to no music, but still they dream of having us for their daughters, of taking us home and seeing what, given the proper tools and rules, we might become. We smoke cigarettes in the bathroom. We've been known to carry gin in vanilla bottles and have a swig or two after lunch.

Mr. Jerman, though, we would be his daughters in a heartbeat. We would change our names, we would all become Jermans. We would let his wife, Emily Jerman, be the mother of us all. We see her rarely, at wind-ensemble concerts, dances, and field-hockey games, standing on the sidelines behind the opposing team—tiny, thin Emily Jerman, always looking so cold that we want to build a fire right at her feet. Emily Jerman, always wearing one of her husband's sweaters, smiling at us, leaning her thin bones against her husband's arm and talking into his ear in a voice we've never heard but guess must sound like baby birds. We want to be like her, so we steal our fathers' sweaters, our brothers' sweaters, our boyfriends'. We let ourselves grow thin. Emily Jerman and Bryan Jerman. We say their names over and over at night into the darkness of the Upper Five Dormitory where the air is already hazy with girls' breath. We pass his name between the beds—*Have you had Bryan Jerman yet?*—like he's something you could catch.

In the morning when we wake up, their names are still hanging over us, and it's still November, always November. November is by far the cruellest month at The Columbus School for Girls. By November nothing is new anymore, not the teachers, not the books, not the rules and the bravest ways to break them. November is Indian summer, and then it's rain. November, Mr. Jerman says, is longing, and we agree. We long for Thanksgiving, but we don't know why because it will only lead to real winter, killer winter, when nothing moves. All month we long to go back to the days when our school uniforms were new and tight across our hips, when our notebooks were empty, when no one had discovered us yet.

"Girls," Mr. Jerman says in the middle of this cruel November, "I have been thinking about you."

We could say the same thing, especially since he has been reading us Emily Dickinson these past weeks. We have come to think of Emily Dickinson as Emily Jerman and vice versa. We whisper about Emily Jerman's closet full of white dresses and her strange ideas about certain birds and flowers and angleworms. We think this must be what Emily Jerman does all day in the bungalow behind Lower Four Dormitory: she writes hundreds of poems on the backs of Columbus School for Girls memoranda that Mr. Jerman has folded and torn in quarters, just the right size for one of her poems about the yellow daisies beheaded by winter, that white assassin.

"I have been thinking," Mr. Jerman says again, "that we need to do a little more exploring. We have been sitting like bumps on logs reading these poems when we could do so much more."

We look at him, making our smiles bright and trusting the way we think he must like them, letting him lead us on.

"I could take you to Emily Dickinson's house," Mr. Jerman says, and we lean forward over our desks. It feels like he's invited us into his own home. "If you're interested, I can call up there this afternoon. We can take one of the school vans. I'm sure my wife would love to come along too. She's always wanted to go there."

We can imagine. We can imagine Emily Jerman going to the home of her namesake, her other, her true self. We can imagine our own selves being the Jermans' daughters for a whole weekend, far away from The Columbus School for Girls, deep in what we think must be the savage jungle of western Massachusetts.

—

Mr. Jerman, we hear, has a hard time convincing the headmaster to let us go. We listen to them discuss it late the next afternoon while we're waiting for tardy slips.

"Bryan," the headmaster is saying, "think about it. All of *them*. And just you and Emily. What if something happens? What if one

of them goes berserk? Or gets arrested? Or smuggles along contra-
band?"

"Leo," Mr. Jerman says, "nonsense. The girls will be perfect
ladies. It will be good for them to get out, see some more of the
world. And Emily will be along to take care of any, you know, girl
problems."

"I just don't think so," the headmaster says. "I'm not sure these
are girls you can trust."

"Rust," we say.

"Of course I can trust them," Mr. Jerman says. "That gin at
lunchtime business is all a made-up story. They're chafing at the bit
a little, that's all. This trip will be just the thing. I've told their
parents to call you about it."

"Oh, God, Bryan," the headmaster says.

"Oh, God," we say.

"Girls," the headmaster's secretary says, "you know there's none
of that on school grounds."

The telephone on the secretary's desk rings in a stifled *brrrr*.
We're sure it's our parents, all of them making one huge impossible
conference call to tell the headmaster to keep us at this school
forever, until we grow old and die. We can't stand it anymore. We
forge the signatures on our tardy slips and beat it to smoke cigarettes behind Lower Four Dormitory. From there we can see the
Jermans' bungalow, and we keep smoking until Mr. Jerman comes
home. We think his shoulders look awfully slumped, and we notice
too the way the fiery late-afternoon light seems to have taken all the
color out of his face. The front door opens, and Emily Jerman is
standing there, a yellow halo surrounding her whole tiny body from
head to toe. When she reaches up to touch Mr. Jerman's face, we
try to look away, but we can't. Our eyes have become hard, cold
points of darkness, fixed on them, on their tenderness, and learning
it. Emily and Bryan Jerman go inside their bungalow and the door
closes behind them. We watch them move from room to room past
the windows until it's so dark we have to feel our way back to

Upper Five Dormitory, crawling on our hands and knees, lighting matches to see what little of the way we know.

At night we dream Emily Jerman has come to stand at our bedside. She is putting small pieces of paper under our pillow, Columbus School for Girls memoranda, torn in quarters. *Lie still,* she commands. *If you move, they will explode.*

The next day is Saturday, when we always have detention, and then Sunday, when we have Chapel. The opening hymn is "A Mighty Fortress Is Our God." Mr. Jerman has told us you can sing most of Emily Dickinson's poems to the tune of "A Mighty Fortress Is Our God," so we try it. The headmaster glares at us; beside his head is the word RUST, like the balloon of talk in a comic strip. We sing to him, enunciating like there's no tomorrow, and he watches our mouths move, trying to discover our blasphemies, the mystery of us. Was there ever one of us he understood, he must be asking himself, was there ever one of us who did not have a black heart and carry a knife in her teeth?

—

"Girls," Mr. Jerman says on Monday morning, "grab your coats and hats, pack your bags. It's all set. We leave Friday afternoon. Friday night in Pennsylvania. Saturday at the Emily Dickinson Homestead."

We're stunned, and then we cheer until Mr. Jerman's eyes move from our faces and out to the middle distance. We turn in our desks to see Emily Jerman standing at the window. She waves to us and moves off across the garden.

"She wanted to get a look at you," Mr. Jerman says, his voice strangling in his throat.

We watch Emily Jerman—us and her husband—we watch her as she gathers wood for kindling: birch, alder, even green pine. Her arms are full of wood and purple thistles, her red hair falling forward to cover her face and throat.

Oh, Emily Jerman! Her name rises, almost to our lips. We burn for her, all day long, wherever she goes—our long hair fallen like hers, in flames.

—

By the time we're ready to leave Friday afternoon, it's getting dark. The Jermans are going to drive three hours apiece to get us as far as Harrisburg, Pennsylvania, where we've got rooms in a motel. We look out the windows and watch the back of Emily Jerman's head. She has said hello to us, but nothing after that. She rides up in front next to her husband, and sometimes their arms touch, his right and her left across the space between the seats. We stare at them when this happens, our eyes glittering and hungry. We play charades. By the time we get an hour out of town, all we can see is night rising on the soft shoulders of the road and our own faces reflected in the windows. The highway is our own hair streaming behind us, and the moon is our eye. For miles and miles there haven't been any lights. We're all there is in this world, just us and the Jermans.

In Zanesville we stop for supper. Mr. Jerman drives off the highway and through a web of back streets to a Chinese restaurant, "The Imperious Wok," he calls it, glancing over at his wife, who turns to him and smiles. When we get to the parking lot, the marquee says THE IMPERIAL WOK, and we laugh, but we don't get the joke. For a minute it makes us wary of the Jermans, for having secrets between themselves, for having a whole history we can never know. Inside, Mr. Jerman explains the menu and shows us how to use chopsticks. He is amazed that we've never had Chinese food before. He toasts us with his tiny bowl of tea.

When the waiter comes, Emily Jerman orders a cocktail. Mr. Jerman looks at her and raises his blond eyebrows but doesn't say anything. We realize this is the first whole sentence we have ever heard Emily Jerman say: *I would like a double vodka on the rocks.* Her voice is surprisingly low and sweet. We have always thought she should have a high voice to go with her tiny frail body, but instead it's a voice like being wrapped in a smoky blanket. We hope she'll keep on talking. Right now we want to be Emily Jerman's daughters more than anything else in the world.

The waiter brings our food, announcing each dish quietly, with a question, like he's trying to remind himself what it is. After each name, Mr. Jerman says, "Ah," and his wife laughs, a low, thrilling laugh, and we know we're going to have to spend all night in our motel room trying to imitate it exactly. She orders another double vodka.

"Dear," Mr. Jerman says, "who's going to help me drive for the next four hours?"

"We will," we say, reaching into our coat pockets for our driver's licenses. We hand them over to Emily Jerman, who looks at the pictures and then up at us, squinting her eyes to get the true likeness.

"Seventeen," she says. "Damn. I remember that." Then she laughs her low laugh—like a car's engine, we think, finely tuned.

Mr. Jerman hands around the dishes of steaming food. We still don't know what any of it is, but the smells are making us not care, they are like nothing we've ever known. We feel a little drunk now, chasing gobbets of meat and snaking onion around on our plates with these wooden knitting needles. A triangle of bright red flies from someone's plate and lands in Mr. Jerman's tea bowl, and grains of rice ring our placemats where we've let them fall. We lean our heads back and drip noodles into our mouths, noodles that taste like peanut butter. We lick the plum-sauce spoon. We take tiny little sips of tea. We watch Emily Jerman get looped.

"Seventeen. Oh, God, do I remember seventeen. It was before you," she says to her husband, leaning against him in that way that makes us stare at them with hard bright eyes. "I was at The Columbus School for Girls, can you imagine? Things were by the book then: no drinking gin at lunch, no blouses open down to here, no overnight trips. The goddamn earth was flat then. That's why it's called The Columbus School for Girls, to show how far you could go in the wrong direction."

"Emily," Mr. Jerman says, exactly the way he says the name in class, like he's a little afraid of it.

"Oh, don't Emily me, sweetheart," she says thrillingly, her low laugh like a runaway vehicle. "I'm just giving your girls some true history, that's all."

"What was it like?" we ask.

"The same, really. We read Emily Dickinson too. Or some of us did. 'A narrow fellow in the grass,' " she says, to prove it.

"What house did you live in?" we want to know.

"Cobalt," she says, naming a dormitory we've never heard of. "But the boiler exploded and it burnt to the ground ten years ago. Nobody likes to talk about it."

We glance over at Mr. Jerman, who seems lost to us, shaking his head.

"A girl nearly died," Emily Jerman says, looking us straight in the eye. "And the gardener did die. They were, you know, in her room. It was a big scandal. Hoo boy."

"Emily," Mr. Jerman says in a way that lets us know everything his wife is saying is true.

"He loved Emily Dickinson," Emily Jerman tells us.

"Who did?" her husband says. But we already know who she means.

"The gardener. He'd been to see her house. He had postcards. He gave me one."

"You never told me that." Bryan Jerman stares at his wife. Already we're miles ahead of him, and we can see it all: the girl who is Emily Jerman grown young, and the gardener there beside us, then the two bodies tangled together, singed, blackened by smoke.

"Fortune cookies!" Emily Jerman cries, clapping her hands. "We'll play fortune-cookie charades. It's just like regular charades, only when you get to the part about movie, book, or play, you do this."

She brings the palms of her hands together, pulls them in close to her chest, and bows from the waist. Mr. Jerman is smiling again, looking at his wife like he can't believe how clever she is. The fire, the girl, and the gardener drift from the table, guests taking their leave.

"A bit of mysterious East for you," the waiter says. "Many happy fortunes."

Look below the surface, truth lies within. Unusual experience will enrich your life. Positive attitude will bring desired result. Time is in your favor, be patient. The rare privilege of being pampered will delight you. The fun is just beginning, take it as it comes. Beware of those who stir the waters to suggest they are deep.

Our charades make Emily Jerman laugh until tears come to her eyes and run down her cheeks into her mouth. We watch her taste them and she watches us back, holding our eyes just as long as we hold hers. Then Mr. Jerman tells us it's time to get *on the road again,* singing it like Willie Nelson. Out in the parking lot he takes his wife's hand and presses it to his heart. Light from the Imperial Wok falls on their coats, turning black to tender purple.

"See?" he says, and together they look east to where the lights of Zanesville die away and there's only stars and West Virginia and Pennsylvania and finally the great darkness of western Massachusetts. We stare at them, our eyes going clean through their bodies. Then we look east too, but we can't for the life of us tell what they're seeing.

Hours later we wake to hear Emily Jerman singing along with the radio. "And when the birds fly south for a while," she sings, "oh, I wish that I could go. Someone there might warm this cold heart, oh, someone there might know." Her voice breaks on the last line, and we close our eyes again.

At the Holiday Inn in Harrisburg the Jermans unload us one by one, right into our rooms, right into bed. We stay awake as long as we can listening to Emily and Bryan Jerman in the next room, imagining we can hear the words and other sounds that pass between them when they're all alone.

In the morning it's Scranton, New York City, Hartford, and on into Amherst. Emily Jerman looks terrible, her hair hanging loose, her skin the color of old snow, but she drives first and Mr. Jerman takes over after lunch. Then she stares out the window. We think something has happened to her during the night. At first we believe it has to do with love, but soon we see how wrong we are, how lost, and for a split second we wish we'd never left The Columbus School for Girls. We've been moving east with Emily Jerman, weightless, like swimmers, but now she's holding on to our uniform skirts, and she's dragging us under. When we get to the Dickinson Homestead in the middle of the afternoon, the air is so wet with snow that we're having to breathe water, like the nearly drowned.

Emily Jerman hasn't said a word all day, but when we're all out of the van, she tells us she's going to stay put. She's been moving too fast, she says, and now she needs to sit for a while. Mr. Jerman hands her the keys, squeezes her knee, and leads us inside the house. We try to catch a glimpse of her out the window as we're standing beside Emily Dickinson's piano, listening to Mr. Jerman make introductions.

The tour guide tells us she is the wife of an English professor who studies Emily Dickinson, and for a whole year when they were first married, he would talk about her in his sleep. That, she explains, is how she learned most of what she knows about the poet, by listening in on her husband's dreams. She looks straight at Mr. Jerman.

"It's how most husbands and wives come to know anything at all," she says.

He stares back at her out of his great blue unblinking eyes, and for the first time ever, we think he looks bullish and stupid. It unhinges us, and we have to sit down on Emily Dickinson's chintz sofa.

The professor's wife keeps talking. She tells us what belongs to Emily Dickinson and what doesn't. She lets us touch a teacup and hold a pair of wine glasses the color of fresh blood. We feel as though they want to leap out of our hands and smash on the floor. We want to throw them down to get it over with, and we can almost feel their smooth coldness leaving our hands—the same way we think about standing up in Chapel and shouting out something terrible. Then we wonder if we haven't already done it. At that moment the back door opens, and Emily Jerman walks into the hall. The professor's wife drops the guest book and its spine breaks. Pages and pages of visitors wash over the floor.

"See, Bryan," Emily Jerman says to her husband, "I told you I shouldn't have come."

She picks up the pages of the guest book and walks over to the piano. She stays there with her back to us for a long time. We can tell that she is crying. We want Mr. Jerman to do something, but he stays with us, listening to the tour guide wander through all her dreamed facts, and we hate him for that.

Upstairs we see the dress and the bed, the writing table, the window that looks out over Main Street, the basket used to lower gingerbread down to children in the garden. We stick our noses inside like dogs and sniff to see if the smell of gingerbread is still there, and we tell each other that it is. When the guide's back is turned, we touch everything: the bed, the shawl, the hatbox, the dress, even the glass over the poet's soft silhouette.

We watch Emily Jerman move down the hall and into this room like she's walking in a trance. We see her eyes are red and her face is swollen. The professor's wife is talking about incontinence, and then about the Civil War, but we don't know how she got there. We watch Emily Jerman, more whisper than woman's body, a sensation in this house, a hot spirit distant from her husband and from us. We stare at the two of them, and all at once we know we will never remember anything Mr. Jerman has taught us, except this: that the world is a blind knot of electric and unspeakable desires, burning itself to nothing.

—

As we're leaving, the professor's wife makes us promise not to miss the graveyard, and we assure her we wouldn't dream of it, we tell her that we have already dreamed of it, just like her husband, and she tells us to button up our blouses. It's cold out, she says.

"We'll save that for tomorrow," Mr. Jerman says. "It's too dark now."

"Oh, no," Emily Jerman tells him, the light beginning to come back into her voice, "it's perfect now, perfect for a graveyard."

She takes the keys out of her coat pocket, unlocks the van for the rest of us, and gets in behind the wheel.

"I know the way," she says. "I already looked on the map."

Emily Jerman makes three left turns and we're in West Cemetery, where it's pitch dark. Mr. Jerman asks if she knows where the grave is, and she nods, but drives us once around all the graves anyway. When we come back to the entrance road, she pulls a hard left and drives up on the grass. There in front of the van's lights are three headstones behind a black wrought-iron fence.

Emily Jerman climbs down quickly and opens the van doors from the outside. We're surprised by how strong she is, how determined she is for us to be here. She leads us to the graves, pushing us a little from behind, pointing to the marker in the middle. "Called Back," it says. She shows us all the offerings there—dried flowers, coins, somebody's ballpoint pen with its red barrel looking like a swipe of blood.

" 'Just lost when I was found,' " Emily Jerman says behind us, " 'just felt the world go by, just girt me for the onset with eternity when breath blew black and on the other side I heard recede the disappointed tide.' "

"Saved," Mr. Jerman says. "It's *saved*, not found."

"Just lost when I was fucking *saved*, then," his wife calls back.
" 'Therefore as one returned I feel odd secrets of the line to tell.
Some sailor skirting foreign shores.' "

We've turned around to look for her, for Emily Jerman, but
she's standing in between the van's headlights, leaning back and
against the grille, so we can't see her, only the smoky mist her
breath makes in the cold as she speaks.

"Do another one," we say, but she won't.

"That's my favorite," she says. "It's the only one." She tells us
to leave something at the grave. She says it doesn't matter what.

There's nothing in our coat pockets but spare change, wrappers
from Starlight mints, and our driver's licenses. We don't know what
to do. We can feel panic beginning to take fire under our ribs, and
we look up first at the evening sky, clear and blue-black, then across
the street to the 7-Eleven, where the smell of chili dogs is billowing
out the doors. We lean over and take hold of the hems of our
Columbus School for Girls skirts. We find the seam and pull
sharply upward and then down, tearing a rough triangle out of the
bottom of the cloth. Cold air rushes in at our thighs and between
our legs.

"Girls!" Mr. Jerman says, but his voice gets lost in the sound of
his wife's laughter.

"What a waste," he says, but we tell him it isn't. At The Columbus School for Girls, sewing is compulsory, the needle in our sides,
and we know that with an extra tuck and the letting out of one pleat
at the other seam, our skirts will look exactly the same again.

At dinner Mr. Jerman hardly says a word while his wife orders
double vodkas and tells us more about her days at The Columbus
School for Girls.

"Those graduation dresses you have now," she says, "they were my idea."

We look at Mr. Jerman, who nods his head.

"I just couldn't stand the thought of black robes, and so I drew up a pattern and took it in to the headmaster, who's dead now, by the way, and what a blessing *that* is."

"What did he say?" we ask.

"He said absolutely no, he wasn't going to have a bunch of girls traipsing around in their nighties. He wanted us fully covered. But I went ahead and made one dress and wore it every day. Every day for all of March and most of April. I got detention every day, too, and served them all, and finally he gave in."

We wonder why Emily Jerman would now be passing the rest of her life at a place that had treated her so badly. We think she must love Bryan Jerman beyond reason. We can't imagine that she wants to go back tomorrow, not any more than we do.

"It was a beautiful place then," she says. "The gardens were kept up. Outside was like Eden. The gardener could do anything, bring anything back to life. He was a genius."

"Emily," Mr. Jerman says, "I believe you had a crush on that gardener."

"Darling," she says, "we thought you'd never guess, didn't we, girls?"

His laugh dies to a choking sound as his wife stares at him, breathing hard and smiling like she's just won a race. The silence is terrible, beating between them, but we won't break it. We want to watch and see how it will break itself.

"To the new girls," Emily Jerman says finally, toasting us with her third vodka.

We can see how, inside the glass, our own faces look back at us for a split second before they shatter into light and fire and gluey vodka running into Emily Jerman's mouth.

—

We don't know how long we've been asleep at the motel in Northampton when Mr. Jerman comes to wake us up. It's still dark outside. We have been dreaming, but we couldn't say about what. Mr. Jerman stands beside our beds and reaches out to turn on the lamp. When he can't find the switch, he takes a book of matches from his pocket, lights one, and holds it over our heads. We think maybe we have been dreaming about that, a tongue of flame hissing above us, or about everything that is going to happen now.

Mr. Jerman tells us to put on our shoes and socks, our coats over our nightgowns, and then he leads us outside, down to the parking lot where the motel's airport van is waiting. The heat inside is on high, so we can barely hear what passes between Mr. Jerman and the driver, except when he says he couldn't very well leave young girls alone in a motel, now, could he?

We know they're taking us back to Amherst, and when we pull into West Cemetery, we know why. There, exactly where Emily Jerman had parked it in the early evening, is our school van, the lights on, shining on the wrought-iron fence and the three head-stones behind it. Emily Jerman is standing behind the fence, her right hand curled around one of the thin black posts rising up to shoulder height.

Two West Cemetery guards stand off to her left, motionless, watching, their bodies balanced slightly ahead of their feet and their heads hung down as if they had been running and then had to stop suddenly to keep from going over the edge of the world.

"Girls," Emily Jerman says when she sees us standing with her husband. "Look at you, traipsing around in your nighties. How far do you think you're going to get in this world dressed like that? You have to learn how to keep warm. When I was your age, I learned how. When I was your age, I was on fire. On *fire,* do you understand?"

We do. We see the two bodies pressed close, Emily Jerman and the gardener who could bring almost anything back to life. We hear his whispering and smell her hair in flames.

Mist rises in front of the van's headlights. The cemetery ground between us and Mr. Jerman looks like it's burning, but this does not surprise us. It only makes us curious, like the night birds that rise now from the leaves to ask *whose fire? whose fire?* and then drop back to sleep.

We know what will happen next. Mr. Jerman will walk through this fire, and it won't consume him. He will move past us toward his wife, and we'll feel his breath as he passes, sweet and dangerously cold. This time, we'll look away when they touch. We won't have to see how they do it, or hear what words they use. We know what we need to know. This is the new world.

AISLE HELP

Carol Jane Shelley hates it when the brides-to-be come in with their husbands-to-be in tow. She'd much rather have the brides-to-be all by themselves so they could talk things over in private. She's come to know that the brides want her more for sympathy and consolation than for advice. All they want is to rail against their mothers-in-law awhile, say how awful the color aubergine is and how it's every damn where this year, including every single article of clothing in their mother-in-law's wardrobe. Sometimes they sit down and whisper how it's all turning out to be a bad idea. Their eyes fill with tears, and Carol Jane keeps the Kleenex handy for any bride who comes in pretending she's lost her voice. And once it happened that a boy was in to have his dating-service video done and an inconsolable bride-to-be looked up at him, and he at her, and damned if one wedding wasn't called off and the planning for another begun right there in the space of ten minutes. It was the kind of ten minutes Carol Jane used to live for. It justified her very being, and she'd go home at night and say to Bently, see, that's the reason to have a wedding consultant and a dating service under the same roof. We're going to have to expand the office.

Bently would just kiss her and shake his head. He would sit down in front of the television. She's happy, he would think to himself, and sometimes he felt that was all he wanted from his life.

Aisle Help is the name of Carol Jane's wedding-consultant and dating service. It was the name Bently came up with two years ago when they'd been in love for three months and Bently had decided to become Carol Jane's savior. She was doing temp work and trying to buy herself a car, but she wasn't saving much. Everything she made got spent on rent, the movies, dinners downstairs at El Azteca, and little presents for Bently—flannel shirts, cartoon mugs that gave useless advice. Bently decided he had to step in and pay off Carol Jane's credit card bills, and from then on she felt like she'd been reinvented. Then Bently sat her down and told her what she was good at: talking to people, herding groups around, visualizing stuff in her head, creating a scene.

"What do you mean, creating a scene?" she'd said.

"Just that," Bently had told her, calm as anything. "You can see how something's going to turn out before it's even started. I can too, like it's unrolling in front of you, like a movie. I've watched you when it's happening."

Carol Jane considered this for a moment and had to agree. "When I look at people, most of the time I don't see what they're doing right then, I see what they're about to do," she said. "It's kind of spooky. I live in the future, I guess."

And that's when Bently started coming up with names for a dating service and wedding-consultant business: Don't Do It, they said at first, laughing. Next, Just Say No. Then, Veiled Threats, Beware the Brides of March, and Brides Tread Revisited, specializing in remarriages. When Bently hit upon Aisle Help, Carol Jane felt another huge weight lifted off her shoulders.

She thinks about Bently now, imagines the future spread out between them and her own hands trying to reach across that gulf and bring him in closer. She shuts her eyes tight against the rest of what she sees.

Tonight Carol Jane hands Bently a check for two hundred dollars.

"The last of it," she says, smiling and trying to look him in the eye.

"Almost two years to the day," Bently says. "I have to tell you, honey, when I loaned you that money, I thought it was the last I'd see of it. I thought, she'll take this, and in the morning, it'll be *hasta la vista*."

"Here I am, still," Carol Jane says, thinking how the words taste like pennies in her mouth. She looks at the parts of Bently's face she used to love, and now the cut of his chin, the rise of his left cheekbone makes her sick, but she doesn't know why. She feels that with this check she's handing him back his heart. Why do people fall out of love? People with no good reason to?

She wonders this in the gigantic quiet between them, wonders when exactly she got tired of Bently and his ways, which aren't bad compared to some ways she's heard of. He doesn't drink much or chase after other women. He's mostly soft-spoken and kind. She wishes she had a sister because then she might fix her up with Bently and send them happily down the aisle. She thinks Bently is better than she deserves, thinks the words "good catch." Carol Jane is starting to operate in the language of her brides-to-be, and it scares her. She knows it means she should take her own best advice.

⎯

"I still don't understand why you want me to do this," Bently says as he sits down in a chair opposite the video camera. He's come into Aisle Help in the middle of the afternoon on his day off, a little drunk.

"Because I'm not very busy today, and you always said you wanted to see how the whole show works," Carol Jane says, "and I'd like to have a video of you to keep around."

"So you can play it three times an hour when you miss me."

"That's right. And maybe show it to the girls who come in here."

The light runs out of Bently's face.

"Why would you want to do that?"

"No reason," Carol Jane says, hiding behind the camera's one good eye. She's had the crazy idea of showing Bently's video to some of her customers. Maybe they'd call him. He's joked about it himself. She thinks that would certainly be going out with a bang, closing the business and auctioning off the last man to the highest bidder.

"How can you run a place like this," he says out of the blue, with his back to her, "and not be married yourself?"

"How can you run a slaughterhouse and not go under the knife every day? It's about as logical."

Today, though, is a bad day to be talking about marriage. Bently's spent the afternoon in the bar at El Azteca. While Carol Jane sights in the camera, he comes up behind her and bumps his hips against her backside. It makes her feel warm, flustered. She can smell beer on him, that soft, sour smell, like a baby.

Why in the world don't I love you anymore, she thinks, and then whirls around to look at Bently, afraid this time she's said it out loud. Bently has his hands crossed over his heart. She directs him to the client's chair, sits down across from him, and punches the remote-control button. She hears the video camera click on.

"Tell me a little about yourself," she says, "starting with your name and occupation."

"I'm Bently Harrison," he begins, "and I'm a pharmacist. At the Treasury Drug in Brookhaven."

He looks away from the camera at Carol Jane and grins.

"That's for anybody who wants to get a look at me in my native habitat," he says.

"Never had anybody do that before. Not a bad idea," Carol Jane says. "Now. What do you like about your job?"

"Mostly everything," Bently says, his eyes moving off Carol Jane's face. "I like mixing and counting. I like the way the pills look moving through the dosage counter and out the chute, and the noise they make going into their plastic bottles. There's something reliable-sounding about it. I guess that's pretty dumb."

He looks at Carol Jane.

"We'll edit that part out," she says. "Now, tell me what you like to do for fun."

"You know what," Bently says.

"Tell it to the folks at home," Carol Jane says, trying to be playful, trying to make a joke, pointing over her shoulder at the video camera.

"I like to read spy novels, watch TV, and play pool, especially with Carol Jane's family, who are good sports but take their shots too fast. I like to fish."

"What do you look for in a companion?"

"Are we talking male or female?"

"Either. Both, actually, might be helpful."

"In a male companion, I look for somebody who's like me. In a female companion, I look for somebody who's like you."

"Who?"

"You."

"Me?"

"You."

Carol Jane isn't sure whether this will make Bently sound charming or desperate. She decides she'll need to do some fancy footwork with the fast-forward.

"What qualities would you look for in the perfect mate?"

"Yours," Bently says, smiling wildly into the camera.

"What made you come into Aisle Help today?"

"You were here. I knew I'd find you here."

The telephone rings in Carol Jane's office. She flips off the remote and tells Bently she'll be right back.

In her office she picks up the receiver and hears the dial tone. She sits for a long time with the phone held to her ear, listening to the buzz, until it turns to a high squeal. The sound reminds her of the voice of a former bride-to-be who called off her wedding and sent the ring back to the groom C.O.D. She didn't even insure it, and she wrote "costume jewelry" where the mailing receipt asked for the contents of package. Carol Jane told Bently this story, and they laughed about it, about the way the bride-to-be said she just didn't feel good about the groom anymore.

"I hate this business," she says out loud. She stands beside her desk with the phone still pressed to her cheek, moving it slowly to feel its warmth. "I made it up from nothing, I'm good at it, and I hate it."

She crosses the hall and stops in front of the waiting-room door, checking to see if there are any walk-in customers, even though she knows there won't be. Most people wouldn't think of walking in to a dating service or to see a wedding consultant. It's always premeditated, she thinks, and then the phrase "like murder" comes into her head. She turns and moves slowly back down the hall toward the video room, listening to the noise of her heels on the wood floor.

In the taping room Bently smiles up at her, a smile that's about to turn into a laugh until he gets a good look at her face.

"Bad news?" he says.

"A wedding called off by the bride," she says.

"Traumatic?"

"Bently," Carol Jane says, "I have to tell you something." She leans against the doorjamb and crosses her arms over her chest. "I don't know about us anymore. I just don't know. It isn't working out."

"What do you mean?" he says, half rising out of his chair. "What isn't working out? Tell me."

"I don't know. We aren't compatible."

"What do you mean, we're not compatible? I always thought we were. You always acted like we were."

"You care about details, and I don't give a shit. You save money and I spend it. You want to stay in this town, and I'm dying to get the hell out. Your parents don't like me. They think all I wanted you for was to loan me money to open this stupid goddamn business, which I now detest."

"And you're about to prove them right."

"Is that what you think too?"

"Listen," Bently says, closing his eyes and shaking his head from side to side. "This is all too much, being bushwacked this way. I'm going home now. We'll talk about it there. You finish up your day and come home. Then we'll straighten things out."

"I don't know," she says.

"You know why you hate this business?" Bently says. "Because you're always on the outside. You're always just the architect. You never get to live in the house."

—

Bently moves in with his sister, O.J., and her husband in Brookhaven, where it's an easy walk to Treasury Drug. He spends his first days away from Carol Jane trying to think of everything that might have gone wrong.

"Maybe it isn't anything you did," O.J. says.

"It's never what you do, it's what you leave undone," says Steve, O.J.'s husband. "Nine divorce cases out of ten, the wife wants to plead neglect, until we can come up with something juicier."

"You win those cases?" Bently says.

"Steve always wins," O.J. says. She crosses the kitchen to stand in front of her husband and adjusts his tie. They're exactly the same height, and the ends of their noses touch. Then she places her hands under his elbows and lifts him six inches off the floor. She does this twice, then lets him back down and gives him a kiss. Bently thinks what a strange couple they make, his sister the body-builder and her husband the lawyer.

"Come with us to the gym after work," Steve says to Bently, who nods his head once. "You look like you could use a little exercise. Take your mind off things."

Steve offers him a ride to Treasury Drug, but Bently says no, he'd rather walk. At the bottom of the driveway, though, he regrets it. This is the neighborhood Carol Jane grew up in, and they've been through it together a thousand times, wandering the streets, the lake, and the golf course, talking about how they'd grow old together. She'd have her gray hair caught at the nape of her neck and walk ahead silently, while he'd be always running to catch up with her, always jabbering, trying to get her attention and keep it.

These thoughts make him sad. He imagines the nape of Carol Jane's neck and how it spreads out to make her shoulders. She insisted it wasn't a neck right there, but a throat. It was a prettier word, he'd agreed, a word that served her better.

Just west of Peachtree Street Bently crosses through the parking lot of Dunkin' Donuts, where he and Carol Jane sat in his car on Christmas Eve two years ago and exchanged presents. He gave her ten silver dollars, one each for the weeks since they'd met. Now he forgets if it really was ten. Forgetting makes him sad. Remembering makes him sad.

"But what else is there?" he says outside the mirrored glass doors of Treasury Drug. He believes it's the wisest thought he's ever had.

The checkout girl, Mary Wayne Johnson, is already sitting on her high stool behind the cash register. She looks up when Bently comes in, says hey, and pretends to go back to her book, but Bently can feel her eyes on him all the way past stationery, gifts, and greeting cards to the pharmacy counter. He knows she has a kind of crush on him. On her break she always wanders back to the pharmacy to ask about generic brands, dosages, new drugs, what's being tested. All day long she'll call on the intercom phone with customers' questions, instead of letting them talk to him directly. This makes his work much more confusing than it has to be, but Bently puts up with it for reasons he doesn't quite understand. She interests him in a vague way. She always dresses completely in black, in stirrup pants and turtlenecks, or sleeveless T-shirts in warm weather. She wears large bright earrings and bracelets made of papier-mâché or stuff that looks like machine parts. Though she wears no makeup herself, women often ask Mary Wayne Johnson to suggest shades of blush and lipstick. She's told Bently she's an art history major at Oglethorpe University, and she knows color. She brings huge art books to work, books full of glossy reproductions.

Today, during her morning coffee break, Mary Wayne Johnson comes into Bently's office carrying one of these art books.

"Dalí," she says. "Salvador Dalí. You know him?"

Bently nods. "He does those clocks," he says. "The ones that ooze. And crutches."

"Very good," Mary Wayne Johnson says, smiling. "Look what I found."

She shows him a two-page glossy, "Pharmacist of Ampurdan in Search of Absolutely Nothing."

"Does this look like anything to you?" she asks. "I mean, why is this guy a pharmacist?"

"Probably because he can't do anything else," Bently says, surprising himself.

"Oh, we are very happy today, aren't we? What's wrong? Trouble with the wife and kids?"

Bently knows it's just her way to chatter like this, but he feels like he's going to cry. He turns his swivel chair away from her and skates it across the floor to the filing cabinet, his legs kicking wildly. He pulls open a drawer, pretending to look for a prescription file, but it's the wrong drawer, and he comes face-to-face with Carol Jane's picture. Suddenly his office is very bright and too hot.

"It's okay," Mary Wayne Johnson says. "It's okay, but you let me know if I can do anything."

Bently hears her leave the office, closing the door quietly, her bracelets jangling on the other side.

That afternoon, as he's filling a new prescription for birth control pills, Bently starts to wonder if Carol Jane's fallen in love with somebody else, and in a huge leap of unreason he thinks maybe this prescription in his hands right now is really for her, only under an assumed name. As he counts out the four foil packets, he curses each one, 28 days of placebos, 56 days, 84, 112, and then he feels ashamed.

"Bently," Mary Wayne Johnson is standing beside him, handing over a small plastic package, "these just came from the main office. You should have a couple extra to take home for your old lady."

It's a metal button for employees' lapels, blue with white lettering. TREASURY DRUG, it says. I'LL HELP.

He turns to look at Mary Wayne Johnson, then bends slightly forward to kiss her on the mouth. She looks surprised, then shakes her head slowly, just once. Bently wonders if she means he shouldn't have done that.

"Thanks," he says. "You think of everything." He forms a sentence about Mary Wayne Johnson taking all the pun out of his life, but he doesn't dare say it out loud.

After work Bently meets O.J. and Steve at the health club in the basement of Piedmont Hospital. O.J. has a free membership because she's hospital staff, and she can have one guest a year. They meet at the registration desk, O.J. still in her whites. Bently thinks how in a nurse's uniform she looks like a normal woman, how no one would ever picture the rippling quads, delts, triceps, biceps, and—even if she is his sister—gluteals. She's been known to lift uncooperative male patients off the ground and carry them into the OR, though that was back in her days as an emergency-room nurse. Since then she's changed her specialty to neonatal care, but she says she could still bench-press a hundred newborns if push ever came to shove.

When they go into the weight room, Bently sees it's empty except for Mary Wayne Johnson, sitting with her arms slung over the bars of the military press. As soon as he realizes it's her, Bently feels naked, and he turns to face the mirror. She's staring at her own reflection, but when she does notice him, she pulls her head back in a gesture of surprise, then smiles and stands up, unhooking her arms from the machine.

Bently takes O.J. by the arm and guides her across the weight room to make introductions.

"Mary Wayne Johnson?" O.J. says. "Great name, a name with a secret."

"Yeah," she says, "on their first date, my parents went to see *True Grit,* and even in the dark it was love at first sight."

She turns to face Bently.

"I've never seen you here before."

"I've never been here before," he tells her. "My sister's the one with the membership."

"Well," Mary Wayne Johnson says, giving Bently a jab in the ribs, "don't try to do it all in one day."

"Never fear," O.J. says. "I'm a nurse."

"Good thing," Mary Wayne Johnson smiles. "He's kind of fragile."

"Don't I know it," O.J. says.

Women have this language, Bently thinks, knowing he's not onto anything new. It's all theirs, and if you're a man, you can't ever hope to understand it. Sometimes you can overhear a phrase or two when a woman is dreaming, but for most of your life as a man, you're shit out of luck. He watches O.J. work her way around the weight machines, trying to remember the ways they talked to each other when they were kids, growing up in the same house, eating the same food, trying to outwit all the same people.

He notices O.J. change the hydraulic pressure on the machines with no disgust or show. Everybody can see she's the strongest person in this room. At the end of her second set of bench presses she rolls her eyes at Bently, and he smiles back, rolling his eyes the same way. Seeing his sister in her element fills Bently with a wave of helpless love for Carol Jane. He lifts the free weights in both hands, feeling the muscles in his forearms and biceps tense and defy resistance. Mary Wayne Johnson crosses the room to stand in front of him.

"I could hear your heartbeat from over across the room," she says, smiling.

"Sure thing," Bently says back.

"Really," Mary Wayne Johnson says. "It gets louder as the blood comes pumping in. The loudest ones are always the best."

—

Carol Jane misses Bently sometimes, and then not. She misses him mostly at night, for his presence, the large fact of him in bed next to her. She's seen in catalogs where you can buy a Bed-mate, a full-body pillow to have next to you while you sleep. In the ads there's always a woman hanging on to her Bed-mate for dear life. Carol Jane hates the ad, hates it especially that the woman is wearing a wedding ring, and that the photographer has arranged things so that her ring catches all the light in the room. She thinks sometimes of calling the catalog's 800 number and ordering the damn Bed-mate just so she won't have to look at the ad anymore.

She's thinking about Bently and the Bed-mate now, standing in the doorway of her old room, staring at the bed she used to sleep in before she moved into her own apartment. She's come over to her parents' house for dinner, take-out pizza, and then they're all going to play pool. She's steeling herself to lose graciously. Bently was the only person able to beat the team of her father and mother. Part of Carol Jane wants to go call Bently and invite him to come along. He could be here in five minutes, from just across the golf course at his sister's house. She's suddenly overcome by the memory of having crushes on boys in high school and trying to figure out ways to bump into them without making it seem like anything more than an accident.

When she hears the doorbell ring, Carol Jane wanders back into her mother's kitchen. Six months ago she had a dating-service client, a painter who delivered pizzas at night, after it was too dark to work on his canvases. Even though she knows it's a long shot, she thinks maybe he'll be the one delivering their pizza tonight. She's felt in the last half hour, since she phoned in the order, a kind of aching need to see Mike Fiumi the painter, to take him as a sign of her success, her ability to do right by somebody, even if not by Bently. Mike Fiumi was the best client she'd ever had. He found his dream girl so fast Carol Jane felt obliged to cut his fee in half. And he called Carol Jane back twice, after the first date and again four weeks later, to say they weren't rushing into anything, Mike and his dream girl, but he knew she was the one, and that without Aisle Help he never would have found her. He sends Carol Jane coupons for free pizzas about once a month. They are using one of those coupons tonight. She suddenly wants to go watch Mike's dating-service video, to see what one half of true love looks like, and then maybe she'd watch the video of Mike's dream girl, study them both, figure out how hearts can work not like machines but like motion, like irresistible force.

After supper Carol Jane, her parents, her brother, and his wife drive to Buckhead Billiards. Carol Jane rides with Jimmy and Linda, whose wedding she planned three months ago. Linda, Carol Jane thinks, is wise without having the faintest idea that's what she is. She knows exactly how to handle Jimmy. She tells him to stop whining, then picks up his hand and kisses the palm. She does everything without guile. She once told Carol Jane that marriage was 50 percent work and 50 percent future returns.

"Marriage is a rock and a hard place," she'd say, or "Marriage is two blind people walking along the edge of a cliff. Marriage is Christmas morning."

She didn't explain that one, but she knew she didn't have to.

Tonight in the car, Carol Jane stares at the back of Linda's head and thinks her to be even wiser than usual.

"We have to psych them out," Linda is saying to Jimmy. "We have to destroy their concentration."

"Or we're going to be like lambs at slaughter," Jimmy says. "What did Bently used to do to beat them?"

"He was just good," Carol Jane says, "that's all it ever was."

Since Bently's not there to even out the teams, they play two against three, Carol Jane's parents against their children and their daughter-in-law. Carol Jane's father is not a man given to conversation, except when he plays pool; then he lets out bits and pieces about his days in Chicago pool halls.

"The Jeffery," he says to his wife. "Remember that one?"

She nods and starts to name the people they played with.

"Did you ever lose, Dad?"

"Never."

When his wife goes to the ladies' room, Carol Jane's father lowers his voice.

"The only time I lost bad," he says, looking at Linda, "was playing with a woman. We called her Jeffery Lou because that's where she played. She was always alone. I was there that one night without your mother, and I got nervous."

Carol Jane doesn't want to hear any more, not why her father was there without her mother, not what it was about Jeffery Lou that made him nervous. She feels herself on the brink of something terrible, and so she steps back to lean against the wall and hold her beer bottle up to her forehead. Her mother comes out of the ladies' room and looks at the faces of her husband and her children. She looks at Linda last.

"You all look guilty," she says. "You've been moving things around."

—

When Carol Jane leaves her parents' house, she drops in at Aisle Help. All evening she's had to fight off the desire to go watch Mike Fiumi's video and Bently's, the one they never finished, and now she's lost the battle.

Inside the office it's pitch black and too hot, smelling vaguely of Mexican food from El Azteca downstairs. Carol Jane moves to the window and opens it even before she turns on the lights. She leans sideways, facing into the cooler night air and allowing herself a view of the parking-lot entrance. She has a notion that Bently will drive in. He'll get out of his car and stand in the parking lot, looking up at her. For a few minutes, longer than either of them might have expected, they won't say anything. Then Bently will come upstairs to her office. Carol Jane doesn't know what will happen after that, but she thinks whatever she and Bently say to each other, the words will be exactly the ones each of them needs to hear.

She turns on the light in her office, then walks down the hall to the video library, a six-foot-deep walk-in closet with wall-to-wall shelving. The videocassettes are arranged alphabetically, Fiumi a little to her left and Harrison just about dead center, opposite the door. Carol Jane picks out the two tapes, feeling their heft in her palm, as if they're a measure of food or drink. She walks across the hall into the video room and slips the first cassette into the tape player, then sits down in front of the television set. When Mike Fiumi's face blossoms onto the screen, she gasps in spite of herself.

"Tell me a little about yourself," she hears her own voice coming from where she sits off-camera, sounding high-pitched, like a child's, "starting with your name and occupation."

"I'm Mike Fiumi," Mike is saying, "and I'm a painter. I do mostly still lifes and landscapes. Houses too."

"Houses?" Carol Jane's voice says.

"The outsides, like with ladders and cans of Pittsburgh Paints. Sandblasting and weatherstripping. I also deliver pizzas at night."

She switches videos, from Fiumi to Harrison, and fast-forwards through Bently's questions. Bently looks away from the camera, and right then Carol Jane freezes the frame. She walks over to the television to get a closer look at his face, stilled that way, a way she's never seen it before now, except when he's asleep, and then his eyes are closed. Six inches from the set, she can make out herself reflected in Bently's pupils. She's amazed at her own smallness, and to see herself this way makes her think of an incubus or a succubus or the devil that might sit on your shoulder and whisper into your ear. She unfreezes Bently, and she can see her reflection move in his eyes, nodding for him to go on.

"That's for anybody who wants to get a look at me in my native habitat," he's saying.

"Never had anybody do that before. Not a bad idea," Carol Jane says. "Now. What do you like about your job?"

"Mostly everything," Bently is saying, his eyes moving back to the camera. "I like mixing and counting. I like the way the pills look moving through the dosage counter and out the chute, and the noise they make going into their plastic bottles. There's somethng reliable-sounding about it. I guess that's pretty dumb."

Carol Jane fast-forwards.

"In a female companion, I look for somebody who's like you."

"Who?"

"You."

"Me?"

"You."

"What qualities would you look for in the perfect mate?"

"Yours."

"What made you come into Aisle Help today?"

"You were here. I knew I'd find you here."

There's the distant sound of a telephone ringing, and Carol Jane knows this is where they stopped filming. Bently's face dies away, but only for a second.

"Surprise," his voice is saying. "You're still on the phone, so I thought I'd keep going. I'm not sure why you wanted to do this, but there are some things you need to remember. Remember who named this place and remember how. Remember my name. Bently Harrison. Say it, no, whisper it, to yourself. Right now. Remember how many times I've asked you the question I'm about to ask again right now. Will you marry me? Remember what Linda says, marriage is a rock and a hard place. Remember that I'm the rock. Remember not to take your shots so fast."

When the TV screen goes dark, Carol Jane imagines it's Bently leaving the room. She thinks of him going the way night goes, not in big pieces so you can see it happen. You feel it go little by little, maybe like blood feels draining out of your veins, hard to put back in, but not impossible.

WHO IT
REALLY WAS

I'd never have believed a girl like Eileen Neal could fall in love with a boy like B. T. Washington Kemp, in a town like Atlanta, Georgia, but she did, and fast, like she wanted it to have already happened before anybody caught on and made a move to stop her. In the end she stopped herself, but not in time. And she didn't stop me, though I think she knew she couldn't. Eileen and I, like most of the girls we grew up with, have long histories of secret love. We all learned early to dissemble, to digress, to live for the cover of darkness. We might call you on the phone, just to hear your voice, then hang up without speaking a word. We would never wear our hearts on our sleeves or give out our names to strangers, and so I will not give you mine.

B. T. Kemp was a new boy in the senior class at my brother's school. I heard about him because my brother always made any new kid, no matter how old, his personal mission. He had a soft spot for them, for the way they stood in the middle of the cafeteria on their first day, mesmerized by the spoons and forks, looking like lunch was something they didn't have at the old school. He thought new kids were exotic. He took them to be messages from other worlds, and he'd talk for hours about their accents, their clothes, their haircuts. That fall the new kids were a big part of Harry's report to me, which he gave daily, since for the the first time in our lives we were at different schools. We had come to be a distraction to each other, the teachers at my school said, mainly because I liked to pull him out of class whenever I thought he needed fresh air. And he needed it often. Every time I'd glance into his homeroom, he'd have this look on his face like he was choking, and I'd say, excuse me, Miss Brandau, can I talk to my brother? And she'd start to say no, but he'd be halfway to the door, and then there was no stopping us. My school had grown even more afraid of brother-sister teams after a pair of them called in a bomb threat one day when there was a test they hadn't studied for. We never worried about tests, Harry and I. Tests are the easy part. It's what you have to learn on your own that causes all the trouble.

From what I heard, B. T. Kemp wasn't the average new kid. He arrived suddenly and late, in October, and then he was from Boston, Massachusetts, a city that might as well have been on another planet. Harry told me this new kid said he knew some Latin, and the first thing he did was drive down to the state Latin contest in Macon, unofficially, and then he won three first prizes. Eileen was there too, but she never mentioned it until later.

"He looks like he'd know Latin," Harry said. "He has a kind of foreign way about him."

B.T. explained to everybody his initials stood for Booker Taliaferro, and the guys started calling him "The Book." Harry said B.T. just smiled and shook his head.

The other seniors asked B. T. Kemp over to their houses on Saturdays, but he always said he had work to do at home. For a while we thought he was just shy, then that gave way to thinking he'd heard what everybody was saying about him. News like that travels fast. Harry said it made you take a long look at him, and then you'd come around to believing it was true, that B.T.'s mother was a white woman who had married a black man, and not long before B.T. and his mother showed up in Atlanta, his mother had left his father standing alone between Northern Avenue and Castle Island, where the Charles River empties out into Boston Harbor. I know the exact location because I've stood there myself and listened to B. T. Kemp call Eileen's name out to sea. And that's where I left him too, with my name caught in his throat, rising to his lips, maybe, by now, lifting him over the stars.

Eileen wouldn't go anywhere with us that fall. It used to be we always spent our Saturdays together, Eileen and I, Eileen's older brother Jerry, and Kayann Norris, who'd been Jerry's true love since third grade. Jerry said Eileen slipped out of the house early Saturday mornings, walked off up the street toward town, and stayed gone until supper.

"I have to get away by myself and think," she said whenever Kayann and I asked where she'd been.

"Think about what?" we said.

"I don't know. The future. Don't you ever need to think about the future?"

"Come on, Eileen," Kayann said. "You know and we know it's not the future."

"You don't think I'm telling you the truth?"

Kayann looked at me, rolled her eyes, and we let it drop. We were standing at the bottom of the driveway, watching Eileen walk back up the hill toward her house. I was struck by this picture of her, struck deep in my heart by the sadness of it. Even after Kayann turned away, my eyes still followed Eileen's white blouse as it grew fainter and fainter, a light dimming by small degrees until it opened up again into the front door of her house, then went out for good.

"Those Neals," Kayann said finally. "I don't know if there's any sense in that family." She meant Eileen, but I knew she was also thinking about Jerry. "Jerry's got this idea in his head these days," she went on. "Now, don't fly off the handle or yell." She stopped walking and turned to face me. "He wants us to elope. It's so we can be together and all, but there's more to it than that. He says if we don't do something now, we'll be headed down this one road for the rest of our lives."

"Kayann, are you crazy?" I did yell, there in the dark. "You aren't going to do it, are you?"

"I imagine it all the time. I hate the thought of everything laid out in front of me like a map. You know what I mean, the kind of life where the most important thing is having a flat stomach. Sometimes I can see it coming at me like a freight train."

"I think you're nuts."

We were walking back to Kayann's house, cutting through side yards and scuffing the leaves under our feet. There'd been a spell of Indian summer the last few days, warm weather hanging on for dear life in what was supposed to be the beginning of winter. You waited for the chill to snap back into the air, waited and waited, laying out heavy sweaters and long socks at night, knowing full well the weather would break the one day you weren't prepared.

"You surprise me," Kayann said sharply, then the tone of her voice eased up. "I heard about two kids at North Fulton who eloped, and it's stuck in my mind all these years. I even remember their names were Angel and Angie. Angel was the boy and he was ROTC, which you might not have thought. The way it went was they left on a Saturday morning and drove to a town called Hollywood, Georgia, way inside the Chattahoochee National Forest. They lied about Angie's age and asked around until they found somebody who'd marry them. It was a justice of the peace who was also a retired ship's captain. Ship's captains are just as good as justices for marrying, and they knew that. These weren't your average high school kids. They'd been around, they'd seen *Love Boat.*"

She jabbed me in the ribs, and her laugh came out sounding like a bark.

"Anyways, they went back to their parents' houses like nothing had happened. Then on Monday at school they told everybody and Angie showed off her wedding band, which was Angel's school ring turned around backward. Of course it got back to their parents, and boy, you can just imagine. But they wouldn't get it annulled, and since she was seventeen and he hadn't taken her across state lines, there wasn't much anybody could do."

"But you and Jerry wouldn't come back."

"No, we couldn't. We'd move up north."

"Where? Out in the woods?"

"Maybe," she said. "It can be done. I heard a story about the troggs, these kids in England who left civilization and went to live in caves. Troggs for troglodytes. They had a whole society, and they were happy for years, until somebody discovered them and tried to bring them back."

"Seems like you've heard a lot of stories."

"That's right," Kayann said. Her voice was blade-sharp again, but then it softened like before. "Seems like all I do these days is hear stories about people and file them away for later."

When we got to the Norrises' yard, Jerry was waiting for us. He said hello to me and reached out to touch Kayann on the arm. It was only for a moment, like he wanted to make sure she was flesh and blood. *Hey, you,* he whispered, and then his hand dropped back down to his side. Kayann wondered out loud if we should do anything about Eileen, but Jerry said no, sooner or later she'd tell us what she was up to, or else we'd figure it out for ourselves. We headed off in different directions, me up to Roswell Road and the two of them back into the woods behind Kayann's house. After I'd hiked twenty yards, something made me turn and watch them move along the edge of the trees. The evening opened up like it was a door, and I could see the moonish glow of Jerry's blond hair, but I couldn't make out Kayann at all.

When Mrs. Neal called me up to talk about Eileen and where she'd been disappearing to, it was almost a relief, even though I didn't have much to tell her.

"All right, then, fine," she said like she didn't think she should believe me, "I can appreciate a confidence between you, but please just tell me one thing. Has she said anything to you about colleges? Do you know for sure if she's sent off for any applications?"

I said I was sure she had. I remembered seeing her carrying an armload of college bulletins and application forms. We all got them from the school counselor, more than we could hope to keep track of. We were always dropping them in the halls, leaving them in the cafeteria or at each other's houses. They were getting to be a kind of trail we'd laid out for ourselves.

Mrs. Neal's voice sounded tiny and strangled as she talked on about Eileen. I was standing in the kitchen watching my mother make out her grocery list and search through a black-and-red wallet for discount coupons. She held up one for cereal, and I gave her the thumbs-down.

"You used to love that kind," she whispered, and she was right. There were whole years when I wouldn't eat anything else.

I started thinking about those years, partly because Mrs. Neal was talking about them into my other ear. She was saying this was all funny to her because we never used to be out of each other's sight, Eileen and me.

Before school we'd get coffee at the Majik Market, and those little boxes of cereal. You could slit open the box and the foil liner, pour in the milk, and eat it that way. Instead of milk, we used the coffee creamers, since they didn't cost anything. There were plastic spoons in a tub on the checkout counter. We'd eat leaning against the back bumper of somebody's car, watching traffic make the turn onto Northside Parkway, imagining ourselves free of home, of school, free of our sixteen-year-old lives, even free of each other.

My mother stood at the back door making signs to tell me she was going to the store. When I waved, she smiled and held up her left hand, fluttering the thumb against the tips of the other four fingers the way people do when they're telling you about somebody who talks too much.

After Mrs. Neal said goodbye, I lay back on the kitchen table and closed my eyes. The house was perfectly still. The Formica's coolness slowly worked its way through my shirt to my spine. I was trying not to think about anything, not Eileen or Jerry and Kayann, not the rest of our lives. Far away, up on Peachtree, there was the metallic ring of a man's voice coming through a loudspeaker. I couldn't hear what he was saying, but it must have been important. I wondered that his voice could be carried so far, through so many trees, and it seemed to me then that if only I could hear those words, they might keep me from breaking apart inside. I thought I'd never felt so empty as I did at that moment, and it made me dizzy, so that I snapped open my eyes, hoping that the light of my mother's kitchen might fill me back up.

Harry was standing in the doorway watching me. I asked him one of those stupid questions, like how come he wasn't outside on such a nice day, just to make sure my voice still worked, and he blinked and wrinkled his forehead like I was speaking in a foreign tongue.

"I miss you getting me out of class all the time," he said.

"It wasn't all the time," I said back, hating the mean sound of my voice, and then trying to make up for it. "Only every other day."

"We about drove them crazy," he said. "Didn't we?"

I sat up on the table and took a good look at Harry. He had come all the way into the kitchen and was leaning against the wall by the telephone, staring like he could see right through my skin, deep into my heart and hear all its sad talk.

"A kind of funny thing happened yesterday," Harry said. "Remember B. T. Kemp?"

I nodded.

"He asked if I knew you."

"What did you say?"

"I said yes."

"What's funny about that?"

"Then he asked what you were like."

I thought Harry would start smiling then, but he didn't. I shrugged my shoulders and stared off past his face, waiting to hear the rest.

"I think he has a crush on you," Harry said.

"He doesn't even know me."

"Mom and Dad will go berserk if they find out."

Harry had just learned to appreciate the word *berserk,* and he used it for everything, whether he needed to or not.

"Just calm down. He doesn't have any crush on me. He's never even seen me."

"Oh," Harry said, not believing it for a second.

"What else did he say?"

"That's about it. He hangs around my locker a lot, though."

Right then I wanted to cry. All along this is what Harry really intended to tell me, that he had a new friend, a new kid, the best of all the new kids. I was glad for him, and then sorry for myself, mysteriously robbed first of Eileen and then of Harry. The thought made me lie back down on the table and cover my face with my arm.

Then there was a knock on the door and Eileen's voice muffled through the glass, asking if I was okay. When I got up to let her in, she walked past us, through the kitchen and down the hall to my bedroom, and I followed. She closed the door and sat down on my bed with her back against the wall and her calves and feet hanging over the side. She wrapped her arms around the pillow and pressed her left cheek against it, her face turned away from me. It was then that she told me about B. T. Kemp.

She said he wasn't like anybody she'd ever known or would ever know in this life or any other. She was sure of it, had been sure since she first laid eyes on him at the Latin contest where he walked off with all those first prizes. She told me she knew all about his mother and his father, and it didn't make any difference.

"But it will make a big difference to Daddy. And Mother too. She won't say anything, but she won't have to. He'll do all the talking."

There was nothing for me to tell her. I knew she was right.

"Of all of us," Eileen said, "you, me, Kayann, I was always the biggest snob. Stay with your own kind, I used to say, right along with everybody else. It's like I just woke up. Everybody says there's all these rules you have to live by, but it isn't true. You get right up close to breaking one of them, and you find out there isn't a rule, just empty space."

I was thinking how in all the years we'd known each other, I had never once seen Eileen cry. Filled with tears, her eyes got to be the blue of a doll's eyes, the kind that are painted on the face, not set in and glittery, but all blue hardness and no depth. All that time in my bedroom she didn't close her eyes once or put her hands over her face. She kept looking at me; even when I walked across the room to get her a wad of Kleenex, I could feel her eyes watching for some kind of sign. When I sat back down beside her, the weight of our bodies knocked us shoulder to shoulder, and we stayed that way without moving apart. When I finally did move, her eyes were still on me, even as she asked if it was all a hopeless mess she'd fallen into. I stared back into that impenetrable blue and lied, and told her nothing was ever hopeless.

We still didn't meet B. T. Kemp until Thanksgiving, actually the day after, in Chastain Park. When he got out of the car, I understood what Eileen meant when she said B. T. Kemp was not like anybody in this life or any other. And I fell in love with him myself, right then. There was a beautiful confusion about his face, like his features had been thrown from a distance and hadn't quite settled yet. His hair and skin were exactly the same shade, a deep caramel color that made him seem like he'd feel warm wherever you touched him.

"You're Harry's sister," he said to me. "I'd know you anywhere."

"I'd know you anywhere too," I said.

"Kind of a shock, isn't it?" he said to all of us, "that it's me, and I'm flesh and blood?"

It sounds mean to repeat it now, but that's not how B. T. Kemp intended those words. He was referring to himself as Eileen's long-held secret, not as the half-black boy who might have shocked us and would certainly shock our parents if they ever found out about him. All that afternoon in the park he kept his arm around Eileen's shoulders, and he told story after story about Harry— Harry in class, out of class, Harry in the cafeteria, on the football field. That was the way B. T. Kemp made me love him, by being fond of my brother. He had gotten Harry to love him first, and in my mind, there was a kind of connection, you might call it guilt by association, the most tender crime in the world.

—

When college acceptances came in the early spring, it looked like I would be going to the University in Athens and so would Kayann, unless she and Jerry Neal eloped. Eileen was accepted at the University of Massachusetts in Boston, and so was B. T. Kemp. She kept it from her parents for a week, then one Sunday night when Kayann and I were at her house, she broke the news.

"Mmmm," her father said, "and where else?"

"It doesn't matter," Eileen told him, "because that's where I want to go."

"Eileen," he said, "that's silly. Why would you want to go all the way up there?"

"It's a good school."

"Not as good as some others."

"Well," Eileen looked at us and let out a long breath, "my mind's pretty much made up."

Mr. Neal settled his eyes first on me, then on Kayann, thinking we must have had something to do with this strange notion of Eileen's.

"We'll discuss it later," he told her.

"There's nothing to discuss," she said.

I knew this bravado was for us, and it made me feel guilty, like it was more than we deserved. I turned away from them to stare out the dining room window at the darkness. It lightened to a velvety blue-black over the rectangle of the Neals' backyard, a different texture hanging in the air and off the limbs of the trees. Kayann seemed to notice it too. She put her hand up to the glass and held it there until Mr. Neal told us it was late and we should think about getting ourselves home.

They never did discuss it, but the next we heard, Eileen was having to help her father paint the house on Saturdays, Sundays, and every afternoon after school. He had her high on a ladder doing the second floor and the attic dormers. She said once she climbed up there, she stayed and she never looked down.

It was in the wake of all this that Kayann and I talked to B. T. Kemp for the second time. We'd seen him with Eileen, but only for a minute or from a distance, and then he had always disappeared. But one day there he was, waiting for us on Cochise Drive, across the river from school. Harry told him the track coach let us run the neighborhood streets in pairs, and that Kayann and I liked Cochise for its roller-coaster hills. Everybody else on the team thought we were crazy, but that meant we had the whole street to ourselves every afternoon.

We didn't think much of a car, a blue Falcon, parked at the bottom of the last hill. We stopped across the street and shook out our legs, drawing in huge gulps of air. B.T. rolled down the window and smiled at us, then let the smile drift off his face.

"Hey, there," he said. "Sorry about stopping you like this, but I wanted to know about Eileen. I could have called you, I guess, but I didn't know how you'd like that."

"It's okay," I told him, "Eileen's doing all right."

"She's pretty much a prisoner," Kayann said.

"I know," B.T. said. "They've got her painting the house, so I drive by there sometimes. There's this big space between the second-floor windows, and I keep hoping she'll write a message in the paint, my name or something."

We smiled and shook our heads.

"Her parents won't even meet me. They won't have me in the house." He stopped talking and looked at us, weighing some possibility. And then he said it. "Yours probably wouldn't either."

"Maybe not," Kayann told him, and knelt down to retie one of her shoes, "if you act that way."

"Eileen's parents are pretty strict," I said. I had this feeling I wanted B. T. Kemp to go on talking, keep telling us these truths. I wanted to touch him then, like I wanted to back in Chastain Park in November. The idea caught me by surprise, but I reached into the car anyway and took hold of his shoulder.

"I guess I just don't know what to do," he said. "I can't believe my mother wanted to come here."

"Why did she?" Suddenly I wanted to hear about his mother.

"She visited once and liked it."

"I understand that happens to a lot of people," Kayann said.

B.T. didn't seem to have heard her. He turned to look out over that last hill on Cochise, toward the Chattahoochee River, across to school and the football field. He stared hard through the new leaves of the trees like Eileen might be over there at that very moment.

"Tell her," he said, still facing away from us, "tell her to hang in there. Tell her that's what I'm doing."

"We will," Kayann said. "We should be getting back."

"Tell her everything's going to be okay." His voice had a clear, far-off sound to it, like a bell ringing in another town.

Eileen's parents kept her at home for three weeks, until she had what her father called a change of heart.

"More like a transplant," Kayann told me. "She's saying she'll go to school anywhere they want, and that she's calling it quits with B. T. Kemp."

"Just like that?" I said. "Are you sure?"

"Just like that."

"Do you believe her?"

"I have to say I do. Wait until you talk to her. You'll believe her too."

It was a few days before I saw Eileen. The third week of her confinement coincided with spring break, and her parents took her and Jerry up to Raleigh to visit their grandmother. When I did see her, on Monday morning, she was at her locker, kneeling in front of it, slowly extracting loose sheets of notebook paper. I stood beside her until she looked up.

"Hey there," she said.

"Hey, yourself. How was Raleigh?"

"Fine. Everybody's fine."

There was a pause while she unfolded a page from a yellow legal tablet and read it over, then crumpled it into a tight ball.

"So?" I said.

"So what?"

"Eileen, quit acting like I'm some stranger."

She looked into her locker as if the whole world was in there. I could tell she was trying not to cry.

"Come on," I said, "let's get out of here."

In the parking lot she handed me the car keys. Once we were out of the school driveway, I pulled the steering wheel hard to the right and made the tires squeal, but we were across the Paces Ferry bridge before anyone had time to think of following us.

"I hope that left huge skid marks," she said. "The kind they can never get rid of."

We headed straight up Paces Ferry Road toward Vinings, past the fire station and the 7-Eleven, around the corner into the middle of town. To our right was Nellie Mae Rowe's house, something of a landmark in those days, with its front yard full of lights and signs, tin cans, Christmas ornaments, painted figurines, woolly lambs, donkeys, black Sambos and Virgin Marys with their eyes closed and hands folded. Eileen told me to pull into the gravel drive in front of the house. We both stared out our own windows for a long time.

"Remember when you first came out here?" she finally said.

I did, but I could tell she wanted to remind me, so I kept quiet.

"You came out here," she said, slowly and precisely, as if she were giving me dictation, "to interview Nellie Mae Rowe for the school paper. We were in the tenth grade, and both of us were in love with John Wall. You got to come out here with him, and you interviewed her and he took pictures. You stayed out so late your parents came looking for you. But you were here at Nellie Mae's, and John Wall was holding your hand, and it was the only place where you didn't think I'd find you. Remember?"

I remembered like it was the day before, like it was still happening.

"And after that night," she went on, "he was all yours. I decided it wasn't worth the trouble."

"Why do you bring that up?" I said.

"Because we're here."

I didn't think it was much of an answer at the time, but I've come to believe Eileen was seeing the future, and she knew how the story would end.

"It was too hard," she said, "with B.T. and my parents. I'm sorry, but it was."

"You don't owe me an apology."

"Maybe you could do it, but I can't. I don't want to struggle all the time. I could see what it was turning into, constant struggle. I just want things to be easy. I don't want to go out and change the world. I just want everybody to be happy, that's all. Is that so much to ask?"

"Not at all."

"The worst of it was the night before we left for North Carolina. I don't know what got into him—B.T., I mean. I guess he felt like he had to do something. He drove up the driveway and walked around to the back door. I was doing the dishes, and I heard him introduce himself and ask if I was home, then my father's voice, calling for me. There was this funny catch in it, like he was trying not to laugh out loud. When I got to the door, he said, 'Eileen, this boy tells me he knows you, but I believe he's mistaken. Isn't he mistaken, dear? Answer me.' "

"And you said you didn't know him." I could hardly recognize my own voice saying the words for Eileen.

"Yes," she said. "Yes."

I didn't know what to tell her.

"The look on his face," Eileen said, "it was just awful. It was like I was killing him. And then he turned around and walked off to his car. He called the next day, called and called until I answered the phone, and asked why I said I didn't know him. He said, so is this the way it is, and I said yes, this is the way it is."

"Eileen," I said.

"I must not have really loved him," she said, but the words and the sound of her voice made me think she did, and would for a long time.

—

From that moment on, it was as if B. T. Kemp had been swept off the face of the earth. Only Harry still talked about him, but always about what they used to do, conversations they had had a month ago. Once I tried calling his house, just to hear his voice, and a woman answered, his mother, but I couldn't speak to her. I listened to her say hello over and over, until she got tired of the silence and hung up. Every afternoon during the rest of track season, as Kayann and I sprinted to the end of Cochise Drive, I imagined B. T. Kemp's Falcon would come flying over the last hill. It never happened.

"You'd think he'd come back and talk to us," I said one day in May.

"You know what I think?" Kayann said, "I think you're hoping he comes back. You want him to come back. All this time, you're so quiet about it. You're so quiet about everything, but who it really is that's in love with him is you."

I couldn't deny it, and after that we never ran on Cochise again.

Harry reported that at graduation B.T.'s name got called, but no family stood up and nobody stepped forward to receive the diploma. The principal looked down at his roster, said the words *in absentia,* and put the diploma back on the table. Harry said the applause was louder than for anybody else, all the teachers stood up and so did the graduating class. He tried to tell me that he did too, but his voice broke. When I moved to put my arm around his shoulders, he shrugged it off and bolted out the back door.

The story came to be that B.T. Kemp's father drove down from Boston and in the middle of one of those warm May nights climbed in his son's bedroom window and carried him off, probably back up north. His mother disappeared too, but for her there wasn't any story. Harry said she died of grief, but I didn't believe him.

"A person can die of grief," Kayann said. "You'd probably find out it's what most people die of, if you could ask them right there at the end."

"Well, not me," Eileen said. "I'm going to die of happiness in my own bed, in my own house, someplace far away from here."

We were staying outside by then, late into the night. It seemed like darkness was the only thing that could hold us, keep us near each other. Every night that summer I wondered if Kayann and Jerry would elope, if they'd get up and walk off into the woods and never come back, but they didn't. The reason is, I understand now, that Kayann became beautiful. All of May, June, and July, I watched it happen, like a tree coming into leaf. More and more, her beauty took every ounce of attention she had, and Jerry drifted through the neighborhood looking lost. He had the face of someone who should never be alone, his pale hair and skin making it seem like he'd vanish into thin air if a strong, beautiful girl like Kayann wasn't there to hold on to him. In the end those evenings still opened up like they were a door, but the truth is that the darkness hid us from each other, so that to move in any direction was to risk being lost forever.

Evening always seems to me like a curtain now, never a door, and tonight it's veined by trees, some of which still hang on to their leaves for dear life, even though it's November in New England. I know that's not how it's supposed to work, most people talk about leaves hanging on to the tree, but I wonder.

I stayed with Kayann and Eileen a year in Athens, then came to Boston to finish school. As soon as I got to town, I looked up Kemp in the telephone book and called them all until I found B. T. Kemp. We met at Fanueil Hall, at the oyster bar where he worked, and he told me that I still looked like Harry, but I had become beautiful. After that, B.T. came to my dorm room almost every night for two years. Often his hands would be cut from opening oyster shells or holding other kinds of fish by the gills. The gills are sharp along the edges, he said, sharp where it's a matter of life and death. Sometimes he would hold me and cry out Eileen's name, and once he was there when she called to wish me a happy birthday. They were singing to me over the phone, Eileen and Jerry and Kayann, Happy Birthday to You, while B. T. Kemp unbuttoned my clothes.

"Is there somebody there with you?" Eileen said, hearing the tiny catches in my voice, recognizing them.

"No," I told her. "It's just you and me."

Last week I sent him away for good.

"I don't really know you," I said. "When you close your eyes, it's not me."

"Who is it?" B.T. said.

"It's Eileen. Isn't it?"

"Yes," he said, "and sometimes when I'm on my way to see you, I pretend it's Eileen who will be here. And my mother too."

"You have to go now," I said, and he did.

I think I am dying of grief.

Tonight there's an early snowfall in Boston, and I've gotten myself caught in it coming home from the library. I slow down, then pass my dorm, cross Storrow Drive, and sit on a bench for a long time, listening to church bells mark the hour. The snow comes harder, and I think about B. T. Kemp, who has probably seen a whole lot worse weather than this. I imagine him somewhere nearby, counting the time in this town, thinking of Eileen or maybe not, and for a split second I see it all, the way it might have been, and then his face disappears again, hidden by the curtain of evening. Tomorrow I will pick up the telephone and dial his number, just to hear his voice. When he answers I won't say anything for a moment, then I'll hang up. He'll hope it was Eileen, but he'll know, just as you do, who it really was.

CALLED BY
NAME

"Kayla Vane," is all Truman Suter ever says into the phone when he calls, or all he has a chance to say before I hang up on him. It makes me hate the sound of my name, to hear it in his voice, hate it more than I do already. *Kayla Vane* is the name a stripper might make up for herself, a stripper in a small-town revue who's moody and has a gift for lying and, I've come to think, one bad eye, which she winks at you when she makes a joke. It's the name of a woman who's never satisfied, who has to have the *la-di-da,* the rings on her fingers, the bells on her toes. Still, you want to trust a woman called Kayla Vane, if only to prove you're not afraid of her. You want to believe her promises, but the truth is, you shouldn't.

I take the phone off the hook in case Truman Suter tries to call back, get up from my desk, and start switching off the computers, moving slowly down the aisle between carrels, checking each screen for the messages my kids usually leave at the end of the day. *Thanks, Miss Vane. See you tomorrow, Miss Vane.* Now that it's the end of the school year, they're brave: *To be continued in Vane. Miss Vane isn't,* which took me some time to understand. I think about how I first imagined them, last September, as I drove west from Atlanta toward the dry circle on the road map that called itself Pueblo, Colorado, the truck loaded with computer-literacy manuals and software. I was learning Spanish from Berlitz tapes. Speak Spanish Like a Diplomat! the plastic tape cases said. All I had to do was Speak Spanish Like a Librarian! I wondered what the difference was, and I still do.

For all those miles, I imagined myself walking between rows of

Mexican children, *los niños,* with their hair the color of blacktop, touching their bony shoulders, *hombros,* to praise them or gently correct their mistakes, *errores,* leaning in close so that my face and their faces are reflected together, smiling into the monitor screen. I imagined they would come to love me, even if they didn't at first, and at the end of the year they would beg me to stay forever.

After fourteen hours on I-20 and U.S. 87, I stopped at a bar in Wichita Falls, Texas, where I got friendly with the bartender. He told me not to even think about driving all night because there wouldn't be enough gas stations open between Wichita Falls and Pueblo.

"But I'll be late," I said. "I'm supposed to be there tomorrow."

"I'll bet you," the bartender said, smiling, "there's other people in that town can switch on a computer."

"Not like I can," I said, not meaning the words the way they sounded, feeling too tired to make them come out right.

"Well, well," he said, setting his hands on the bar shoulder-width apart and leaning in close, "buy you another beer, genius?" He told me then his name was Mike Oakley.

After last call came and went, Mike Oakley asked me to stay on for a nightcap, and I went home with him, but I had to keep my eyes closed all night long. Mike Oakley reminded me of my father, who's been dead for a year now, if my father had been shorter and dark-haired, if my father had been a student in accounting at Wichita Falls State College. In the morning he packed his gear, his accounting textbooks, and rode with me to Pueblo. Even back then I knew he'd be with me forever, till death do us part, and I warned him, I told him the truth at a truckstop in Boise City, Oklahoma. *Mike Oakley,* I said, *I'm just like my father, who toured north Georgia trying to get country boys to hear God calling them to the priesthood. He worked to make bad boys good, and then one day after a week of these trips up north, he went around behind the garage and shot himself. I'm just like him, Mike, so don't let me out of your sight.*

The last thing I do before leaving the computer room is hang up the phone. I stare at it hard, willing it not to ring, but it does anyway, and I answer. Truman Suter is saying my name. I tell him to leave me alone, that I don't want to talk to him, but he's not listening.

"You know that's not right," he says. "Why can't you just admit it?"

"Goodbye, Truman," I say. I hear my voice shake, and damn it, so does he.

Outside the library I feel better, in daylight, in public, where Truman Suter wouldn't try to touch me. I walk hard and mean so that the heels of my boots ring on the pavement, and I think about Mike Oakley who gave me these boots, bought them from Truman Suter's father, really from his mother, whose legs had gotten too big to fit into them. We went into Suter's House of Guns one night before Mike left, to look at hunting rifles, and there were Mrs. Suter's boots, red-and-tan Frye's, size 5½ B.

"Nobody has feet this small and legs this big," Suter said, pointing to his wife.

"Nobody but me," Mrs. Suter agreed.

"But that's why I love her," Suter said. "Ain't a woman alive can dance the way she can, I'm telling you, lifting one of them little feet into the air and still can balance."

After Mike paid for the boots, Suter took my hand and said if I ever needed anything while Mike was away, I should come in and ask for him special.

"And wear them boots," he told me, "so I'll know right off you're Mikey's girl."

I think about writing Mike in Harlingen, Texas, and telling him about the trouble with Truman Suter, but what would I say? Baby, I got lonely one night, and called up your buddy Truman Suter. I won't ever be able to explain why I wanted him so bad, and now I'm sorry, but he sure as hell isn't, and he's got this way about him, it scares me, how his eyes can get almost transparent, blue like clear water, and his voice goes flat and soft like he knows he's going to get what he wants. And Mike, I'm pretty sure there's consequences, you know, tiny but growing and growing, the kind you have to live with forever. Say it, Mike, Kayla's baby, the way you'll be talking about it for the rest of our lives. Make it so you guessed and not that I told you so.

But when I do write, I never say any of this, just ask about Mike's father, Mike Oakley senior, about soybeans and cotton, tell him when I'm coming out to see them. His father will most likely be dead by then, his cancer rotting him from the inside, quickly now and thoroughly. He's a big man, according to the pictures Mike keeps in his wallet, a big man who's been taken down inch by inch for two years and now felled like the huge oak he is.

At home I turn on the evening news and sit down with a beer. For a while nothing on television gets into my head, it's like watching with the sound off, and then suddenly the beer takes hold and makes all the news seem deep and true and aimed right at your heart. Even a story that isn't news, a story about a girl teaching her own father to read, brings tears to my eyes, reminding me of last February 22, when the morning newscaster announced the date and I teared up just this way. I couldn't believe it was just the fact of George Washington's birthday until I remembered that in grade school February 22 was Father's Day, and all the fathers took time off from work, came to school, and sat beside their children in tiny chairs, listening to stories about themselves, watching their children work. Later the fathers wandered the halls, looking at their portraits in crayon or tempera paint or charcoal, greeting other fathers and talking about what smart, good-looking kids they had. My own father seemed huge to me. In his suit he was strangely formal and distant, so that I held on to his hand and made him stay and stay, for assembly, for lunch, for gym class, forever. In the end he had to leave without telling me, sneak away while my back was turned.

When the news is over I think about supper and decide not to bother. Food makes me sick most of the time anyhow. Another beer would fill me right up, the carbonation settle my stomach.

Walking to the kitchen, I feel the bones creak underneath my skin, and it makes me move slowly and deliberately. I like knowing how I'm put together on the inside, but these days I know less and less. At night sometimes I lie awake in bed counting my ribs and waiting for my breasts to grow, my belly to tighten, rise, and grow round. I imagine Truman Suter's baby is the moon caught in my belly, trying to lift me over the stars.

The phone rings then, and on the other end is Mike's voice saying *Kayla,* and I know from the sound of it he's calling to tell me his father is dead.

"He's gone," Mike says, and for a while that's all. There's a sound between us like the ocean, rising surf that dies down and then rises again. All I can say is his name, *Oh, Mike, Oh, Mike,* but he pretends I've asked a question.

"We're doing okay, I guess," he says. "He went easy, Kayla. It was in his sleep, about three hours ago. The people from the funeral home just got here. I thought I'd be glad it was over."

I can hear his voice breaking, and I tell him it's good that his father went easy.

"Kayla, I want you to come out here. I mean, if you can. We want you to, and I need you to. Then we'll drive back together after things settle down. Can you come? I want you to be here."

I think about Mike and his brothers, picture them standing around their father's bed, holding their hats and not crying. They're keeping their eyes open because they're trying to memorize their father's face. It's something the living need to do. I put myself in Harlingen with them, standing at the foot of Mike Oakley senior's bed, watching Mike junior and his brothers. They all need a woman now, three living men without wives or mother, one dead man lying between worlds.

"Yes," I say to Mike, "I'll come right away. They already have a substitute for me at the library. I can leave in the morning."

"It's eighteen hours."

"I know," I say. "I can drive it straight through."

"Kayla," Mike says, "listen to me. Take two days. Stop in Dallas, maybe. And be careful. Promise me."

"All right," I say, knowing I won't stop, and knowing that I stopped being careful a long time ago.

"Kayla, I love you."

"Yes," I tell him. "Yes. See you soon."

I sit back down at the kitchen table, smoking and thinking about Mike's father, wondering where he is now, if right this minute he's slipping out from between layers of blankets and layers of flesh, if he's left his house to stand looking out over his thirty acres of land that belongs half to another man, somewhere in Illinois, and half to that man's sister, somewhere in California. I wonder if he's holding out his arms and saying, *This land which was never mine now doesn't belong to you, Mikey, you, Tommy, you, Ben,* naming his sons. *I give you all I have, which is nothing.* And then he goes and lies down under the shade of the only tree in that field. I wonder if he closes his eyes. I wonder if he takes a bottle out of his coat pocket and drinks and closes his eyes again.

I imagine my father appears and sits down next to Mike Oakley senior, the blackened patch around the bullet hole still visible on the right side of his face, the powder burn and dried blood. I see my father as I memorized him, only now he's turning himself, angling to hide the blasted-out part of his forehead. Mike Oakley senior hands Jimmy Vane the bottle, and Jimmy Vane keeps hold of it awhile. They don't talk to each other. They don't need to right now. Jimmy Vane leans the dark side of his face on Mike Oakley's shoulder. He keeps his eyes open, my father does, taking in the length and breadth of the fields that Mike Oakley doesn't own. I think he's waiting for me to appear on the far horizon. Lately it seems like I'm always about to meet my father, around every corner, or I think he'll be sitting in the truck when I come out to leave for work in the morning. He's waiting for me to tell him there's going to be a baby. He wants to be the first to know.

This is the barter we've been building up to all these years, the fair trade, my first bad secret in exchange for the first one he told me. We were driving home from the hardware store, where he'd gone to buy a new mailbox for the rectory at Our Lady of the Assumption after vandals had shot out the old one. He was talking to me about his work, traveling from Atlanta to Cumming to Dahlonega to Blairsville and Hiawassee, giving lectures, encouraging young men to search their hearts. "Called By Name," his talk was titled, because that's how you know if God wants you to become a priest—you hear your name in God's voice. My father kept his eyes so firmly on the road that I had to check every so often to see if I was missing something. After a while I couldn't help myself and asked if he ever felt it, called that way, and he said no, it was pretty quiet in his heart. And then he looked at me, finally. *It's pretty empty in there,* he said. That was his secret.

If he was going to smaller towns up in the Chattahoochee National Forest, Elijay or Wiley, or especially, he said, a town called Tiger, he carried a small pistol under the front seat of the car, on the driver's side. If he stayed overnight, he kept it on the bedside table. He said sometimes those north Georgia mountain boys put up a hell of a fight before they gave in to God's calling, and he wanted to be prepared. He said, *You should have one of these, and I'll teach you to shoot it.* He said, *You might have some trouble with boys yourself one day.*

I go out to cash a check at the Safeway and walk five blocks to Suter's House of Guns. I get there faster than I think I'm going to, and then I have to stand on the sidewalk, looking in Suter's windows for signs of Truman and trying to catch my breath. But it may not ever be caught, so I go on in. I've never been here on a Friday night, which is Suter's busiest time of the work week. Mike used to bring me in on Saturday afternoons when Truman was working, and they'd laugh about the whole male adult population of Pueblo spending the day in the bars or watching TV or both. Mike and Truman knew everybody in town, Mike because he tended bar on weeknights and Truman because his father would always cut you a good deal on a firearm.

Tonight there are four other customers standing at the counter, admiring the handguns, but you can tell their real interest is in the big-ticket items, shotguns and rifles lined up on a high shelf along the south wall of the store, close together like pickets in a fence.

"But what would really keep him away," one of the men is saying, "is a Belgian Browning over/under, a pigeon-grade lightning model, twenty-eight-inch barrels, choked improved cylinder, modified with a single trigger, fourteen-and-a-half-inch length of pull."

All the men laugh, shake their heads, and say, *Shoot, Bob.*

I walk over to a revolving case of Buck knives, thinking to get one to take to Mike, and leave without seeing Suter, but the man at the cash register, who isn't Truman or his father, walks around from behind the handgun cases and asks if he can help me. I turn around to face him, letting my eyes drift over and stay fixed on the closed door that leads to Suter's back room. He asks if I was wanting to see Mr. Suter about something. When I nod yes, he tells me to go on back, Suter's on the phone, but I can wait. Behind the door there's the low growl of a man's voice. It stops after I knock, and then the door opens. Suter looks blank at first, then smiles.

"Mike Oakley's girl," he says. "Kayla."

I tell him that's right, and he invites me into the office, walks back around his desk, and sits down. He picks up the receiver and rolls his eyes toward the ceiling at the same time. He smiles at me again, but it's a grimace of clenched teeth. I wouldn't want to be whoever's on the other end of this call.

"Okay," Suter says into the receiver, "sorry. Tell it to me one more time."

He listens, shaking his head.

"No, sir," he says, finally. "That ain't legal in this state. Sorry. Yep. Have a good one."

He hangs up the receiver and his eyes move to my face, trying to get an impression. Like any man who's used to handling guns, he doesn't want to be the first to make a move or ask a personal question.

"That boy on the phone has been trying to get a permit to carry a concealed weapon for two years now. Got a record as long as my arm, harrassment, DUI, hunting out of season. A model citizen. I ain't the sheriff, though, just a deputy, so it won't be up to me. Anyways. How're them boots holding up?"

"Just fine," I say. "Mr. Suter, I need you to sell me a firearm."

"A handgun?" His eyes move to something on the wall just to the left of my face.

I say yes and reach into my purse for cigarettes, then shake the pack, glad to be doing something with my eyes and hands right now. Truman favors his father, I can't help noticing. He has the same bottomless blue gaze, that look that says he knows what you want before you know it.

"You just tell me one thing," he says. "You tell me you ain't wanting to get yourself a firearm because you're mad at somebody."

"No, sir."

"And you ain't mad at no police?" This question makes Suter smile.

"No special one."

"And you ain't fixing to send it through the U.S. mail, not to Mikey or nobody else?"

"No, sir."

He takes some paperwork out of his desk drawer.

"You'll need a permit, and you have to have a photo."

"I do," I say, showing him the strip of four photographs from the booth at Pueblo Mall. "Which one do you like best?"

Suter smiles again and runs his index finger down the strip. He taps the second one, where I've used the scenic background—a view of the Rockies in winter—instead of the plain blue velveteen curtain. He opens the ink pad on his desk and holds out his hand, palm up. It's the move of somebody either asking you to take a walk with them or showing you they've got nothing to hide. He holds my hand in both of his and folds the fingers into the palm so that my index finger is pointing straight at his chest. He rolls my finger across the ink and onto the form, then hands me a premoistened towellette. When I open the foil package, the scent of lemon rises over the desk like a veil between us.

"Weight?"

"Ninety-five."

"Hair?"

"Brown."

"Eyes?"

"Hazel."

"Occupation?"

"Teacher."

"Reason for issuing?"

"Protection."

Suter looks at me then, thinking I might want to say more, might want to without being able, and it's like the moment right before a first kiss when the will to do it and the desire become one and the same, and then nothing at all. For one tiny pulse of a second, I think I will lean over the desk and kiss Truman Suter's father and tell him about his son and me. Then he lowers his eyes, says not to worry, the sheriff will sign the form, send it up to Denver, and I'll most likely get the permit in about two weeks. He tells me to try not to get arrested before then.

Suter stands up and motions me to follow him out to the store.

"How's Mike doing?"

"He called tonight. His dad just died. I'm going out there tomorrow."

"Poor Mikey. Tell him I was sorry to hear it."

"I will."

"Poor Mikey," he says again.

In the main room of Suter's, Truman Suter is now working the counters. He's surprised to see me, and then his expression changes to that willfulness I know. On Truman it's the look of a man who's sure a woman won't refuse him or can't get away from him, not this time, not ever. He comes over to watch his father talk me through my purchase, a .380 automatic that Suter says I'll come to like the feel of, even if I don't right now. I try to put myself so that Suter's body is between his son's and mine, and when we cross the store to the cash register, I make sure Truman Suter doesn't get behind me. I pay Suter in cash for the gun and a box of bullets, one hundred and thirty dollars, six twenties and a ten.

"Want a lesson?" Suter says, and I tell him yes, thinking he means to give me the lesson himself, but instead he tells Truman to take me around behind the depot, where he says there's bright lights and nobody to bother us.

We walk back through Suter's office and outside into full darkness. I'm working hard to make sure my face says nothing, but when we're out of sight of Suter's, I stop. Truman walks a few paces on.

"What's the matter, Kayla Vane?" he says when he realizes I'm not right behind him.

"It's okay," I say, "I don't need a lesson right now. I need to get home. I'm waiting for Mike to call."

Truman laughs, one short *ha,* and holds his arms open wide.

"Kayla," he says. "I won't touch you if you don't want me to. I promise. I *swear.*"

"No, Truman."

"Come on, Kayla. You know and I know you have no idea how that thing works. I'll show you and that'll be it. Then we'll both go home."

I have no good reason to trust either Truman Suter or myself, but I let him lead me down the alley behind Main Street until it crosses to the railroad tracks. We turn left when we come to the tracks and walk along beside them for a quarter mile, past the last

of the houses in the neighborhood where my students live. I'm glad
it's dark. I wouldn't want any of them to see me like this, with
Truman Suter, with a gun, walking out of town.

We stop under the last light pole, where six-foot-high embank-
ments of dirt and dry grass rise up on either side of the tracks.
Truman shows me how to work the magazine, fit in seven bullets,
and slide it back into the gun's handle. Then he tells me to take out
the magazine, eject the chambered bullet, and do it all over again.
He makes me run through the whole operation three more times,
until the movements come easily and I don't have to look at him
to see if I'm doing it right.

"Good," he says. "Now. We forgot to bring earplugs, so you're
going to have to tough it out. Won't be time for earplugs anyways,
if you got to use this gun like you think you might."

He shows me how to stand, facing down the tracks away from
town, and I imagine a train coming at me, a speeding train I have
to stop with this one bullet. I thumb off the safety, sight in the
imaginary train, hold my breath, and squeeze the trigger. The force
of the explosion sends my arm jolting up into the air.

"Jesus." I can't help myself.

Truman Suter smiles and tells me to keep firing, he says I'll get
used to it, and I pull the trigger six more times, getting used to it,
as fast as I can. I realize too late that the magazine is empty and
Truman is standing behind me. Though we aren't touching, I can
feel the radiating heat of his body. Then his arms go around my
waist, his grip is hard, the muscles ropy along his forearms.

"Kayla," he says in my ear, "for old time's sake."

I look down at his arms crossed over my belly, and everything
slows down until I seem to be picturing us from a distance, Truman
Suter's arms locked around some other woman, his thighs pressing
against the backs of her legs. His right hand on my belt buckle is
as still as if it's in a photograph. Then his hands move, trying to
figure out how the buckle works. It seems to take a long time, but

I bring the butt of the gun down hard against his fingers. He yells and lets go.

"Get away from me now, Truman, and nobody will know."

Truman Suter stands still for a few seconds, holding his own hands, then takes a step backward. It's in this step he loses that willful look, and I know he won't bother me now. I reach down for the box of bullets.

"I'll know," he says, "and if Mike ever comes back here, he'll know."

"He already knows," I lie. "So go on and get the hell out of here."

I stand there watching him go, holding perfectly still until he's out of sight. A tiny hand dips and rolls in my gut, and I know what this must mean. Truman Suter's baby is waving goodbye to his father forever. He comes from a long line of women who send their men away, and it's never too soon for Truman Suter's baby to learn this. *Jimmy Vane,* my mother said, *I never want to see your face again,* and he walked out the back door and around behind the garage, and made damn sure she got her wish.

—

I run my eyes along the two shelves at the back of Walgreen's, beside the pharmacy counter, where the druggist can keep watch over women like me. The names on the boxes might make you think of school supplies, except that they all have a competitive sound, like they're for junior high girls who've gotten ahead of themselves, or want to: Advance, Fact Plus, Clearblue Easy, First Response, Answer, Q-Test, Clearplan. I want whatever's smallest, least involved, and I like the name Clearblue. If there is a baby, this is what it looks like inside me right now, a blue knot of cells, an idea making itself over and over again, clearer all the time.

Back home, I sit down at the kitchen table with the pregnancy test and the .380, and try to write a letter to my mother. *Dear Mother, I'm leaving for Texas in the morning. I'm in love with a boy named Mike Oakley and his father just died in Harlingen, and we're going to get married. There's a baby on the way.* I wonder at that last sentence, writing itself so easily, and its question runs the whole way up my backbone in a cold arrow. I touch a corner of this letter to the tip of my lit cigarette and watch the paper burn without creating fire, just a brown stain that moves upward and inward until I'm not holding on to anything.

Dear Mother, I'm in love with a boy named Mike and I'm going to Harlingen, Texas, to be with him. I don't know when I'll be back here, or if. Dear Mother, Sorry I haven't written in all this time. Dear Mother, If it's a girl, I'll name her Jess, for you.

All my dreams tonight are about babies, hundreds of them, dark-haired and dark-skinned like my students, climbing out of Mrs. Suter's boots. Some can walk and some can only crawl, all of them moving through the long tunnel of this house toward the front door. They are trying to turn the knob, open the door, and let themselves out. Some of the older babies jump up and hang on to the screen, their fingers turned into claws. Soon I find that not all the babies are at the front door, some are crowded into the bathroom, leaning over the toilet to see what's inside, or trying to pull themselves up onto the rim of the tub. There are more babies in the kitchen, bent to look under the sink like tiny workmen, a chain of them pulling on the refrigerator door, reaching up over their own heads into the silverware drawer. Everywhere in this house the screechy pitch of baby voices seems to rise higher and higher but doesn't. It's like walking through a factory where marbles are being blown from glass and rolled along conveyor belts, or maybe it's ball bearings, or hooks and eyes, some kind of small moveable part. I walk carefully and silently among the babies, trying to save them from themselves, trying to remember all their names.

When I wake up, the last of the babies is stealing out of the bedroom. In the bathroom there are no babies, and the Clearblue Easy test is set up like I left it before I went to sleep. All I have to do is pee into the biodegradable cup and dip the tester stick in. I make a pot of coffee for the Thermos and light a cigarette at the other end of the house, worrying about what cigarette smoke might do to the test results. I read the road map and stare out the front windows, making deals with myself: If I don't turn around and look during the ten minutes, the results will be one thing. If I do turn around, they'll be the other. I keep changing the terms of the deal—not the turning around, but what it will mean. When the time's up, I can see down the straight sight line of the hallway. The test stick is blue. Blue is yes, white is no.

"Blue is yes, white is no." I say it all the way down the hall to the bathroom door. I promise myself I'll do another test after I get to Harlingen, in a few weeks, so Mike can see.

I believe this test, though. I believe it and I can almost see this baby, a bad baby, Truman Suter's bad baby, but already I don't care. Already I feel his weight, Truman Suter's willfulness inside me in a way he'll never know about. All at once it's as if this baby knows what I know, realizes his own badness and makes himself heavier. I sit down on the edge of the bathtub and think about calling Truman Suter. He'd come over here with his bruised and swollen hands, and I'd tell him, and we'd do it again, make more of this baby the way we made him in the first place, Truman Suter's smashed hands stumbling over my body like a blind man's.

I think of Mike now, and how I'll tell him in a few weeks, tell him and then watch the blue of his eyes, the way his face won't change when I say the words, whatever they turn out to be. He'll take a step backward, I know this much, away from me, as if to get a better look. I know him. I know how in that first second he won't touch me but will leave me to myself, out of awe. It makes me want to drive west, away from Mike Oakley and Truman Suter. I need hours, days, lifetimes on the road to talk to this new stranger. I'll begin telling him my own stories, and when those are done, less than a mile out of town, I'll start in on those of his ancestors. It will be a little one-sided, the rogue's gallery of his making, but it can't be helped.

Tell that one again, I'd say to my father, the one about Fort Hamilton. I couldn't get enough of this story, the way Truman Suter's bad baby won't be able to get enough of me. *It was after the war,* my father said, *after everything, and I was an orderly at Fort Hamilton in Sheepshead Bay. The commanding officer was a British navy captain, and we had prisoners of war there, a few Italians and Germans. One of the Germans had been on a submarine that sank a British ship, and he kept talking about it, talking and talking. He was sweeping the floors, and kept on telling his story, thinking he was a hero. Well, the c.o. heard all the talk, took a gun out of his desk drawer, and shot the German in the head. Turns out the c.o.'s best friend was on that blown-up ship. That guy's brains were all over the wall,* my father said, and his voice cracked like a child's would. *I can still hear the sound of the shot and the sound the broom made when it hit the floor.*

Always he told me stories like this one when we were in the car together. Then he'd remind me to fasten my seat belt. I remember he had a flawless sense of direction; he never, ever got lost. It's impossible not to know where you are, he always said, just impossible.

—

There's no easy way to get to Harlingen, Texas, no direct highways to settle into and ride to the end. Mike's already told me this, time and time again, until I could swear I'm hearing the map in his voice, straight through the phone lines, the roar of two-lane travel on Highway 87, caught behind columns of tanker trucks, whose drivers all seem to be traveling more and more slowly by the minute, maybe falling asleep, maybe listening to slow dance music on the radio, closing their strong arms around the steering wheel like it's their woman, making her a few careful promises, heedless

of time, place, the speed of anybody else on this road, feeling only
the dangerous speed of light.

I have it all on slips of paper, route numbers and the names of
all the towns where I might go wrong: I-25 to Raton, New Mexico,
where I'll head east on Highway 64, waiting for it to become 87,
then 64 again at Des Moines, to Clayton, where the road forks, but
I stay on it to Texline, the Texas line, just what you'd want this
town to be named if the decision was yours, and I believe this is
where I'll start to like Texas, a state that calls a spade a spade. I stay
on 87 to Dalhart, Texas, where I'll pick up 385 through Channing,
Vega, Littlefield, Gomez, after which it's briefly 137, then 87
again—87 my old friend, I'll be saying by that time—at La Mesa to
Big Spring, to San Angelo, to Eden. In Eden I take 83 to I-10 at
a town called Junction and follow it to San Antonio. South of San
Antonio it's I-37 to Corpus Christi, Body of Christ city, then 77
south to Harlingen. Then I'll be lost for the first time in all these
thousand and some-odd miles. I'll find a pay phone and call Mike.
And it's then I'll remember I never told my students goodbye.

—

Our ground time in San Antonio will be brief, I think as I'm
getting out of the truck, just one beer and a chapter of *The Hunt
for Red October* to ease the jangling of local radio stations and trucks
on I-10. This restaurant is called The Midway, midway between
what and what, I don't know, but I like its looks—one story,
painted gunmetal gray, like the color of a battleship. Inside, the
vestibule splits off the family restaurant, with red-checked table-
cloths, from the lounge, which is cool and dark like a cave. I sit up
at the bar, and a waitress reaches in from behind to hand me a
menu. I have to lean forward to read it, angling to catch some of
the light that glows over the bottles of hard liquor on the back wall.

The Midway Lounge is empty except for two men in the booth
directly behind me. The booths are on a raised platform, so in the

mirror behind the bar their heads frame my face, eyes cast down
like they're staring at my shoulders or at my hands folded around
the beer bottle. They talk to each other without looking up, their
lips moving so that the flush of this first beer makes me imagine
it's me they're whispering to. It's one of the triptychs back at Our
Lady of the Assumption in Atlanta, the Blessed Mother flanked by
Gabriel and another angel whose name I can never remember.
Raphael? Michael? The name makes me drop my hand to the top
of my belly, holding on as if this were four months from now and
Truman Suter's baby has grown visible, becoming something to
count on. I've left the .380 out in the truck, and I'm sure that's why
I feel so light now, having driven all this way with the gun lying
across my lap, saying to Truman Suter's baby, *If you're a boy, you'll
learn to shoot this, and if you're a girl, you'll learn even better than if you were
a boy.* I think about the hundreds of babies in my dream and how
hard it would be to love them all. Names run through my head like
a movie of all the boys I've ever known, only boys, always ending
with Mike.

"Mike," I say out loud and think of how he used to laugh about
different kinds of drunks and what they'd do if left to their own
devices: Bourbon walks, beer talks.

"What's that, honey?" the waitress says.

"Nothing."

"Another Bud?"

I tell her sure.

Directly behind me one of the men in the booth slides out and
stands up, so that all I can see in the mirror is his right hand
reaching from behind my head to shake the right hand of the man
still sitting. He crosses the vestibule into the family restaurant, and
the other gets up and comes to sit next to me at the bar, leaving
an empty stool between us.

"I wrote that," he says, pointing to *The Hunt for Red October.*

"Bull," I say and smile at him anyway. It's a lie worth admiring somebody for, and a very small part of me wonders if he might be telling the truth.

"Well," he says, "I could have. He just beat me to it."

"Do you write books?"

"I used to."

"Would I know your name?"

He tells me his name is Bill Holloway, and I do think I might have heard it, or seen it in the library. I say this and Bill Holloway laughs and waves his right hand in the air.

"You don't have to tell me that."

I say I wouldn't if it weren't true.

"I came over here from my table because I have something very important to tell you."

I ask him what it is, and he takes his time about answering. I can tell Bill Holloway is a little drunk, but not in a way that could cause trouble later on. So far he's keeping the polite distance between us.

"About this time last year," he says, "I came in here and right where you're sitting there was a girl who was a Mormon and running away from her daddy, who was a drunk and a polygamist, and I said, honey, can you be a Mormon and a drunk too, and she looked at me right like you're doing now, and she said the smartest thing I ever heard anybody say. She said you can be any damn thing you want. How about that for smart? Do you think it's true, you can be any damn thing you want?"

"Yes," I tell him. "Yes, I do."

"I would've married that girl to help her get away from her daddy, if I didn't have a wife already, but I'm telling you this because you're wearing that same look she had."

There's something about this conversation I want to stop but can't. It reminds me of talking to Truman Suter before things got too personal.

"What look is that?"

"Tender and bad. Like you know a secret nobody else knows and you're thinking about killing somebody over it."

"What happened to her?"

"Don't know," Bill Holloway says. "She got in her car and drove away. I told her to write when she found work, but you know people never do that when you ask them to."

The waitress walks down the length of the bar, shaking her head and smiling at me. She asks Bill Holloway if he wants another beer like she knows the answer is going to be yes, which it is. I tell her nothing for me, thanks.

"Is Mr. Hollywood bothering you? If he is, you just let me know," she says and moves off toward the kitchen.

"Hollywood?"

"It's not what you think," he says. "I did a made-for-TV movie once, out in L.A. It wasn't any big deal; there were lots of them awhile back. Disease of the week, they called it out here."

"Cancer?"

"No, cancer's been done. Mine was a living-will type situation. You probably never saw it, though. Ninety percent of the TV stations in South Texas wouldn't air it. Folks around here think you belong to God right up to the bitter end. He's got himself a big plan, and you got to be part of it no matter what."

"What do you think?"

"I'm with Evangeline Keck, did I tell you her name? Evie Keck, the polygamist's daughter. You can be anything you want."

"Evangeline is a nice name," I say, the accent falling harder on *Evangeline* than I mean for it to.

"You in the market for names?"

"Not really."

He stops talking for a minute and looks at my reflection in the mirror behind the bar.

"Where you headed, honey?"

"Harlingen."

"Got a boy there waiting for you." It's not a question, but I answer it anyway.

"Words to the wise," Bill Holloway says. "Don't drive into Harlingen, Texas, alone after dark unless you know exactly where you're going. It gets dangerous at night with all the drug dealers up from Matamoros and Empalme."

"Thanks," I say. "That's just what I was going to do, drive right into town. But now I won't."

"Unless you got a gun."

"Unless I have a gun."

I take a five-dollar bill out of my wallet and put it down on the bar.

"I'll walk you out," Bill Holloway says.

When we get out to the truck, Bill Holloway wants to stand and admire it for a minute. He says it looks *soft*, marveling at the word itself and how it could describe a red truck. I unlock the door and reach under the seat for the .380.

"I'll be okay in Harlingen," I say, and Bill Holloway takes a step backward when he sees what I'm holding. "It's a gun."

"This woman calls a spade a spade," he says, laughing. "What's your name, tough gal?"

I tell him.

"Kayla Vane," he says. "Kayla Vane surely is the name of somebody who calls a spade a spade. Tender and bad, Kayla Vane. You look out now, Kayla Vane, I'm going to put you in a movie sure as I'm born. Kayla Vane, does your mother know you're packing a pistol? I'll bet your mother calls a spade a spade too."

I say goodbye to Bill Holloway, reaching up at the last minute to give him a kiss on the cheek. I want to tell him no, my mother doesn't know I'm packing a pistol. I want to tell him she wouldn't want to know, and she wouldn't call a spade a spade either. She never did when she had the chance. She lied and said it was an accident, the gun just went off in his hand while he was loading it or cleaning it or something, she didn't understand guns. She said this over and over to everybody, nurses, priests, relatives. For a while she said it to strangers at the A&P, other women caught with their fingers bruising a tomato, peering into the window where the bacon shows its true colors.

Then she decided what happened was God wanted Jimmy Vane back, called him by name, she said, to be in His most blessed priesthood. *Yo, Jimmy Vane,* I'd say, doing my best imitation of God. *Jimmy Vane, I'm calling you. Jimmy Vane, up here, on the double.* I'd say it at the kitchen table, all through supper, until she cried and said she hated me, ran into her bedroom, and slammed the door. When I left for Pueblo, she called out through that closed door, *Write when you find work.*

In dreams you can love them all, the baby, his father, the husband, his father, your father. It's only the world that makes you choose, and name your lovers and your children. I promise Mike I'll be his until death do us part, and he promises to never let me out of his sight. We go out dancing every week before the baby comes, and I wear Mrs. Suter's boots, and it's just like Suter said; *Even with one foot off the ground, you still can balance.*

We name the baby Truman Michael because I have told Mike a story about how Truman Suter taught me to shoot a handgun so well that it saved my skin outside The Midway Lounge in San Antonio when a man named Bill Hollywood tried to press his luck. I subscribe to *TV Guide* so that I'll know ahead of time if there's going to be any made-for-TV movies about polygamists or women traveling alone and if my name is on any of them.

Truman Michael is, as I predicted, a bad baby. He never sleeps. He chews everything until it gives in to him: my breasts, his bedclothes, his plastic spoon and the rim of his plastic cup, the *TV Guide.* I sometimes call him Jimmy after my father, even though

Mike says it will make him crazy to be called by a name that isn't his. I say it won't make him crazy, and anyway, he can be whatever he wants. Each night, in the dark of his tiny bedroom in Harlingen, Texas, I tell him he must outlive me, children must outlive their parents. I tell him he must never go to Pueblo, Colorado, and if he has to, he must under no circumstances buy firearms there. I tell him he must be kind to women and try not to eat with his hands. When the phone rings and somebody from the Harlingen Volunteer Fire Department says my name, which I never changed, at the beginning of his sales pitch for raffle tickets, well, you can imagine. *Kayla Vane.* It's always Truman Suter's voice.

Truman Michael is colicky and only sleeps, when he sleeps, in a moving vehicle, so we drive all night, just the two of us, because Mike has to get up early. The baby closes his blue eyes, and he turns away from me, toward the passenger-side window, filled now with stars and moonlight, his head pressing against his carseat. When I bring him into the house, I see the markings of sleep all up and down the right side of his tiny face, the skin shiny and wrinkled like he's been burned there. In the dark I call him Jimmy and tell him the story of the first long drive he ever took, I sing him the lullaby of it, how his face was pressed the same way against the inside of my womb, when I tried to imagine him but could only see the round faces of my children in Pueblo, Colorado, whom I had left without the least goodbye. I promise I'll never do him that way, leave without telling. I promise he'll be the first to know.

FAYE GOLD'S
STORY

"I wanted to be a trucker or else one of those nurses who get to fly from city to city with nothing but their whites and a hair dryer. I used to picture myself traveling out of Atlanta, which is where I come from, to Roanoke, Atlanta to Memphis, Atlanta to Charlotte, Atlanta to Charleston, just in time to save victims of Hurricane Hugo. So now when my kids in Paradise Day Care say they want to be nurses or drive trucks when they grow up, I look after them especially hard. I tell them it means they can go anywhere. I tell them a sick person or a cross-country haul is the hand of fate, and it offers itself every day all over the world. I've tried to help them learn to follow the hand of fate like a road map. That's probably the exact lesson I was giving when Eddie Ransom drove into town on his Harley, cursing his brother-in-law and looking for his momma's grave.

"You could hear the bikes from about a mile off, and so by the time they got to our block, my kids had jumped up from the story circle and run for the windows to see what in the world could be creating such a racket. I couldn't even make myself heard to call them back, but it wouldn't have made any difference. It was two men on motorcycles, and they slowed outside the front walk, then swung down the far alley and rode right onto the playground. The smaller man parked a respectful distance from the swings, but the big man glided in and leaned his bike on the jungle gym.

"By then my kids were out the back door, and I was right after them. They ran until they got to just out of reach of the two men and stopped, quiet and starting to put their fingers in their mouths and suck on them the way kids will when they're waiting for something to happen.

" 'Kickstand's broke,' the big man said, 'and anyways, the last time I saw a woman pretty as you, I rode off with the damn thing down and about killed myself. My name is Eddie Ransom. This is my brother-in-law Tommy. He's a damn idiot.'

" 'Eddie, the graveyard's supposed to be right here, over where those kids are standing,' Tommy said.

" 'See what I mean?' Eddie Ransom looked back at me.

"I could tell right then Eddie Ransom was what you call a cool customer, the kind with a dark heart; it will win you points in heaven if you can resist him for twenty-four hours. He had Irish looks, black hair and blue eyes and the high coloring of men who have spent years drinking and working outside.

" 'I'm not an idiot,' Tommy said. 'I'm just trying to help you out, Eddie damn Ransom, and that's the thanks I get?'

"He turned to me.

" 'Ma'am, was there before or is there now a graveyard on this property?'

" 'I don't think so,' I said and couldn't keep myself from asking why they were so interested.

" 'We've been sent out by my wife to search the world over for hers and Eddie's mother's grave,' Tommy said.

" 'That part's actually the truth,' Eddie told me, 'and my mother once lived a half mile away from here, in 1954, and so I believe that gets us into the realm of possibility.'

"My children had recovered themselves enough to start moving in the direction of Tommy's motorcycle. Although it was the closer of the two, Eddie's scared them, and you could see why. The way it leaned against the jungle gym, a fancy round one called a geodesic dome, that Harley looked like some strange axis, leaning on the outside of the world instead of on the inside where it should be. It was force against force, and even a four-year-old knows better than to disturb such a balance."

"Well, then what happened?" Marie Shepherd says, pulling on a T-shirt now that the sun's going down. She's sitting out beside the pool at the Crown & Rose Motor Inn, in Colorado Springs, where she's stopped for the night on her way to California. It's five-thirty in the evening, the cocktail hour, and so she's drinking Diet Pepsi with a little rum poured in to kill the taste, and reading a Robert Ludlum spy novel. She's alone there, except for five women, all in their sixties or seventies. They're seated around a white wrought-iron table playing what sounds to Marie like five hundred rummy. She thinks they have the most gorgeous hair she's ever seen, as long as hers is, and piled on top of their heads or hanging down their backs, raven black, auburn, chestnut, fiery red, not a single gray strand among them.

Ten minutes ago one of these women, her straight black hair layered and full around her face, came over and sat down beside Marie. She adjusted the shoulder straps on her bathing suit and introduced herself as Faye Gold. She told Marie she had once taught a grown man to read using Robert Ludlum novels.

"Got so he could have found his way around Washington, D.C., better than the damn Secret Service, just from reading about spies and Republicans," Faye Gold had said.

"Really?" Marie had asked her.

"You're not Secret Service, are you?" Faye Gold said, taking off her sunglasses and narrowing her eyes. "There's lots of military in this town. You got to be careful."

"No," Marie told her, "I'm just passing through."

"Going where?"

"California."

"Sorry if I'm being nosy, but all by yourself to California?" Faye Gold said.

"Yes," Marie said.

"Aren't you scared?"

"Not when I'm driving. The scary part is stopping every night," Marie answered, surprised she would say these things to a perfect stranger.

"My Eddie used to tell me the same thing. He was a trucker. He said when you're driving, you start to think you've outrun your destiny, but as soon as you stop you see you haven't outrun it and you never ever will. Still, Eddie always got on the road the next morning believing destiny was no match for him and his eighteen wheels. He had to learn all over again every day."

The Eddie she means is Eddie Ransom, and the tale she's about to tell, Faye Gold wanted to warn Marie before it got going full tilt, is a love story unlike any she's ever heard before.

"So Tommy the idiot says he's going to get them some lunch and information at the 7-Eleven they passed up the road because he says there's no 7-Eleven anywhere that doesn't have that certain wise kind of vagrant sitting there and buying Slurpees all day. I thought that was right smart for an idiot and let him go.

"And it's getting to be noontime, so I hustle my children back into Paradise and start handing out their peanut butters and American cheeses. Eddie Ransom is no paying customer, so I let him kind of fend for himself. Pretty soon I see he's sat down at one of the little desks and he's turning over the pages of *101 Dalmations*. One of the boys has sidled away from his lunch to stand beside Eddie.

" 'Who's that gal?' Eddie asks, pointing to the first full-page glossy of Cruella de Vil.

" 'She's Eviletta,' the child said, proving he'd gotten the gist of the story if not all the details.

" 'What's her problem?' Eddie asks.

" 'Read it to me,' the child says.

" 'I can't read,' Eddie says.

"Having navigated his way through this one before, my child goes and gets a shorter book.

" 'Sorry, tiger, I really can't read,' Eddie Ransom says, and there's something in his voice that makes everybody in the room believe him.

"I shoo the child away and ask if I could give Eddie Ransom something to tide him over until Tommy gets back. I always carried an extra sandwich to work in case one of my children hadn't got their lunch that day. Eddie says no, he can wait for Tommy, he's been doing it most of his life anyways. I go back to giving my children their milk or juice, but I'm thinking about Eddie Ransom's momma's grave. Then it hits me: He could use the phone book to look up the cemeteries in town; there weren't but two city cemeteries, and then the Shrine of Rest that takes care of folks who don't go for the underground option.

"He smiles then, Eddie Ransom does, that big toothy open smile of his, and says, yes, ma'am, if I could write down the numbers for him, but otherwise a phone book wouldn't be much use because, like he said before, he really can't read.

" 'How'd you get here, then?' I say. I didn't have much in the way of manners in those days. Not that I'm any Emily Post, but I do better with strangers than I used to. Anyways, he says Tommy read the signs and signaled at the exits, and all in all, he was pretty reliable. But a week earlier old Tommy decided to drag-race with an unmarked police car, and they'd spent the night in jail in Abilene.

" 'Kansas?' I say.

" 'The very same,' Eddie says. 'We enjoyed it so much, we stayed an extra day waiting on Western Union. And the police there liked us as much as we liked them, so they let us go on all the tours and such. They were celebrating eighty-five years of Eisenhower, and they took us to see a gal doing Mamie Eisenhower, and it stuck with me for a long time—poor Mamie, left on the home front while Ike goes ripping off to Europe. It makes me think it's true what they say, it's the woman next to him that makes a man great.'

"And damned if Eddie Ransom's eyes don't shine, and the way he's looking at me, I know he means every word. It makes me hope

Tommy would never come back, if I own up to my thoughts right
then. But of course there was Tommy standing in the doorway with
two giant Slurpees and a white paper bag that smelled like chili
dogs. My children's heads whipped in that direction like they were
on strings.

" 'We'll just go on outside,' Eddie said, and so they did.

"It was mighty hard to keep my mind on those children all
afternoon. Something about Eddie Ransom had got deep down
inside me, and I was petrified he was going to leave to go find his
momma's grave, and I'd never see him again. But he didn't go.
Tommy left and came back two separate times, but Eddie stayed,
stretched out under the shade of a cottonwood on the edge of the
playground.

" 'He's still there, Miss Faye,' one of my children would whisper
from time to time. They made me pull the story circle over close
to the window, so Eddie could hear too. That afternoon I read
them *101 Dalmations,* which I usually try to steer them away from,
because it's so long and they get fidgety, but that day they were rapt.
Rapt. Once or twice I looked out the window and thought I saw
Eddie smiling, but I couldn't be sure, and afterward he never would
allow he'd been listening to that story at all.

"When I took my children outside again after nap time, he came
and sat beside me on the steps and talked about where he'd come
from in West Virginia, a town between Highway 220 and Smoke
Hole Caverns by the south branch of the Potomac River. His
brother owned a hunting lodge back there and got half his face torn
off by a bear. Last spring, he said, he was out visiting his brother
and saw a girl lose her fishing reel in the river, raise her arms to
heaven, and jump in after it. He tried to save her, but it was
snowing hard and he lost her in the current. It was something about
that girl made him decide to finally humor his sister and set out to
look for his momma's grave, something about her arms raised up
that way, with the snow coming down like a curtain between him
and her.

"And just then, when Eddie Ransom looked like he was about to bust out crying, Tommy comes driving up and says he found it, Evergreen Cemetery on South Hancock Avenue.

" 'You found her *grave*?' Eddie says.

" 'No, but I talked to the boss man, and he says by his records, she's there, with all the other Ransoms.'

" 'You idiot,' Eddie says, standing up like he's going to take a swing at Tommy. 'The Ransoms are in goddamn Georgia. She's with the Palmers if she's with anybody.'

" 'Oh,' says Tommy, climbing on his bike and heading back east out to Evergreen.

" 'Maybe you should go with him,' I say to Eddie.

" 'No,' Eddie says. 'How's he ever going to learn to do anything if I don't let him mess up some?'

"By the time Tommy gets back, I'm handing over the last of my children to their parents and wondering am I ever going to see Eddie Ransom again. With an honest-to-goodness ache in my heart, I lock up real slowly and and turn around to say goodbye.

" 'You want to ride along, Miss Faye?' Eddie Ransom says, calling my name like my children do. 'We're going back out to Evergreen to have a look.'

"I allow as how this might be kind of a private moment for the two of them, but Eddie says no, I know about as much of the story as they do, and anyways, right now I could show them where to get supper and they'd buy me mine as thanks for letting them park in my playground.

"And that's why Eddie Ransom came to Colorado Springs, to find Kitty Palmer Ransom's grave, which he never did. And the reason he stayed is that as we're turning the corner at Platte and Nevada, on the way to have supper, we got stuck behind a trucker trying to make the same turn. Eddie Ransom leans back and says to me, what's with that guy, and I read right off the side of the truck, UNITED STATES TRUCK DRIVING SCHOOL INCORPORATED, COL-

ORADO SPRINGS, COLORADO, 1-800-555-SEMI. At the restaurant Eddie tells Tommy he thinks he might stay in town and enroll.

" 'You can't do that,' Tommy says. 'You can't even read.'

" 'I'll learn,' Eddie says. 'Anybody can learn.'

"In the Super-8 Motel, somebody has left *The Gemini Contenders* by Robert Ludlum in the nightstand drawer, right next to the Gideon Bible. That very night Eddie picks it up and makes Tommy do the first paragraph with him. Even if he was an idiot, Tommy had a heart of gold, and they do not only the first paragraph, but the whole first chapter over the next two days.

"This was sixteen years ago. After I married Eddie Ransom, he set about learning to read in earnest. We got through all of Ludlum and then started in on Frederick Forsythe. We were making our big move to John le Carré when Eddie stopped his rig to help a man in a wheelchair change a tire on I-70 and got hit by a drunk driver. Eddie was driving for an outfit called England Transport that has big shiny silver trucks, like the whole rig is wrapped in tinfoil. I expect that drunk driver got mesmerized by the shine of Eddie's truck, and he just couldn't keep away."

—

"We meet here," Faye Gold says, putting her sunglasses back on, "at the Crown & Rose once a week to play cards. We don't generally talk about the dead, even though we're all widows, and some of us kind of recent at that. But we all have a lot in common anyways. We like to grow our hair long and color it back to its natural shade, and we like to take a drink now and then and stay out in the sun so long our skin gets like leather, and it's funny too, but we all like to talk to strangers."

"I'm not a widow," Marie Shepherd says, wanting to offer something of herself as Faye Gold has just done, "but I guess I'm an orphan. My father died when I was ten, and my mother died two years ago." She stops talking and looks at the widows, their beautiful hair, their expectant faces, and she can't help herself. "My mother," she continues, "drove up onto the railroad tracks in Saratoga Springs, New York, got stuck, and couldn't get out in time. It was the Christmas season, and the trunk was full of presents she was out delivering. We found one of her fruitcakes a half mile off, sitting right-side up just below the mailbox of people we didn't know. My brother Sargent and I saw it as we were driving to the funeral, and we didn't say anything about it."

"That's a good one," Faye Gold says, and the Crown & Rose Widows nod their heads in agreement.

"We'll make you an honorary member," Faye Gold says, "and we'll take you out for supper."

"Will you do me a favor first?" Marie says. "Will you cut my hair?"

"Trim it, you mean?" Faye Gold says, reaching over for a hank of hair that lies curled at Marie's waist, and examining it for split ends.

"No, I mean off, all of it, gone."

The Crown & Rose Widows gasp, but Faye Gold is skeptical. "Why would you want to do that?" she says.

"I don't know exactly," Marie says. "I need a change."

"What do you think, Laverne Hall?" Faye Gold says to the Widow beside her.

"I'd say this looks like a five-woman job," Laverne Hall says.

One of the Widows gets a pair of sharp scissors from behind the motel's front desk and lays newspaper along the concrete walkway in front of the door to Marie's room. They pull the desk chair outside and sit Marie down in it.

"We don't have a mirror for you, honey," one of the Widows says.

"That's just as well," Marie tells her. "Anyways, I trust you."

"Big mistake," Faye Gold says. "But such is life. Now, I think we chop about eight inches, and then see where we are."

Marie closes her eyes, feeling the Widows' hands in her hair and listening to the *schush* of the scissors. It reminds her first of her own mother giving her haircuts when she was younger, and then of her first boyfriend and the excited, tentative way he used to put his hands in her hair, holding it up to the light and testing its weight. Marie thinks she's falling in love with the Widows, and then, in the next moment, she's almost sure they're not real women standing behind her, just hands moving and cutting the way the wind does through trees in full leaf. She can feel her head getting lighter, rising right up off her shoulders, into the cloudless sky over the Crown & Rose's swimming pool.

Laverne Hall is the Widows' own personal clairvoyant. She also teaches aerobics, and her tank top and bicycling shorts reveal the figure of a thirty-year-old, right down to the sculpted arm muscles and sinewy calves. She has black hair, pulled back from her face in a tight braid, and Marie notices the roots are flawlessly dyed. Of all the Widows, Laverne Hall's face shows the most age. Marie decides she looks like an eagle, and in certain kinds of light she might be mistaken for Lady Bird Johnson.

Laverne Hall's aerobics classes run four times a week at the Slender You Spa on Palmer Parkway. One of the classes is for widows only, and Laverne plays the *William Tell Overture* to work on the widows' quadriceps and hamstrings. Then she plays Vivaldi at 45 rpm to get the widows' heart rates up. It works every time. She plays *The Four Seasons,* spring when it's spring, summer when it's summer, and so on. The Widows always look forward to the day when Laverne will sense a change in the air and move them on to the new season.

Laverne can look in the mirror while she's doing the runner's stretch and tell right off what's going to happen to you.

"Darlene Orr," she might say one afternoon, "you're going to trip off the sidewalk on your way out today, I can just see it."

And then it would happen, just like Laverne said. Privately, Darlene Orr believed Laverne picked on her because her left leg was two and a quarter inches longer than her right, and it made her prone to falls and spills.

"I'm getting a message," Laverne says now as the Widows continue to work on Marie's hair. "Let me go get my antenna."

She walks back to her lounge chair, reaches into her handbag, and pulls out a necklace of stones that look like amethyst, each one the size of a pecan and wrapped around its middle with silver wire. She slips the necklace over her head and adjusts the stones on her bosom.

"My antenna," she says again to Marie. "Got it at a garage sale, but it doesn't care where it comes from."

Laverne sits down in a white metal pool chair opposite Marie. She twists and squirms to get comfortable, then lights a cigarette and closes her eyes. Her hands make convulsive movements like she's feathering through the pages of a book. One eye opens to look at Marie, who thinks at this moment Laverne seems owlish or sleepy, she doesn't know which.

"We'll just look and see what's happening," Laverne says.

The Widows whisper to Marie that she should reach up to touch her hair and see where it is now. Marie feels the blunt and thickened ends hanging just off her shoulders, and for a second she thinks she'll cry out loud. The sound of her mother's hairbrush passing down over her ears, the flutter and rip of a bird taking wing, and the smell of her mother, which, in her adult life, Marie realized was lipstick and old perfume, these things come rushing back to her. Her heart contracts a little, and then she's all right. Darlene Orr holds up her compact mirror.

"Shall we keep on?" she whispers, and Marie nods.

Laverne frowns and shakes her head.

"Darlene, hush," she says, "I'm getting a message."

Darlene Orr sticks her tongue out at Laverne.

"Very funny, Darlene," Laverne says, without opening her eyes.

In the compact mirror, Marie can see the Widows behind her, smiling, trying not to laugh out loud.

"Marie, Marie," Laverne says. "Marie, there has been a person in your life, important, name beginning with the letter R."

"That would be my father," Marie says.

"And we know he's dead because you told us so back before we started in on cutting your hair. This R. is somebody still present in this life, somebody who's still got ahold of you. And that may well be your daddy. You know, the dead do us that way. So watch out for this R. You work in an office?"

"I used to," Marie says.

"You quit?"

"Yes."

"Well, good. Good because what you were looking forward to was back trouble. From sitting all day. Watch out for your back anyhow, though. You carry too much. You carry loads no woman should be carrying by herself. Let's see, Marie, Marie. You're on your way west, now, is that right?"

"That's right."

"And I see you going out there to have a lot of babies. I see those babies all around you hanging on to your clothes. Oh, golly. They all have on little blue sunsuits. Are you going west to have all those babies?"

"No, ma'am," Marie says, "at least not yet. Right now I'm just going."

Marie looks into the mirror of Darlene Orr's compact. The Widows have cut her hair shorter in front, so that it hangs almost over her eyebrows. She feels like the eyes that look back into hers could belong to anybody.

"You're going to leave your husband," Laverne is saying.

"I don't have a husband."

"The man you live with, then. You're going to leave him."

"I live with my brother," Marie says.

"I guess that's different," Laverne says. "You can't very well leave your brother, now, can you?"

"Not this particular brother."

"No, not this brother," Laverne says. "He's a sensitive one, I see now. He's a kind of poet. Everybody thinks he's crazy. Everybody but you. Is he coming west with you?"

"Yes, he's going to come out as soon as I get settled."

"He misses you. I can tell you that. But he'll be all right. Now, let me ask you something else. Where is your momma buried?"

"Upstate New York," Marie says.

"Where *exactly*?" Laverne presses her.

"Near Ticonderoga, a town named Schroon—that was her name, Marie Schroon. It was everybody's name there."

"You need to go see your momma's grave one more time, like Faye's Eddie did, or send your brother. You need to. I don't know why. You'll find out when you get there."

"I already know why," Marie says, closing her eyes too so that the two women are looking at each other without seeing. "It's because Schroon Lake is washing away its banks, washing into the graveyard. She used to have a pretty good view of the water from her and Daddy's plot, but now it's a little too close for comfort."

"That's right," Laverne says. "You're going to have to go back. You're going to have to move her one last time. That's why you came to us today."

"And had my hair cut?" Marie says. "By the Crown & Rose Widows? What's the meaning of that?"

"It was too long," Laverne says. "It gets tangled up underneath. It falls into your face during aerobics classes and makes your eyes tear up for no good reason. It gets caught in car doors. It blows in your eyes when your're driving, when you need to be able to look down the road and see what's coming. That's why you came to us today and had to endure the story of Faye Gold's life."

"Thank you very much, Laverne Hall," Faye Gold says, "but the story of my life isn't over yet, not by a long shot."

"And nobody knows that better than I do," Laverne says gently. "Go on, Faye, tell her the rest of it."

"Laverne predicted Eddie's death," Faye Gold says to Marie, "practically to the day. I remember exactly how you put it. You said *predecease.* And then the day he died, even before I got word from the highway patrol, Laverne came to the house and said it had happened. Didn't you?"

"It's the honest truth, Marie Shepherd," Laverne says, "but that's not all I predicted, is it?"

The two Widows look at each other, and Marie feels the great tenderness between them. She wishes Sargent were here because she knows she will want to speak to someone about this moment for many years to come.

"No," Faye Gold says, her eyes still locked with Laverne's, "that wasn't all. You also told me I was about to have company. And I did. Lordy, for days. The house was filled with people and casseroles and molded Jell-O salads. But you said it was company I wouldn't be expecting."

"Why do people always bring molded Jell-O salads when somebody dies?" Darlene Orr says.

"Hush, Darlene," Laverne says, "hush and just think about it for a minute. A Jell-O salad with pieces of flora and, on occasion, fauna floating in it. It's perfect, it's the way the dead hang in suspended animation for a while before they leave this world forever. Go on, Faye."

"But that wasn't the company you meant," Faye Gold says. "Two weeks after the funeral a girl walks up to the front door of Paradise Day Care, where I still work after all these years—not a girl, a young woman—and says she's Eddie Ransom's daughter. Even if she hadn't said a word, there wouldn't have been any doubt in my mind. She looked just like him. I'd spent half my life looking at parents and their children, and I'd gotten good at the little twists and turns of resemblance, but I tell you, she was the spitting image."

"How did she find you?" Marie says.

"The way you might guess. Her momma had died the year before, and going through the papers she put two and two together. Her momma and Eddie died on the same day, a year apart."

Behind Marie, the Widows sigh deeply.

"That part gives me gooseflesh every time," Darlene Orr says.

"It must have made you feel strange," Marie says.

"It sure did," Faye Gold says, "at first. But then it made sense to me that a big voracious man like Eddie Ransom would have these other connections to the world. And then his daughter became a kind of wonderful puzzle to me. Every day I'd notice some new way she was like Eddie, without ever knowing him. She even had his voice in a female register. Her name is Frances. It was her momma's name too."

"Did she stay?" Marie says.

"Yes, she did, and I don't know what I would have done without her. Eddie Ransom was the great love of my life, and after he was gone, I didn't want another man. I was too old for another man, but I wanted somebody I could tell Eddie Ransom's stories to. I needed to talk about him for a while, and Frances wanted to hear. Women are good for each other that way. I never met a woman who didn't like to listen to a good story. There's something in a woman that wants to learn new stories and put them away for later, like a savings account. I don't know what they're being learned for or saved for. That part's beyond me."

"Laverne probably knows," Darlene Orr says, and Marie is amazed to hear true reverence in her tone.

"No," Laverne says, "I don't know the why of anything. I know the how and the what and the when, but not the why. I don't know why Eddie Ransom's daughter showed up on Faye's doorstep, and I don't know why you showed up here today. I may tell you I do, but the truth is, the why of things is always smoke and mirrors."

"Can I ask you one more question?" Marie says to Laverne.

"Shoot," Laverne says.

"Will my life be happy?"

"Marie, Marie." Laverne closes hers eyes. "You will achieve peace and great dignity. But happy? Let's see."

"I can tell you a story about happy," Faye Gold says, "same as a story about love. Laverne's about to say it's up to you. She's about to tell you that in this life you choose happiness or love, sorrow or an early grave. But there's always the hand of fate to contend with. I can tell you right now none of us would have chosen to be widows, not even Laverne her very own self."

"True," Laverne says, opening her eyes.

"So, happiness, love—" Faye Gold says.

Marie leans forward in her chair, waiting for Faye Gold to finish the sentence. There's silence in the fading daylight around the Crown & Rose swimming pool, a quiet that seems to sweep from the darkening blue of the chlorinated water, straight west through Manitou Springs, up Pike's Peak and over it, clear to California. Marie waits until she realizes the Widows are no longer standing behind her. They're shadows now, sweeping up the cut swaths of her hair, rolling up the newspaper, returning the scissors to the motel office. Laverne is taking off her antenna, folding the string of beads in half and half again, like they're a scarf or a shawl. The Widows know Faye Gold isn't going to finish her sentence, not now or ever.

Marie thinks about getting on the road tomorrow morning and not stopping again until she comes face to face with the Pacific Ocean. She recalls what Sargent said to her on the phone last night. He said he misses her, that he never knew he could be so lonely before now. He said feeling this way reminds him of something he's never told Marie, that one night years ago he overheard their father say to their mother, *You are so beautiful, I never knew what it was to be happy before now, I never knew how to love before you.* Tonight Marie thinks about the truth of what passed between her father and her mother, between Eddie Ransom and Faye Gold. All over the world no one knows these things, how to love, or how destiny can't be outrun. Everyone is just learning.

CLOSE
TO FALLING

Just before they hit Amarillo, Texas, heading west on U.S. 40, Juno Reinhart's father tells her he wants to run up to Colorado Springs for a visit. He calls to her from the back of her pickup, where he's been riding for the last two days, prone and pissed off, his broken leg resting on top of two stiff pillows. They're twenty-three hours out of St. Louis, where Mack Reinhart, hoping to outrun creditors, a bankrupt travel business, and a wife, flipped his Ford Taurus into the median strip on Interstate 70, and lived to tell the tale. When Juno arrived at the hospital and saw her father, her first thought was that he'd been thrown into bed, flung into traction, by some huge explosion in his life, and the sheer truth of that thought made her weak. So when he asked, she agreed to drive him the rest of the way to California. There was business to attend to out west, he told her, then wouldn't explain.

"Damn it, Dad," Juno says now. She pulls her truck off the highway and turns around to face him. "I'm doing you a favor. This isn't a tour bus. I'm not your chauffeur. And enough mystery. What the hell's in California?"

"You are what I say you are, and you'll go where I say you'll go," Mack Reinhart tells his daughter. "No more questions. None of this is any of your affair."

"How come you never want us to think you have a life?" Juno says. "Why does it all have to be such a big goddamn secret?"

Mack Reinhart turns to face out the back window of the truck and doesn't say a word. Juno feels like the fifteen she used to be, not the twenty-five she is. She remembers fifteen as the worst year of her life until now, a year full of reprimands and silences just like these. She remembers how she couldn't wait to drive.

Sometimes, for an hour or so as she heads toward Colorado, Juno tries not to worry about her father and all his losses, his desperate trip west. She tries not to think about herself either, but it's a losing battle. She's pretty sure she's pregnant, but she's not telling anybody yet, least of all her husband. The highway ahead of her, endless and bleak in the late haze of summer, comes to seem like her nightly phone conversations with him. His voice rises up at her now, through the floorboards of the truck; it becomes the knocking of the motor, the small changes in pressure and temperature that are supposed to keep good machines running. He doesn't understand why she's making this trip, and he's stopped trying to. Last night their conversation wasn't about the road or her father. He didn't ask where she was calling from. He talks to her now, Juno thinks, like he doesn't realize she's gone. He doesn't know she's in love with somebody else, he doesn't imagine she's carrying a child that isn't his.

She wants to think with the mind of a pioneer, a woman pioneer, traveling a hundred and thirty years ago, leaving her life behind and gathering it up at the same time. A woman pioneer astounded by the Rockies but not for very long because she has to keep busy rolling out bread dough on the wagon seat, turning sideways to knead and flatten so that she's seeing this landscape just as it passes, always in that instant. She's not looking backward or forward, and she wants it that way.

Juno once read about such women in a collection of manuscripts in the New York Public Library—the journals of Jane Cazneau, Lodisa Frizzell, and Adrietta Applegate Hixon, three women traveling to California on the Oregon Trail. She says their names over and over. She imagines the first Mormons too, coming over the Wasatch Mountains in Utah; she pictures Brigham Young's thirteen wives getting their first look at that huge lake stretched out before them, then rushing down to it, only to get a mouthful of salt.

She thinks that the land she's traveling through now is still the same rough country, still rife with sudden injury and hard betrayal. At the Western Auto in La Junta, Colorado, where Juno and her father stop to buy motor oil, the manager looks out the window at Juno's truck, says, "Fucking truck caps," and holds up his right hand, brushing it close to her cheek. He's missing all four fingers above the first knuckle, and the wound is new and softly pink.

"When you go to take off the cap," he says, "get a pro to do it for you. Get somebody with block and tackle, or a crane. I tried to do it myself, and this is as far as I got."

"The women love it, though," one of the salesclerks calls out from behind his cash register.

Juno wonders why that would be so, why women would love such an injury, and while she thinks about it, she hears another customer telling another clerk about his girlfriend who had tried to shoot him but ended up shooting herself in the leg.

Later, in a Conoco station, her father reports hearing two boys talk about decorating the top of somebody's birthday cake with Draino. They say it looks just like those sugar-candy sprinkles.

"Should we stop them?" Juno asks.

"I think I did," Mack Reinhart says. "I told them I was a necrologist, and poisoning was the first thing we looked for in autopsies."

"A necrologist?" Juno says, glad for any conversation from her father. "You sure can think on your feet, Dad." She's trying to be kind. "Glad I have you out here to protect me."

From Pueblo, Colorado, it's a straight shot north through more dangerous, empty country to Colorado Springs, where Mack Reinhart spent 1954 as a cadet at the United States Air Force Academy. They'll take the tour, find a motel, eat supper, and then Juno will call her husband. She'll have all that time to decide what to say, how to explain this accidental falling out of love, how to tell him she's not coming back.

—

"How does it look, Dad?" Juno calls to her father, and Mack Reinhart reaches his hand through the slider, leaning forward to get a grip on her shoulder and looking north up I-25.

"It's just the same," he says. "It was just this kind of weather when we drove in from Chicago, only we were coming from the other direction."

Juno can hear a tremor rising in her father's voice. She's heard this story a thousand times, how her father grew up in Chicago with his Aunt Marnie and her cousin Florence, then left to seek his fortune in the West, came out with Aunt Marnie's sweetheart, a teacher at the Air Force Academy named Jack Emerson.

"Tell me about this sweetheart," Juno says.

"I haven't thought about him in years," Mack Reinhart says, "but the long and short of it is, he got mixed up with a married woman, an officer's wife, no less, and everybody in Colorado Springs knew about it, everybody except the officer whose wife it was, and of course Marnie back in Chicago. You used to see them at Mass on Sundays, all three sitting in the same pew. It went on the whole year I was there, and then he broke off his engagement to Marnie in June. Last I heard of him, he married a Japanese woman and they started a lingerie business."

"Didn't you ever ask him what the hell he thought he was doing with Aunt Marnie?" Juno says, feeling a small guilty contraction around her heart.

"Once. Got my arm broken too."

Juno's seen a photograph of her father with the wrist-to-shoulder cast, in his dress uniform, his good arm around her mother's waist. In front of the camera they looked like other people, Juno always thought, not her parents, not anybody she'd ever known or ever would. She feels this way about her father now, has felt it with every mile, the veil of their shared history dropping off, so that they've become almost strangers to one another. She thinks of her mother and then of her own husband, two people left behind, alone with albums and drawers full of photographs that don't give anything away, don't even offer any clues.

Just south of the academy gates they can see cadets running parachute exercises, chutes opening like ashy blossoms and swinging slowly down out of the sky. The sight makes Juno feel dizzy, and then, for some reason, sad.

"You need to call home, Dad. It's been two days."

"I know it. I don't need you telling me what to do."

"So, when will you?"

"I'm not sure when."

"Tonight?"

"Maybe. Just you let me handle it."

"I want you to promise me."

"Well, I won't promise you, you hear? Anyways, it's between your mother and me, and you just keep out of it."

Juno jams on the brake and pulls the truck off the highway onto the shoulder. She feels her stomach heave again and barely makes it out of the cab to lose her breakfast on the side of I-25. When she's sure there's nothing left, she walks back to the truck and leans against the door on the passenger side. It's the third morning in a row she's been sick this way, and she knows what it means.

"Honey," her father says, his voice coming from a long way off, through the closed door and the rolled-up window, "if you're feeling bad again, we can go to a motel and rest."

"No, I'm fine," she says, turning halfway around and staring north down the highway. "Just humor me a little, Dad, okay?"

For the rest of the drive to the academy, Mack Reinhart speaks gently to his daughter, talking about his nine months as an officer-in-training, but Juno isn't listening. She keeps driving, aware of the road, aware of the other drivers, but some part of her has gone way down inside her own body and is moving around quietly, checking for other signs of what she now knows to be true and real, knows with the certainty she's heard other pregnant women talk about: *Something twisted itself under my heart, a fist clenching, an eye opening, and then I knew.* She thinks that she makes old Jack Emerson look like a saint.

At the north entrance to the academy grounds they stop at a guardhouse, and a uniformed cadet hands them a brochure and wishes them a good morning. They drive on and make the turn past the B-52 bomber display. Juno can hear her father laughing quietly, and she asks him what's so funny.

"I had this idea," he says. "I know it's stupid, but I had this idea the guard would recognize me."

Juno smiles into the rearview mirror and then asks her father if he wants to stop and take a look at the B-52s. She reads to him from the brochure: "the backbone of America's manned bomber force for more than a quarter of a century." Mack Reinhart says absolutely not, that it's the place he wants to see, not the machines. He says most people in America get the two confused.

They wind down the driveway past Falcon Stadium, over Academy Boulevard, and uphill to the Visitor's Center, where Juno parks and helps her father out of the back of the truck, over the tailgate, and up onto his crutches. Just as it's happened at every stop they've made, people nearby quit whatever they're doing, even unloading their own children, to watch in awed silence. Juno wonders if all these people think her father is a celebrity, some kind of magician, a Houdini come up from hours or maybe even days underwater, bound in chains, hobbled by his feat but still alive. She knows her father loves every minute of it, hobbled by his feet, she thinks, as he struggles and grimaces with pain, then throws his shoulders back and swings off on his crutches, slow and stately. Even if his audience is only the attendant at the gas station where they've stopped for a fill-up, Mack Reinhart moves like he's a war hero. Everyone who's watching him now believes this to be so.

Inside the Visitor's Center those who wish to take the guided tour are directed into the Falcon Amphitheater. Juno and her father move down the left aisle to the front row, where Juno sees two seats together. A chubby teenage girl in tan shorts and a pink LaCoste shirt is explaining the layout of the academy grounds. She's an officer's daughter, an Air Force brat, she says, and she knows the place intimately. Juno doesn't like the way she says that word, *intimately*. She doesn't think the girl's father would like it either.

"The altitude here is seven thousand, two hundred eighty feet above sea level," the officer's daughter says. "If you experience difficulty breathing, please take your time and rest often. We'll be walking a third-of-a-mile nature tail uphill to the Air Force chapel. The gentleman on crutches down front might want to take our courtesy vehicle."

"No thank you, ma'am," Mack Reinhart says loudly, then lowers his voice. "These legs can make it just fine."

Juno looks at her father's face in the shadow of the amphitheater and thinks she might cry. She sees he's trying so hard to belong here, not to let on that he didn't make it for longer than a year, and wouldn't have made it now either because he's such a stubborn son of a bitch. She watches him smile and nod as he listens to Air Force history and Air Force lore, indistinguishable now in the darkness surrounding them. When the lights come up again, Juno notices her father's hands are curled into tight fists, and she wonders which she should believe, the sleepy smile on her father's face or what she sees in his hands, the punch waiting to be thrown.

As they file out of the amphitheater toward the nature trail, she thinks her brother should be making this visit to the academy with him now, maybe even this whole trip, or it should be her mother, but somehow it's come to be Juno who's bearing witness to her father's defeats, his unraveling. She feels that new certainty rising in her belly, in her womb, all over again, and stranger than ever. She sees herself and her father facing each other across a desert of their mistakes, and she wonders about all they're going to have to say to each other in the days to come.

"The first-year cadets are called doolies," the officer's daughter is telling them, "from the Latin *doulous,* or slave."

"You bet your ass," Mack Reinhart says, and a few of the tourists walking ahead of him laugh.

"Hazing is an acknowledged part of life for doolies," she continues, narrowing her eyes against the crowd like she's looking for campus activists and bleeding-heart liberals to challenge the justice of what she's just revealed. "They must walk along the white bricks you see below, and if asked to, they must move double-time. When passing an upperclassman or woman, doolies must call out their names and hometowns, as fast and as loud as they can."

So that's it, Juno thinks, that barking out of names and addresses is what makes it sound like there are arguments going on all over the place.

"This is very progressive," she says to her father as they're walking down the hill toward the Air Force chapel. "I've heard they chain women doolies to the urinals in the men's bathrooms."

"Let me tell you right now, girl," her father says in a tough-guy voice she's never heard before, "the men who would chain a woman to a urinal are the men who never make it, the men who nosedive, the men who bail out, the guys who choke and forget to open their chutes."

"Do you really think anybody forgets to open a parachute? Maybe it's justice."

"I know they forget."

"How do you know?"

"Because I saw a guy have it happen to him exactly that way. A buddy of mine. He was so taken with the view he forgot to pull the rip cord."

Mack Reinhart throws off his daughter's arm, which she has been holding under his elbow, and he tries to move out ahead of her. For a second she lets him go. The air feels sharp, like it's hardened and cracked into small pieces, then reformed itself whole around her face.

"Did it happen to you?" she says, the realization and the question coming at the same time. "Is that why you left?"

"It wasn't my kind of place. Maybe I was too dumb to keep up with those smart guys, I don't know. I'd already met your mother. It didn't make any sense to stay."

"But what about the guy who was so taken with the view? Did he die?"

Her father keeps silent.

"It just didn't open?" Juno says.

"I don't remember."

"Come on, Dad. You wouldn't have mentioned it just now if you didn't remember. You were right there, you said. You saw the whole thing."

Juno stops, but her father stumps along ahead of her.

"I'm sick of trying to care about your life," she calls after him. "Go ahead and be so damn mysterious. It doesn't make any difference to me. It doesn't matter."

These last three words come out as a shout, and other members of their tour group turn to look at Juno and then at her father. She can feel their disgust, she can hear them: Look at that young woman, yelling at her poor injured father. Mack Reinhart swings steadily ahead on his metal crutches, up the steps and inside the Air Force Academy chapel.

"It doesn't matter," she says again, more quietly, but he's way out of earshot now.

"You know why there's seventeen arrows on top of the chapel?" the guide is asking. "You won't believe it, it's so simple. There's seventeen because that's how many there was room for. No big deal, no hidden meaning. I've had people say to me, come on, now, that's not the real reason, but I say, Hey, buddy, if you don't believe me, you can call up my dad."

When she's inside, standing at the back of the chapel, Juno can see her father sitting by himself in the second pew. Okay, she whispers to steady herself, just go and sit down next to him. Her father is silent, staring straight ahead.

"Look at these," he says quietly when Juno's beside him. "Kneelers only the Air Force would have."

The two of them pull at the wooden slats underneath the pew in front of theirs, but nothing moves. As their tour guide passes by, she tells them not to bother, these aren't kneelers, she says, they're hat racks. She turns to face the pews and starts to explain how the building houses three individual chapels, the one they're now seated in, for Protestants, another for Catholics, and the third for Jews. Each chapel has a theme, and she invites members of the tour to guess what the theme is here in the Protestant chapel.

"Falling," Juno says out loud, realizing that she's also instinctively raised her hand to be called on. "I bet the theme here is falling."

"No," the guide tells her, "but you're real close. Anybody else have a guess? No? No takers? It's propellers."

"Now, how is that close to falling?" Juno whispers to her father, and when he turns to her, shrugs his shoulders, and rolls his eyes to the ceiling, she feels the weightlessness of relief. She knows it's okay between them, or it's going to be.

The tour guide points out the pews, the gunmetal-gray strips, like submarine sidings, that run along the tops, and the crucifix over the altar, which is formed by two crossed propeller blades. The organ, she says, boasts the largest and most pipes of any organ west of the Mississippi River. When Juno turns around to look at it, she can't believe how much the pipes look like missiles. She wonders if anybody's noticed it before her, if her whole tour group is making the same observation right now.

The group moves downstairs to the Catholic chapel, where there's also a theme for them to guess.

"Flight," Juno says to her father, thinking of the Holy Spirit, ascension, and the whole Air Force itself. She asks if he hears a steady whirring noise, and he says yes, that it sounds like airplane engines, the way they hum quietly right before taxi and takeoff.

"Any guesses about the theme down here in the Catholic chapel?" the tour guide says, putting too much emphasis on the word *down*. Mack Reinhart elbows his daughter in the ribs and gives her the go-ahead sign, but this time she keeps quiet.

"It's catacombs," the guide announces. She can't conceal how happy it's made her to have, so far, fooled all of the people all of the time. "Catacombs were large underground vaults serving as cemeteries for early Christians, who did not follow the Greek and Roman practices of cremation. They were built in Italy, North Africa, Asia Minor, and other Christian areas from the first to the fifth century A.D. The main catacombs, outside the city gates of Rome, lie twenty-two to sixty-five feet below ground and occupy six hundred acres of space in multilevel passages lined with tiers of niches for bodies. The plaster walls and ceilings were frescoed. Goths and later invaders plundered the catacombs, and by the eighth century most bodies had been transferred to churches. Preservation is now controlled by the pope."

"She's getting a little off-track," Juno says, "don't you think?"

"She's only human," Mack Reinhart whispers back.

The tour guide tells them that the colors of the stained glass in the Catholic chapel—browns and purples and a buttery yellow—were chosen to give the sensation of being underground, and the engineers and the architect designed and constructed special ducts along the walls to bring air in from the outside so that it would sound like rushing water. Then she asks everyone to turn their attention to the stations of the cross that line the walls, and notice how each station has a tiny cross hidden in it, a cross made of gold mined in the state of Colorado.

"It's a symbol," she says, "for the ways the riches of this life are sometimes hidden from our eyes."

"Amen to that," Mack Reinhart says, without looking at his daughter.

The guide leads her tour past the Jewish chapel, which she claims is too small to accommodate the entire group, and Juno will remember later that they never heard what its theme was, and it will happen in the middle of the California desert that she'll feel she needs to know.

Mack Reinhart walks around behind the chapel, and Juno follows him, across the west plaza and inside the Cadet Social Center, where they pretend to be interested in the athletic trophies. They can hear cadets in the snack bar and in the bookstore, the soft hum of conversation. Behind them a cadet is talking to a prospective student and his parents. You get used to the jumps, he's saying. Human beings can get used to anything. It's how they conquer fear.

"Come on," Mack Reinhart says finally, "we don't belong in here."

They stop to rest on a bench that faces south, and they look out over the academy and the whole front range of the Rockies, south to the Sangre de Cristo Mountains and New Mexico.

"I never could have stayed here," Mack Reinhart says, "with or without Jack Emerson."

Juno hates hearing her father talk this way, hates the idea that there are things he can't do.

"He did more than just break your arm."

"He pretty much drummed me out, but I guess he had good reason to." He stops talking and points south toward downtown Colorado Springs. "Right out there. I went out with him on a training exercise, the two of us and four other cadets, and I didn't give you the straight story back there, it was me who got bailed out, on my first jump ever."

Mack Reinhart tells his daughter most guys did their first jump tandem, but he was a daredevil fool, and he wanted to fall for a while before he gave in to the parachute. He turned a somersault, throwing himself out of the symmetrical face-to-earth position. He watched Jack Emerson fold his arms along his side, accelerate, and reach out to pull Mack's rip-cord handle. On the ground he told everybody that Reinhart panicked and couldn't deploy his own chute.

"I went crazy, called him every name in the goddamn book, told him he was trying to make me look like a fool, he was just waiting for his chance, so that if I ever spilled the beans to Marnie, which I had every intention of doing, nobody would believe me, they'd think it was just revenge."

"So you left."

"It seemed like there wasn't much else I could do."

"Why did you want to come back out here now?"

"It's been feeling like a kind of unfinished business. I have dreams about this place some nights, and I dream I'm still in the air, still falling."

He is quiet for a moment.

"We need to write your mother a postcard," he says, getting up from the bench and moving off in the direction of the gift shop.

Juno stays where she is, watching him go. She wonders what other secrets her father's been keeping all these years. She thinks they must number in the hundreds or even the thousands. And why should he tell her any of them? What business is it of hers? Watching his broad back and shoulders, she thinks her father's secrets are like all the grains of sand on a beach, or like the stars at night when you're up this high, this close to the heavens and this far from home.

They exit I-25 at Garden of the Gods Road and drive south to Highway 24. Mack Reinhart wants to see how close they can get to Pike's Peak, maybe even drive the highway to the top. Juno has trouble believing there's a paved nineteen-mile highway to the summit of a 14,110-foot-high mountain. There is a highway, but it's only paved for the first mile, and no one tells tourists the truth about this, thinking it might scare many of them off, which it would. They stop at the tollgate, and Mack Reinhart reads out loud from the Colorado Springs Chamber of Commerce Tour Book, about Zebulon Montgomery Pike, born on January 5, 1779, in Lamberton, N.J.

" 'Began his army career at the age of fifteen,' " he reads, "a real prodigy. 'Headed a search for the source of the Mississippi River, and though he mapped Pike's Peak in 1806, he never reached the summit himself. Died when a powder magazine accidentally exploded during the War of 1812.' "

"Age thirty-four," Juno says, shaking her head.

"Jesus," her father says, "I hope he found the source of the Mississippi, at least."

"Me too. Well, what do you say? To the top of the peak?"

"Why not?"

Later Juno will wonder exactly what she and her father talked about in the two hours it took to get to the summit of Pike's Peak, and she'll finally decide that she didn't talk at all. She keeps her eyes on the road because not only is there no paving after the first mile, but no guardrails either, nothing between them and free-fall into the wide-open space of America. Juno feels queasy, and she wonders if it's the baby or the onset of altitude sickness, which she's heard takes the form of an upset stomach. Her father laughs about having lost his bearings completely, but Juno doesn't think it's very funny. He chatters on, first about the old couple tailgating in the car behind them then about grandparents, and Juno asks her father if he knew his.

"No, they were long gone," he says. "Marnie seemed like the

closest thing I had to a grandmother, but she was about my mother's age. So we didn't think about it that way."

He starts to laugh again, softly this time, and Juno asks what's so funny.

"I was just thinking about the things she said at the very end. She was completely lost, her mind already headed out to wherever before her body had a chance to follow."

"She thought she was in Omaha," Juno says. She's been told this story before too.

"She wondered if she was in Omaha. That's the part I hate to think about. I wish she could have felt sure. I didn't like her not knowing where she was. But before that, earlier in the day, she read us an imaginary letter from Jack Emerson, just reeled it off, something like, Dear Marnie, it has come to my attention, through a relative of yours, that you are in relatively difficult circumstances, related to your health. Every sentence had the word *related* or *relative* in it. And then she looked up at me and asked if that didn't sound just like Jack Emerson. And, by God, it did."

"She just made it up?"

"Out of the clear blue sky, no props, not even a sheet of paper lying around to give her the idea."

Juno watches her father in the rearview mirror. He's laughing so hard tears are running down his cheeks.

"The last person she asked for was my cousin Florence," he says when he's able to speak again. " 'You come here, Florence!' Florence had been dead for almost ten years, but Marnie yelled for her like they were in the same room. She told Florence 'My arm's been burned, but I'll be all right.' "

Juno hears some weight gathering in her father's voice, and she waits for him to explain.

"You were too young to remember any of this," he says. "Florence burned to death. She dropped a match on her housecoat, and it went up in flames."

"Jesus, Dad," Juno says. "I never knew that."

"And Marnie did get burned," her father continues as if he hasn't heard her. "Not too badly, so she was all right. The whole thing was an act of God, it's clear to me now. Your mother and I were coming up to tell Marnie and Florence it was time to pack up and come live with us. They couldn't keep on alone, in Chicago. We were in midair when the fire happened, your mother and me, flying in from Atlanta. Florence died the next day, really of heart failure. The burns didn't seem that bad, but she knew and Marnie knew what our visit was all about, and she wouldn't have wanted to leave."

Mack Reinhart stops talking, and Juno thinks she ought to say something into this silence, but she can't imagine what.

"It was a hell of a weekend." He's laughing again, and Juno thinks maybe he's not afraid to remember all of this, that maybe he's even a little happier for remembering. "It was the same weekend that the South Shore Country Club closed its doors for good. On Saturday night everybody had one last drink and threw their glasses into Lake Michigan. The next morning your mother and I were in the South Shore Hospital getting Marnie's burns taken care of, and there must have been twenty-five kids come in with cut feet. They'd gone in swimming and stepped on all that broken glass.

"When we left the hospital, we went over to the club for lunch, and it was crazy. Everybody wanted a souvenir, and most of the glasses were at the bottom of Lake Michigan, so they made off with the silverware, which was pretty fancy—a lot of initials and somebody's family crest. For every place setting, you could get maybe a teaspoon and a butter knife. It was just wild, just wild. I was never so close to so many things falling apart at once in my whole life."

Until now, Juno wants to say, but she doesn't.

At the top of Pike's Peak Juno and her father and all the other tourists who've made it to the summit are enveloped in clouds and fog shot through with sun, so that the air seems silky, like being caught on the inside of a spider's web. As they're getting out of the truck, a warning from the Park Service comes over the loudspeaker on the roof of the gift shop, telling tourists to beware of lightning, to stay in their vehicles unless absolutely necessary. Juno catches a glimpse of herself in the window of the truck and sees the hair on the top of her head raised straight up by the force of the electricity in the air. There's snow on the ground, and a few flakes of it falling out of the sky.

She walks around to the back of the truck and opens the tailgate. Her father swings his legs around to the edge of the truck bed but makes no move to get out, so Juno sits down next to him. Together they look west, off the summit toward Cripple Creek and the emptied gold beds to the south. The fog drifts in and out of their field of vision, and Juno asks her father if he wants to get out and take some pictures, now that they've come 14,110 feet above sea level. She wants to tell him this is as close to heaven as she's ever going to get, she wants to say those words and have him hold her the way he did when she was five or six, and tell her she was talking a lot of nonsense, the way he did then. She wants to say these things, but then she looks at him and sees how frightened he is to be at this elevation. She hands her father the camera and walks to the very edge of the observation platform and turns around. She's far enough out so that only her toes are touching the cement, and she stretches her arms out for balance, to thwart gravity, and she smiles at the camera for all she's worth, smiles like her life is depending on it.

THE TRUE STORY

There are two ways to tell this story, he thinks, and neither one of them will ever be the truth. There's the way he would tell it, and then there's the way she's going to be telling it to his wife, later on tonight in the far corner of the kitchen or out in the garden in Concord, California, where they're going to meet because he's going to introduce them, his wife and his college girlfriend, who are practically neighbors now, by chance, after all these years.

The hard truth is, when he was in college he'd once let this woman take a punch for him, straight to the jaw, outside the post office on Mt. Auburn Street in Cambridge, Massachusetts. It wasn't even a question of *let;* it had happened so fast he didn't see it coming, the other man's fist, he didn't at that very moment under a clearing sky in February of his senior year know exactly where she was on the sidewalk. Later that night, his arms around her in the dark, he remembered that she had been turning her body, slowly and carefully, turning inward toward him. She had known, even if he hadn't, that the man whose wife he had just insulted in the post office was going to hit him. She had known, and as he touched her fractured jaw, as the half-light of the winter moon came icing through the trees and into the dormitory window, she was turning her lovely body just the same way, turning slowly, so that first her right hip grazed his left hip, then her belly moved across his like lava, steady and hotter than anything he could imagine. The incident outside the post office was slipping from his memory, and he watched it go, like a beautiful woman through a doorway, like a receding train or the sun falling below the horizon, and next, all of

February, his senior year, Cambridge, Massachusetts, gone too like melted ice, melted by the terrible heat from her body, and again he didn't know where she was, though when he closed his eyes, she was everywhere.

It's the story of the post office he thinks she'll tell his wife this evening, after each of them has a couple of drinks and becomes charming to the other. He knows it will happen, has known it for years, and still he's never told his version, never casually in the early days of their marriage—*did I mention the time?* or *once at the post office* or *stamps always remind me of something that happened.* And now he sees it beginning: They will get a little drunk, his wife and his college girlfriend, and eye each other across the room, then they will start to make the kind of circles women make around a party, his wife circling to collect empty glasses and crumpled napkins, and she, she will be moving to look at their art or their photographs, or to talk to his college friends, her college friends, all of them reunited tonight in Concord, California: Brad and Matthew and Jeanne, Elise and Diane, Dan, Tim, Grace, Bernie, who's a priest now, whom she always liked, Jeff, Katie, Ruth, people she hasn't seen in years. They'll end up together in the kitchen, his wife and his college girlfriend, and they'll be sweet to each other and relieved the other is sweet back. They'll try not to talk about him, they'll give it the old college try, but then they'll make themselves another drink, and that's when it will come out, the post office story, maybe, he hopes, he wonders, maybe only part of it the truth.

—

What truly happened was this: He went to the post office to buy stamps, and she went with him to mail a package. She was thinking about the snow coming down, hoping it would fall all afternoon and all night and lock them up in the white of winter's eye where nothing moves. She was also thinking about the letter in his hand, a note to his father, who had, she thought at the time, very creepy handwriting for a man, loopy and girlish. He was thinking about her package, the one she was going to mail, and wondering why she wouldn't tell him, didn't offer to tell him, what it was or where it was going. He was also thinking about buying orange juice and limes at the Broadway Market. He was reminding himself that last week he'd bought too few limes and too much orange juice, and wondering why he couldn't bring himself to ask her about the damn package; what was he so afraid of?

The post office was crowded because it was a Friday and the price of stamps was about to go up. It seemed everyone had a letter they'd put off writing or sending for months, years even, and now the time had come. He also remembers it was a Friday because every Friday afternoon he served his friends drinks in his dorm room, and that's what the limes and orange juice were for. He was good to his friends, liked having them around, catering to them, and that was what she first loved about him, how generous he was, how kind. She once told him this, and now when she thinks of him, which is with only fondness, she wonders if he remembers. The truth is, of all she ever said to him, those are the words he's never forgotten and never will.

The post office was packed, and service was slow. Customers filled the vestibule in a snaking line, and she turned to watch the snow melt off their clothes and form small moats at their feet. As she watched, a child ran in, slipped in a puddle of water, fell and bloodied his mouth. His crying echoed through the huge chamber of the post office, surprisingly, because there were so many bodies to absorb sound, so many bodies wearing so much wool and down. Everyone had something better to do on a Friday afternoon, much better than stand in line at the post office and listen to a wailing child and worry about that child's bloody mouth, or scour the floor for possible missing teeth. Everyone was thinking about his or her letter, long overdue, longed-for, maybe. Everyone was impatient now to send good news in the nick of time, to mail the check, the heirloom, the valentine frayed and fluttering like a real live heart.

He felt for the child, a brave little boy, about five or six; he ached for him, and so he took hold of her hand a little bit tighter, thinking someday the two of them might have such a child, have to console such a child in a post office on a snowy day in February. Not long ago, when they had been out walking together, they'd passed a young mother carrying a child on her shoulders, and he'd said out loud, *I want one,* and the young mother had smiled and said, *It's easy,* and they'd all laughed then, even the child had laughed. Neither one of them even dreamed that someday he and his wife, who would not be her, would have twins and then twins again, that twice he would listen with wonder to two hearts beating in his wife's belly, and later they would all find themselves practically neighbors in Concord, California.

Louder than the cries of the child in the post office on Mt. Auburn Street in Cambridge, Massachusetts, was the sound of a buzzer, and as the child's crying trailed to a cough and a hiccup, the gnaw of the buzzer grew louder and louder, impossible to talk above. By the time the child had fallen completely silent, every postal customer had turned his or her attention to the parcels window, where a scowling woman was leaning on the buzzer, trying to summon, to conjure one of the attendants, all of whom were busy at the other windows.

If he'd thought about it later, which he didn't, he would have said that sympathy for the bleeding child was what made him turn and stare at the woman by the buzzer, stare hard until she felt the weight of his eyes and looked back at him. It was compassion that made him then mouth that particular obscenity, a word rarely, if ever, spoken by a man to a woman in a public place. He would have admitted that it wasn't exactly logical, but he thought the child deserved more attention than the woman at the buzzer did, that faced with a crying, injured child, people shouldn't be as selfish as they were in everyday life. So he turned his whole body toward this woman and waited until he had her full attention, then formed the single word slowly and carefully, his lips moving around the vowels and consonants, his tongue popping off the back of his front teeth to give the final syllable extra force. The woman's own mouth opened and closed, and then she looked away. A postal clerk had lifted the metal screen at the parcels window, and so she turned to collect her packages.

His girlfriend was at that moment stepping up to the counter and handing over her parcel to be weighed. She wanted to put her lips to the manila envelope and kiss it for good luck, but the clerk took it before she had a chance to, took it, looked at the address, and said "New York, New York," and sang the words, *Start spreading the news,* and she wondered, hoped that even this small gesture could be some kind of sign. In the package were ten of her sketches, which she was sending off to a famous artist in New York who had asked to see them. She had written to him ten days before, presented herself and her connections, and his reply, mailed within the week, said, *Let's do it, let's see what you've got. And if they ain't my thing, I'll tell you, and if you don't give a damn what I think, that's just as good. I don't own the art business, but I do have some influence.* And so she had high hopes. It seemed to her then the beginning of something, a force she couldn't name, not her career or her future, much bigger than either of these, and this was why she hadn't told him what was in the parcel. Not telling him was a kind of insurance, in case she was wrong about this beginning, in case the famous artist wrote back saying, *These are not what I had in mind, not what I thought,* or worse, didn't write back at all. If this happened, she wanted to bear it in private, in silence. She hated the way people seemed to announce their failures, tell their troubles, offer their bleeding, oozing, chancrous wounds so eagerly. *Talk is cheap,* she said to her college roomates when she wanted them to leave her alone, and though she had not said those words to him, whose hand she had just been holding, she believed someday she would.

He bought a book of stamps and affixed one to the letter to his father, the letter telling his father about his plans for the summer, which were to stay in Cambridge, work in the library, and live with this girl whose hand he had just been holding. His father would not like it, he knew, not the living with her, not the staying in Cambridge, but he believed he had made up his mind, and he wanted to give his father the next two months to get used to the idea. He knew it could be the beginning of the end with his father, who more and more couldn't understand what the hell his son was doing with his life. *It's February of your senior year,* his father had just said over the phone, *and what plans have you made?* He stood to one side of the counter and looked at the envelope, then unzipped his jacket and put the letter in the breast pocket of his shirt. He told himself he'd mail it outside, at the Broadway Market, back at the dorm, tomorrow, next week, never. He'd never mail it, he thought, and reached again for her hand.

They turned, he and she, down the exit aisle, toward the doors leading out to Mt. Auburn Street. They passed the child who had fallen, and she brushed her hand over the child's hair, which was full of static electricity from his wool cap and so lifted off his head toward the ceiling. The child smiled at her and put his own hand up to feel what was happening, and then he laughed outright. His laughter rose high in the post office, echoing in the air where his cries had just been. Everyone thought again about his or her letter. *Dear love,* they'd written, or, *I am the long lost,* or *I have never forgotten.*

They went outside and down the steps, and she was about to say that it had stopped snowing. The woman who had been leaning on the buzzer stood on the bottom step, holding the hand of her child who hadn't been with her inside. A big man stood beside her, and the woman turned to this man and said, *That's him, he's the one,* and then she stopped talking and cast her eyes down to the top of her child's head. The big man stepped forward, his hands already curled into fists, and he was saying, *Who do you think you are? Who the hell do you think you are, talking to my wife that way?* He followed them along the sidewalk, then moved faster to cut in front of them, blocking their path.

She knew exactly what would happen even before she knew that she knew. She knew the man would try to bring his right fist up suddenly to catch her boyfriend under the chin, and so she began to move between them, slowly, her feet seeming to stay still, her body shifting so that it came to be at a right angle to both of theirs. She did not think about what she was doing or why. If she felt anything at all, it was that she was dreaming, and the air on Mt. Auburn Street had become the syrupy air of dreams. Moving took a long time, and voices sounded slow and hollow and far away.

And so when the angry husband's fist came up, her jaw was right there, her jaw, the left side of her face, her cheek, a gold hoop earring. The punch cracked her jawbone, making a hairline fracture, and knocked her into her boyfriend, into his arms, but it was the last thing he'd expected, to have to hold her or any woman up on Mt. Auburn Street in February of his senior year, and so she slid to the pavement, still conscious, her breath taken away. It was how she felt sometimes when she kissed this boy, that the breath had been knocked out of her; but this was the genuine article, the real McCoy, and she would never confuse the two again.

The angry husband said *Jesus Christ,* and backed away, though his first impulse had been to kneel down in front of her. His left knee had even bent slightly before he realized that kneeling down would make him an easy mark for the boy who had insulted his wife. He moved back off the sidewalk and into Mt. Auburn Street, between two parked cars, and from there he said *coward,* and then, bolder because no one seemed to be coming after him, he called out *chickenshit.* Then he and his wife and their child walked off to their car. They got in and drove away, west on Mt. Auburn Street, so that when they passed by, the woman and her husband could have made an obscene gesture or called out to them, but they didn't.

She, his girlfriend, whose hand he had just been holding, she sat in the snow, outside the post office, for what seemed to him like a long time. She didn't speak, and he was afraid to touch her. She stared at the cars parked on Mt. Auburn Street, and he wondered if she was going to have amnesia, like in the movies, if she was going to turn to him and say, *Who the hell are you?* It flashed into his mind then that he wouldn't live with her in Cambridge, Massachusetts, this summer or any summer. He was suddenly certain of it, and the thought was so new and so strange that he waved it away. People stopped to ask if she was all right, but he waved them away too. Then he whispered to her things he knew to be true: *This is the post office, on Mt. Auburn Street in Cambridge, Massachusetts. It's February of our senior year,* all of it asked as a question she might have the answer to.

As for her, at first she thought she had saved him, saved both of them from the angry husband. Then her jaw, her whole face, began to throb, and she lay down full length to rest her cheek in the snow. She noticed he hadn't touched her, but she couldn't lift her head up off the sidewalk to look at him. She felt she might never move again, might go to sleep right there outside the post office on Mt. Auburn Street in Cambridge in February of her senior year and never wake up. A part of her relished the thought, alone in this cold sleep. Already her eyes were closing, already she was leaving him far behind. Already she knew what would happen between them, and later in the emergency room at the medical center, a week later at the Broadway Market, she looked at him, she watched him mixing drinks for their friends, she saw him as if through the wrong end of a pair of binoculars. And when she turned toward him at night, she had to turn and keep turning because there was such great distance to be covered between his body and hers.

—

Now, in Concord, California, he is watching them, his wife and his college girlfriend, as he mixes drinks for his friends. Still the old troubles, still too few limes, too much orange juice. Nobody drinks screwdrivers anymore, nobody drinks much of anything. Most of his friends take mineral water with lime now—this is California, after all—slices of lime crushed along the rim of the glass, then tossed in with the water. He drinks beer that way sometimes, he's doing it now, watching his wife across the pulpy rim of the glass, thinking how beautiful she looks, how young, in that green dress, the one he's always liked so much because it's sleeveless and cut to show off his wife's shoulders, her back, her shoulder blades. She is a powerful woman, a world-class swimmer who could have, he believes, gone to the Olympics, though she says no. Her event was the butterfly, that oddest of strokes, he's always thought, like an aqua dance, should have been called the flying fish, the sea-creature rag, the mermaid minuet, the Loch Ness fandango. It's sculpted her shoulders and arms, so that he loves to watch her from the back, ironing, folding sheets, kneading bread dough, gathering any one of the four twins up into her arms. He watches her now as she's talking to Jeff about the IRS or the Supreme Court or the Republican party or all three and pumping her right fist into the palm of her left hand to show how it would be if she ran the zoo.

His college girlfriend stands beside Grace, who is seven months pregnant, both of them looking south out of the bay window into the garden. He can hear her telling Grace about planting tomatoes, basil, garlic, growing grapes, pumpkins, about feeding orange trees, about the time a grapefruit fell out of a tree, right onto her head, just like in cartoons. Twice she reaches out and touches her fingertips to Grace's belly, and Grace moves her hand to the exact spot and says, *elbow, knee, foot, head. Ouch,* she says to her belly, *stop hurting your mother,* and then she excuses herself, saying the baby thinks her bladder is a trampoline.

He watches her stand by the window, knowing she's conscious of her place there alone, maybe thinking that if she walks outside right now, everyone will suppose she's had it and is leaving. Then she opens the side door by the window and steps out into the garden. She stops to admire the boxwood, but he knows nobody bothers to admire boxwood, and then he sees her pass the back of her right hand across her face, quickly, so that anyone watching might think she was shielding her eyes from the late afternoon sun, still hot and bright in the west. He thinks she must be wondering what the hell she's doing here, at his house, his and his wife's house, in Concord, California. He thinks she's had either too much or too little to drink. She turns her back to him, and he watches for a sign, a tremor in her shoulders, but she keeps perfectly still. When she comes back inside her eyes are dry, and he crooks his index finger, motioning her over to the bar and reaching to take the empty glass from her hand.

"Another?" he says.

She glances over her shoulder around the room, then back at him. "Just like old times."

"Sort of," he says, and they both drop their eyes. They knew they would have to learn to talk to each other all over again, but now someone's gone and changed the language, making it thin in certain places and dangerous everywhere.

"Nice place," she says.

"We like it."

For a moment he hates her for making him talk this way. He knows that it's never going to be easy between them, and he's sure she'll tell the post office story as soon as she gets the chance. Why should he care? He'll say she made it up, but then when he looks at her jaw, at the left side of her face, her cheek, her gold hoop earring, he's not sure he could call her a liar.

"I hear students get into fistfights over space in your studios," he says, horrified at himself but unable to stop. "I hear some of them are willing to die for you. I hear you're a cult figure, I hear you can walk on water."

"Jesus," Jeff says, holding out his empty glass.

"Now, there's a cult figure," Bernie says, Bernie the priest, who ought to know.

"I *can* walk on water," she says. "You know that."

In March of their senior year there was a deep freeze, ice on the Charles River thicker than it had been in twenty-five years. Still, he knew when he woke in the middle of the night, the thaw would come in a week. The air jangled as if it were filled with bells, and he reached over and gently shook her awake. They put on pants and jackets over their nightclothes and, without speaking a word, walked outside and down to the river. He held her hand, and still silent, they made their way down the bank and onto the ice. Then she moved ahead of him, crossing the frozen river as if it were a room or a street. He followed her, but he did not, for those few minutes, know who or what she was, only that she was walking on water, only that if he let her out of his sight, they would both be lost. She would go under and then he would have to, and the river would close over them.

On the opposite bank she stopped and turned to face him. He took her hand and tried to pull her up off the ice, but she resisted, and when he let go, she started back the way they had come, carefully matching her own footprints, heel to toe. He did not want to cross the river again, he did not see why they had to press their luck. He scrambled up the bank to the footbridge and crossed above her, keeping pace with her, thinking, *This way, if she goes under, I can help.* She did not look up or give any sign that she knew where he was.

He met her on the other side and carried her up off the ice. She was cold, shaking so hard she could barely walk. In the dorm he wrapped her in a blanket and, lying down beside her, put her fingers in his mouth to warm them. Then he said, *Why did we do that?* and she said, as if it were the answer to his question, *You were afraid.*

The truth is, it's really this story he thinks she might tell his wife tonight, and for the first time in his life, he wishes he'd walked back across that river with her, or crawled, or carried her in his arms. This room now, in his house in Concord, California, reminds him of a dream he's had again and again: She is walking across the river, he is following her, he is out of breath, and his wife is swimming beneath them, his wife and their children, all of them swimming easily and happily just below the surface of the water. Their friends—Brad and Matthew and Jeanne, Elise and Diane, Dan, Tim, and Grace, Bernie in his priest's vestments, Jeff, Katie, Ruth—all of them watch from both sides of the river. Then Bernie is standing in the middle of the Weeks Footbridge. He is trying to bless them all, and he would, if they could just stop moving. Now it seems that this dream is about to come true inside his house in Concord, California. There is no ice and no river here, but he is breathless, and she is ahead of him, and just like in the dream, he doesn't know what to do.

—

What happened next was this: In April she sometimes borrowed keys from Tommy, the custodian, and let herself into the basement of her dormitory, then into the storerooms, which were mostly empty but not entirely. Students kept their boxes of books and sheets and winter clothes there over the summer, but she had discovered other boxes that had been left for years and never claimed. She loved going through these, through the ancient class notes and textbooks, and then in April she found a packet of love letters, nearly three hundred pages, handwritten in blue ink on white lined paper. She got the gist, the drift, the trajectory of things after the first fifty pages, that the he would love the she more than the she loved the he, then she took the whole packet down to the river, right under the Weeks Footbridge, and set it on fire. A police cruiser stopped on Memorial Drive, and two officers walked over to ask what she was doing, and she told them the truth, making it sound as if the letters were hers. They told her to be careful, and they let her alone.

When all the letters were gone, she swept the ashes into the river and prodded them with a stick until they sank. She wondered what had happened to these two people who had once, at least at first, loved each other so much, and on her way back to the dorm, she felt like lying down on the sidewalk along Boylston Street and never getting up. It reminded her of being punched outside the post office back in February, and she felt panic. She felt joints, pins, and pulleys coming loose inside her, machinery shutting down forever.

He spent more time in the library, often fell asleep there, and the truth is, that was why he went. He could claim, in fact, to have slept in nearly every library at the college, trying to find the one that suited him best. This proved to be impossible. Some had too little light, too few alcoves, too few books. Others had too much, too many. The libraries that looked out on trees or on the river made him nervous, the changing of the seasons was alarming to him now. Once he saw her walking up from Memorial Drive, and he waved to her out the window. She looked up at him and didn't wave back. Later she said she hadn't recognized him, but he wasn't sure he should believe her.

All this time in the libraries he read nothing except for the first two or three sentences of whatever book lay open on the table or the desk. Then a terrible drowsiness would take hold of him, terrible while he tried to fight it, like quicksand, he imagined, though he'd never know for sure. And that made him tired too: his own certainty that he'd never know the first damn thing about quicksand, that he was destined to live a safe life somewhere in America, in or near New York or Boston or San Francisco, and he was glad, and he hated his gladness.

He sees that she and his wife have gone into the kitchen together, they are leaning against the counter in the corner by the
Mixmaster. It will happen now, she will say, *Do you know how I got
this funny crooked smile? Do you know why my whole face seems to tilt this
way, toward you, even when I'm keeping my chin level?* And just now, as
he's watching them, his wife lifts her hand and touches her own
face, moving the palm of her hand along her jawline, slowly back
and forth from her earlobe to the center of her chin, her fingers
splayed out and held away from her cheek as if they're stiff with
pain.

Later that spring, in the beginning of May, he was coming back
to his dorm room from the library, walking through the basement
tunnels because it was raining outside, one of those spring rains
that transforms the world in the space of a single afternoon, brings
the trees, maples and elms, the flowers in their beds, the shrubbery
into full bloom. After four years he knew exactly how it would
happen, how he'd have to wait through April, wait while the
stubborn ground refused to loosen, the crocuses long gone, so that
late March and April became a kind of desert season, the Mojave,
the Sahara of seasons. But now the wait was over, and he knew that
very evening he and his friends would want to eat supper outside,
would carry their trays out into the courtyard and sit at the top of
the steps, along the low stone wall because the grass would still be
damp. He knew that she would sit next to him, or maybe on the
other side of Dan, but near enough to touch. And then, knowing
all this, he turned a corner, and there she was, walking thirty yards
ahead of him through the basement corridor, stopping outside
the east storage room and unlocking the door. He saw her go inside and heard the door close. He walked faster then, and when he
came to the door, he knew she was standing just on the other side,
he thought he could feel the furnace of her body right through the

door. He knocked and her voice said, *Oh,* like a cry of pain, then, *Just a second,* and he could hear her, not a foot away, hear the odd catch of her breath startled out of her chest. She opened the door, and her eyes went wide. She started to ask him how he knew she was there, but he stopped her. *What's wrong?* he said. He could see she'd been crying. *I don't know,* she said. She took a step backward and turned to face into the storage room, its few boxes lined up against the far wall. *All this stuff,* she said. *I found somebody's love letters,* she said, *and I burned them.* She was crying again, and he moved toward her, put his arms around her, and pulled her back against his chest. He felt her heart beating, knocking against her rib cage like it was trying to escape. He would never understand her, he knew that now, for once and for all. He wanted to be far away, someplace where summer had already come.

—

His wife and his college girlfriend move together out the back door and into the garden, shady and cool on this summer evening in Concord, California. He looks around the den, studying his friends, making sure they're taken care of, catered to for now, then he walks outside too. He follows the two women at a distance, but close enough to hear what they say to each other. Listening to his wife, he makes his own catalog of their garden as she names the flowers—jasmine, hydrangea, lily, peace rose; the vegetables—tomatoes, serrano and early jalapeno peppers, eggplant; the herbs; the four kinds of grapes in the arbor; the wisteria bunched among them like a fifth variety. When he comes close, he hears her telling his wife about the night-blooming cereus she had in college, how she woke her friends up to see it every spring, how she looked forward to that night every year, how it kept a kind of time.

He expects she will turn to him and say *Didn't it?* or *Isn't that true?* but she doesn't, even when he's standing beside his wife, reaching his arm around her shoulders and pulling her close. He wants all three of them to see what they were to each other then and what they are to each other now, and his need for it is so great that he is afraid he'll hold his wife too tightly, dislocate her shoulders, break her swimmer's bones that he believes glow like silver fish inside her body.

"Did she tell you about the post office?" he asks. His wife says no, but she, his college girlfriend, looks at him quickly, then looks away.

"The post office," she says slowly, "I hardly remember. I went there to mail things, I believe. On Mt. Auburn Street."

"The woman pressing the buzzer," he says to jog her memory, "in February of our senior year?"

"What about it?" she says, her gaze moving into the middle distance.

"It was snowing."

"Yes," she says, "it was crowded. Everybody was in a hurry. A man, a man thought you took his place in line, and he waited for you outside. He wanted to hit you, but we kept walking."

"Then what happened?" his wife says.

"Nothing," she says. "He lost interest. I was scared, though. I still dream about it sometimes."

He can see that his wife thinks she's missed something, but she won't dwell on it. He knows this about her. He knows how quickly her thoughts turn to the children, the garden, their life now. He can see clearly in this moment in a garden in Concord, California, how different they are, these two women, and he does not for a second regret anything that happened of its own accord in February and in the rest of the spring of his senior year. He sees the truth about her, his college girlfriend, and the truth about himself. They are both good liars, too good, quick and sly as children, even now. That might have been trouble. They might have fooled each other into thinking all water could be walked on. Together, they might have fooled everyone, all of the time.

He thinks of them walking across the frozen river in March of their senior year and how it was the whiteness, the blankness of the sky that woke him like a beacon in the night, how the silence was already so deep between them that each snowflake seemed to make a sound, calling them outside to listen. When they came down to the river, they saw that the angle of the whole world was different, the drift of the snow had transformed even them, knocked them off their feet and into the dizzy truth-telling of sleepwalkers: *This is where I am going, come if you want, but I don't know you.*

The truth is, they imagined themselves to be lighter than water, lighter than snow, lighter even than the sky in Cambridge, Massachusetts, in March of their senior year. They marveled for the first time over how easily the world could be disguised, even by the weather, then changed forever. *This is where I am going,* they said, each to the other, *come if you want,* and no voice called back, *wait,* or *yes,* but only *I don't know you, I don't know you,* echoing far down the frozen river. And the truth was, the mystery was that for all their sadness, each moved ahead into the thawing world, the ice melted and boomed in the Charles River only seconds later, it seemed, and they reached the shore in the nick of time, just as the broken river throbbed on behind them.

They hear it now, in Concord, California, the river's distant pulse, and they remember how the river boomed like their hearts. They already knew then the truth they know now: how easily, how certainly, these hearts would grow heavier, year after year, how these hearts would weigh them down, even in a garden full of grapes and tomatoes, lilies and roses, in Concord, California, on a summer night, darkening breathlessly and by imperceptible degrees.

DISCOVERING
AMERICA

I. Flatland

In the beginning, Lance di Fabbio is fourteen. She believes she's always been this age, even when she was five and running away from home for the first time, she believes she was thinking with her fourteen-year-old mind, that she was old before her time. She is the daughter of Larry di Fabbio, a baritone and mathematician, who teaches geometry at Lamar High School, in Houston, Texas, 5 classes a day, 25 students per class, 150 students per quarter, 450 students per year. Lance likes to say it that way to illustrate how in exponential growth the world gets bigger and bigger but nothing really changes.

And she's the daughter of Laura di Fabbio, who Lance thinks is quite beautiful. She likes it that she has her mother's coloring: olive skin, icy blue eyes, and straight dark hair, which they both keep long, below their shoulder blades. Lance's mother is ten years younger than her father, who was her teacher in college, a graduate assistant leading a section of basic math. Lance knows that back then her mother wanted to be an airline pilot. She was taking physics and math to learn about vectors and jet propulsion. She believed that the skies were friendlier than anywhere she'd ever been on the ground.

Lance di Fabbio is an unusual name for a girl; Lance is well aware of this, but she doesn't mind. How she got such a name was that it was originally the name of the first-born, the boy-child, her brother Lance di Fabbio, who died in infancy long before she was even conceived of as a replacement. She goes to visit his grave not out of respect but because she can't get over the wonder of it—her name on the marble headstone, surrounded by twining ivy, etched in and already turning green with time. LANCE DI FABBIO, NOVEMBER 1960–JANUARY 1961. "BE PATIENT, FOR THE WORLD IS BROAD AND WIDE." It's the epigraph from Larry di Fabbio's favorite book, *Flatland,* a meditation on the second dimension. Larry di Fabbio liked to think of little Lance offering that advice from the great beyond to everybody who had to stick around in this world.

When she visits, Lance walks to the grave and stands there, saying to herself, *this is you,* and trying to feel moved or pained or frightened. But she never can get to anything more than puzzled pride, as if it's just her name in the newspaper, listed as a witness to a car accident or a convenience-store shooting. She tries to think about the psychological ramifications, as they say on the TV talk shows, how being named for a dead boy has and will damage her for life, but she can't. All she hears is herself saying, poor little Lance, got through his first Christmas in that house and decided he'd had enough.

She leaves the cemetery and walks home the long way, taking her own sweet time. She loves that phrase *sweet time,* and thinks it to be true. Time is sweet, because it's always giving way to more of itself, it never runs out on you, not really, even though people say so. It lies ahead in the distance, a long, flat road full of unknown promise. Lance walks along reasoning like this, making her steps go slower and slower, so that the turn onto Bordley Road and then into her driveway will be a long way off. There is a strange, humid tension in her house these days, and she wants to put off going back there for as long as she can.

She stops beside the vacant lot that stands a block from her house. It's land no one can seem to find any use for, not home builders or commercial developers, not even any transportation people or any franchise people. Every day that she walks by and doesn't see a SOLD sign, Lance is grateful. She stands here now and looks back into the woods that border the lot like a *tonsure*—she's just learned that word—the way monks cut their hair. She knows these woods don't extend very far into the next yards, no more than two hundred feet in any of the three directions, north, south, or east, but she thinks of these woods as endless, impenetrably dark. She walks into the lot to sit at the edge of the trees, the exact spot she came to years ago with a packed suitcase, when she was five and running away for the first time. She remembers that she lost her nerve and went home, leaving the suitcase behind. When she came back later for her belongings, she opened the suitcase and saw that her clothes were crawling with maggots.

Now she lies on her back, so that her face is in shade. She tries to think up other ways to put off going home, but she can't come up with anything. She thinks if she lies here long enough, Hazen Beatty might wander by. She closes her eyes and thinks of Hazen standing over her, his body blocking out the sun. Maybe he would say something sweet to her, maybe he would say he knows how she feels about going home. First she counts to fourteen hundred, a hundred for every year she's been alive, next to ninety-two, in honor of discovering America, then she stands and heads up the street.

It makes Lance sweat cold down the length of her spine just to walk in the front door, past her father grading math homework in his study, tallying scores on his fingers, past her twin brothers, Peter and Paul, playing war games, hunting each other over the bunk beds, in and out of the closet. Lance wonders if it scares them to come face-to-face, each with his own likeness, and have to aim and fire.

In the kitchen, the last room in the house, the hottest and most distant, Lance sees her mother reading the paper, waiting for a pot to boil. She buys four papers a day, the *Houston Chronicle, The Dallas Morning News, The Washington Post,* and *The New York Times.* She hates to miss anything. Lance stands behind her mother and reads over her shoulder.

"The Astros lost again," she says.

Her mother points to the box scores and says the word *smoked.*

Lance's father comes into the kitchen to use the pencil sharpener that's attached to the wall next to the toaster. Then he lifts the lid off the pot on the stove.

"Don't do that," Lance's mother says.

Lance watches a look pass between them and sees it's empty, the way two dead bodies might stare at each other. She thinks what she's discovering now could send any innocent bystander to an early grave.

                        —

This is 1976 in America. Houston, Texas. Lance di Fabbio has just turned fourteen, and Hazen Beatty lives across the street. Hazen's father, Jack Beatty, is a boxing promoter, has been for twenty years, began by trying to get fights for youngsters nobody ever heard of, then fell in with William Faversham and Cassius Clay in Louisville, and after that he was on the six o'clock news a lot but rarely around his own house. Hazen stands outside in the evening, bouncing a tennis ball off the gutter, off the pale-yellow aluminum siding, waiting, Lance thinks, for his dad to come home. Sometimes Lance's father crosses the street to talk to Hazen, about school, she thinks—Hazen is one of Larry di Fabbio's best students. Lance loves to see the smile bloom on Hazen's face when he sees her father coming. She watches Hazen get up a game of catch with his friend John Blades, or chase younger kids on his bike, but more often Lance sees Hazen Beatty using a feint to the belly and a rising left hook on John Blades. Then she hears a screen door slam, and the high voices of their mothers, hauling them outside to apologize.

Lance watches all this from the front picture window. John Blades was the first boy she ever kissed, last year, but while her eyes were closed, she imagined it was Hazen Beatty.

After Cassius Clay hit the big time, Jack Beatty bought a motorcycle, a red Honda 750. He bought a red helmet for himself and recently a child's helmet for Hazen, and they go on rides together.

Juliet Beatty talks to Lance's mother about it, about Hazen's impending death at the hands of his own father.

"He'll get over it," Lance's mother says, and Juliet Beatty looks up suddenly from behind her mouthful of coffee cake.

"Who?" she says. "Get over what?"

"I personally would love to ride on a motorcycle," Lance's mother says.

"Really?" Juliet Beatty says.

"Oh, yes," Laura di Fabbio tells her. "Going a hundred miles an hour. It's a lifelong ambition."

"Really?" Juliet Beatty says again. "I'll remember that in the future."

Lance and her mother walk across the street when Jack Beatty is outside working on his motorcycle. He let them sit on the seat, and he tells them about the engine, about which parts of the bike are the original and which he's replaced himself. He talks to Lance's mother about boxing, about Floyd Patterson, who used to have prophetic dreams before his big fights, about Cassius Clay's first fight at Madison Square Garden, years and years ago.

"I don't like it," Lance's mother says. "It might as well be hunting. It's just two men hunting each other down inside a small space."

"No," Jack Beatty says. "It's nothing like hunting." Lance listens while Jack Beatty explains to her mother the difference between hunting and boxing. He says hunting is a long dream that you stumble through and wait a long time to come out of. But boxing, he says, is being awake, bright-eyed and bushy-tailed. Lance pays close attention. She believes this is information that will be important later on.

"It still looks mean to me," Lance's mother says, "hitting another man that way."

Lance sees Mrs. Beatty watching them from the kitchen window, and frowning when Lance's mother switches the headlight on so that it shines right in Jack Beatty's eyes.

"How about a ride?" he says to Lance's mother.

"Maybe tomorrow," she says, and then Lance thinks she can hear the engine of her mother's thoughts turn over. "Yes, tomorrow. After dinner. Say, seven o'clock."

When Jack Beatty takes Lance's mother off on his motorcycle, they stay gone for two days. They say they rode into the city and got caught in traffic with all the covered wagons coming in for Rodeo Week. It's March, Lance reasons, so this could have been true. Her mother was wearing Hazen Beatty's helmet, and Hazen will tell Lance much later that the smell of her mother's hair stayed in the helmet for years. She senses a change in atmospheric conditions between her mother and father after that; they talk to each other and to her with their backs turned, or looking off in the wrong direction. It's like they've both gone blind, Lance thinks, and she waits for her parents to snap out of it, or else crash into each other in the dark. Lance herself doesn't see Hazen Beatty for a long time. It's as if he's vanished off the face of the earth, or maybe, she thinks, I'm the one who's disappeared over the hard, hard edge of the world.

—

Lance's father starts to talk a lot about the second dimension. Imagine a sheet of paper, he'd say, on which lines, triangles, squares, and other figures, instead of remaining fixed in their places, move freely on the surface, without the power of rising above it or sinking below it, very much like shadows—only hard and luminous edges. Think of it, he tells Lance; In a second dimensional world, rain would come only from the north. In the second dimension, or Flatland, you can't hide anything from anybody in the third dimension, because they can see the insides of things.

"No one could lie and get away with it," he says, raising his voice just slightly.

He gives her his copy of *Flatland* by Edwin A. Abbott, " 'a romance of many dimensions,' " she reads on the cover below the title. " 'I call our world Flatland, not because we call it so, but to make its nature clearer to you, my happy readers, who are priveleged to live in Space.' "

What's so interesting about all that? Lance thinks; the world is in two dimensions anyway—the first dimension is everybody else, the second dimension is you, and never the twain shall meet.

Lance looks up when her mother comes to stand in the doorway and watches her turn slowly until she's in profile, then flex her calf muscles by rising up on her toes.

"What's all this?" her mother asks, and Lance tells her.

"Ah, yes," she says, "*Flatland.* I remember it well. Otherwise known as paradise on earth, the garden spot, God's little acre, another name for Houston, Texas. Where women are needles."

"Laura," Lance's father says, in a voice that promises nothing.

"I'm going to the grocery store," Lance's mother says. "Does anybody want anything? Anything you can't live without? Just name it and it's yours." But she doesn't move out of the doorway.

" 'In Flatland,' " Lance continues reading out loud, " 'there is a constant attraction southward. There are no windows in the houses, because light is always present, inside and out. To wonder about the origin of light would make people go crazy, since there would be no answer.' "

"You'd think everybody would be dying to know?" Lance's mother says. "You'd think it would drive them crazy not to know what was out there?"

"They tax you heavily if you even so much as ask," her father answers.

In Flatland, Lance's father tells her, the houses are pentagonal. The north side is all roof, to keep off the rain, the west and east sides contain entrances, a door for women only on the east and one for men on the west. A house of any other shape is liable to have lines too dim to see in two dimensions, and their points could do serious injury.

"In Flatland," he says, "the men, depending on class, are triangles, squares, or polygons. Priests are circles."

"Really?" Lance says. "But how can they tell, if everything looks flat?"

"They feel each other. When they're introduced, people say, 'Permit me to ask you to feel and be felt by Mr. So-and-So.' And women are straight lines."

This information comes like something Lance has suspected for a long time and is finally finding to be true. A woman is like a road, the way it looks on a map. You can trace her with your fingers, Lance thinks, looking up at her mother, and feel how she's always moving on ahead of you, and you can't do anything except follow.

" 'A woman is a needle,' " she reads, " 'being, so to speak, all point, at least at the two extremities. Add to this the power of making herself practically invisible at will, and you will perceive that a female, in Flatland, is a creature by no means to be trifled with.' "

"Though there are certain exceptions," Lance's mother says, then turns to leave.

The next morning, Lance and her mother are in the kitchen together. Lance is eating breakfast, and her mother is taking the dishes out of the dishwasher, cleaning up the pans from last night's supper. Her father is in the shower, so Lance could ask her mother why she hates Flatland and Houston. She could ask why she fell in love with Larry di Fabbio, her math teacher, in the first place, but she doesn't. Then her father comes out of the bathroom, walks up behind his wife, and circles his arms around her waist.

"What are you doing?" he says quietly.

"I'm putting things away," Lance's mother says back, just as quietly. Then there's a pause. Lance hears her mother draw in her breath and try not to sigh it out too heavily. "That's what the woman does in the morning while the man is in the shower," she continues. "She puts away everything from the night before."

—

There's no way I should be able to remember this, Lance writes in her diary that day, *but I do. I remember the evening in Houston, an orange line drifting in the sky just after sunset, and warm air moving between my dress and my bare legs. I remember taking Dad's hand and walking away from the picnic table in the San Jacinto Battleground State Park. Mother and Peter and Paul, who were three, stayed behind. We were walking toward a set of swings—please, one last swing, I asked him, before it got too dark to see. I was showing Dad how I'd learned to braid a piece of pine straw, I was showing him how I could whistle and snap my fingers, then do both at the same time. I remember how he bent to lift me into the swing, how he screamed, then how close his face fell to mine in the grass. In four days he was well again, home from the hospital. It wasn't even his heart. I believe it was something I did to him, putting a needle in his back that he carried wherever he went, from that day on.*

And about this Flatland. I know what DIMENSION *is, I looked it up. It's the number of coordinates required to describe points in a mathematical object. In this house, we try to live in three dimensions: Mother lives for height, of ceilings, of clouds; Peter and Paul live for width, largeness of extent or scope. They think by being two, they can be bigger. And Dad lives for depth, the part that's furthest from the outside. But he hates it, everything that depth means. That's why he talks so much about Flatland, the second dimension. No elevation, no depression.*

The line of Hazen Beatty's cheekbone is one-dimensional, and right here, Houston, because it's a point on a map, is zero.

This is the last time Lance writes in a diary. She believes she thinks too much as it is.

What happens to her father Lance wouldn't call being born again but whatever the opposite of being born is, not dying, though, but being sucked back in again. He says to Lance that when his time comes, he wants to be prepared, he doesn't want to be in doubt. But she knows what sent him over the edge was the sight of her mother driving up on the back of Jack Beatty's motorcycle. She remembers how the sky behind her mother's head was so clear and blue it looked almost black from a certain angle. Her father ran inside to the kitchen, the bathroom, the bedroom, anywhere he didn't have to see the two of them or discover their secret.

"I heard the voice of Jesus say, Larry, are you a clanging cymbal?" he tells Lance. "And I shot right back, Yes, Lord, I guess that's about all I am these days. And Jesus said to me, Well, then, what are you going to do about it?"

"What are you going to do about it?" Lance asks.

"Jesus knows what I was thinking," her father says. "It's like he's looking into the second dimension from the third dimension. Jesus always knows whatever's in your heart, so even if you try to hide it, you can't."

Lance and her father read scripture every night, from a Bible he's given her. He chooses a passage for the evening and asks Lance and her brothers to read in turn, waiting patiently while they sound out the hard words: Nebuchadnezzar, Gethsemane, Sennacherib, and myrrh. Lance has a white Bible and her brothers have black ones, but they are all three signed on the fly leaf "FROM THY FATHER," in capital letters. They read until one of them starts to fall asleep, and so Lance learns to fake the slurred voice, the sagging eyelids, the sudden drop of the open Bible into her lap. Their mother reads *Time* magazine in the kitchen, snapping the pages at unpredictable intervals and quoting out loud from the "Milestones" column whenever a piece of news strikes her fancy.

" 'Engaged: Elizabeth Taylor,' " she reads. " 'Born: to Jane Fonda, a son.' "

Lance, Peter, and Paul read the Proverbs, the Book of Revelation, and the Book of Job, who, Lance comes to understand, is really everybody's favorite biblical personality. And who can resist him, she thinks, a guy who was good and honest, whose old age is blessed more than his younger days, who gets fourteen thousand sheep and six thousand camels, who has the most beautiful daughters in the land? She wonders, though, about Job's four servants, the ones who say, *I alone have escaped to tell you.* She wants to know why they were spared, and where did they go after they broke the bad news?

In these Bibles, God is called Yahweh, and for a while Lance reads without knowing exactly who Yahweh is. This Yahweh seems to be in a bad mood all the time, and she wishes he'd go back to whatever rock he crawled out from under. His wrath is always kindling quickly, pouring out like fire and making the earth quake. She wants the real God to reappear, as she's heard he so often will, just in the nick of time.

One night in April Lance's mother is especially restless. A woman from the Houston Debutante Society calls to ask whether or not Lance will be enrolling in the dancing class they sponsor, which would be that first all-important step toward her debut when she's nineteen. Instead of giving the woman an answer, Lance's mother tells her a joke.

"What's the mating call of a Houston debutante?" she asks. Then there's a pause. "I gather from your silence," Lance's mother continues, "that you don't know the answer. The answer is, 'I'm so drunk.' "

After her mother hangs up the phone, Lance walks into the kitchen.

"I's okay, Mom," she says. "I never wanted to do any of that deb stuff anyway."

"Lance, honey," her mother says, "you know what the trouble

is? The trouble is that you and I were born in the wrong time, and we're living in the wrong place."

Then Lance's father gets out their Bibles and everybody settles down to read.

" 'Yahweh will speak to them in his wrath,' " Lance's father reads, " 'and terrify them in his fury.' "

" 'Died,' " her mother reads from the kitchen, " 'Howard Hughes. Awarded: Pulitzer Prize to Saul Bellow.' "

" 'Oh, Yahweh, give heed to my groaning, hearken to the sound of my cry.' "

"Disbarred: Richard M. Nixon, in New York, for obstruction of justice. Adultery committed: Jimmy Carter, in his heart," Laura di Fabbio reads, her voice rising.

" 'But thou, Yahweh, dost laugh at them, thou dost hold all the nations in derision.' "

" 'Missing: five-hundred-ninety-foot cargo ship with a crew of thirty-seven, in the Bermuda Triangle. Discontinued: the Cadillac Eldorado, in Detroit,' " Laura di Fabbio shrieks.

" 'Remember this, Yahweh, how the enemy scoff, and an impious people reviles thy name.' "

Lance's father recites this line from memory. Her mother has started to hum a jingle from TV. "Hold the pickle, hold the lettuce," she sings, louder now. "Special orders don't upset us. All we ask is that you let us have it Yahweh."

Lance and her brothers start to laugh, but Lance stops short when she sees the look on her father's face. All the color drains out of it, and he stares straight ahead, into the middle distance. He tries to focus his eyes, but he can't. For a second Lance thinks he is going to die, right there in front of his children. Then he gets up off the couch and walks into the kitchen. She can hear his lowered voice but not the words, and then her mother's laughter. Their parents stay in the kitchen all night while Lance and Peter and Paul doze on the couch. Lance stays sitting up, her Bible still open in her lap, with all the lights on. Her brothers talk in their sleep, but Lance can't understand anything they say.

In the morning their father wakes them gently to say goodbye. He tells them he's going to live at the Trappist monastery outside Houston and prepare to take Holy Orders. This is what he says, word for word, but Lance doesn't believe him. She thinks it can't possibly happen that fast—one day you decide you're called, and the next day they hand you the robe and the sandals, just your size. She believes there should be a waiting period, like for buying a firearm. She doesn't see how anybody could go from being a geometry teacher to being a monk without a couple of whole lifetimes in between. She thinks he is running off, the way her mother did with Jack Beatty, and he'll be back in a few days. But her mother tells her no, this is the real thing.

"The problem is," Lance's mother says, "he never got to travel. He never got to see anything except the inside of a book."

"So do monks travel?" Lance says.

"They wander," her mother answers. "They wander the seven seas, doing their good works, and then when they come to the edge of the world, over they go."

She takes Lance and her brothers to the coast for the weekend, to Galveston and Sea-Arama Marineworld. Lance stares out at the horizon and tries to picture her father drifting in a boat crowded with monks. She imagines them going over the horizon as if it's a waterfall, hears them calling *Geronimo* as they go.

At Sea-Arama Marineworld they see the otters and the seals, the porpoises who are so smart they could take the S.A.T. and go to college. The big attraction, though, is Shalu, a baby sperm whale. At first Lance thinks Shalu's trainer is at least as impressive as Shalu himself. The trainer tells her audience the history of whaling in America, a long story with a moral about how what is hunted and destroyed becomes valued and protected. She tells them how Shalu was found washed up on a beach and not expected to survive. But he did, and after that he kept swimming back to shore and banging his fluke on the beach.

"He liked human company," the trainer says, "so we captured him and brought him here, and he's happy—as a clam!"

Shalu breaches and slams his fluke down on the surface of the water. The audience applauds, but Lance keeps her hands folded together in her lap. She thinks they're all being fed a load of bull. She thinks Shalu probably had a family that these people forced him to leave behind. She believes that somewhere in his tiny whale brain Shalu remembers the past, that he probably hasn't forgotten the history of whaling either. Lance thinks about coming back to Sea-Arama Marineworld in the dead of night and setting Shalu free. She tears Shalu's picture out of the glossy program and puts it in her wallet as a reminder. In the gift shop she buys a book on whales, and she studies it all the way home, memorizing the names of the species and how they're supposed to behave.

When they come back to Houston on Sunday night, Lance is sure her father will be waiting for them, but he isn't. The house is strangely quiet, and Lance thinks she can hear a ticking in the walls, like the whole place is a bomb set to go off any second. As she lies in bed and waits for the explosion, she senses herself drifting under the sheets, as if she's riding the rising and diving back of Shalu the whale.

—

Lance looks at the stacked pyramid of Roman candles and the boxes of sparklers piled on the kitchen table while her father talks to her over the telephone. It's July Fourth, and he's still at the Trappist monastery. Her brothers say they know a kid who's got cherry bombs and will sell them some. Her heart beats wildly at the thought of all that fire and light, and she doesn't want it quieted, not now, not ever. Her father tells her he's started a fast—no solid food—for the souls of the dead and departed, and also to lose ten pounds. The Trappists make a fabulous bread, and a raspberry jam, he says, and he's been eating way too much of it.

"I've gotten to be too much substance," he says.

"No, Dad," Lance says, "you're just right."

"It's all right there in front of you, I just know it," he says. "Meat loaf and turkey in gravy, fried chicken, pork chops, and hamburgers and hot dogs waiting to go on the grill. There's a Waldorf salad, and macaroni salad with tuna and tiny pink shrimps, cole slaw, and green beans cooked for three days in fatback, and always six different kinds of pie. Apple, peach, cherry, blueberry, strawberry-rhubarb, and lemon meringue. You drink mint tea that's the color blood would be if it were clear. All I have is ice water and hot black coffee."

"Dad," Lance says, "your teeth are going to crack if you keep drinking ice water and hot coffee together like that."

"I know," he says, and then he's quiet for a long time.

"Dad?" Lance says, "are you there?"

"Honey," he says, "do me a big favor. Tell your mother I'm through here. Tell her I'll be home tomorrow."

Lance wants to feel relieved, but she isn't. She wonders how it will be to live with her father, if he'll be like a saint, too good to be true. She wonders if he knows her mother hasn't changed a bit. She buys fifteen cherry bombs for Peter and Paul. She lights firecrackers, a hundred at a time, and pretends it's gunfire. She tells herself they're shooting at a gang of guerilla Trappist monks out to steal her father back. She aims the cherry bombs at the monks' imaginary heads and vital organs. Then they all drive out to San Jacinto Park, where the city of Houston puts on a fireworks display for the public, but it's a cheap show, Lance thinks, all single-star bursts of only one stupid color, and an American flag that was mostly a dud.

When her father gets home, Lance is surprised to see that he looks almost exactly the same. He fixes things around the house, changes light bulbs and fuses, and paints the interior. He does all the cooking. He buys a new car and a speedboat, and they start going to Galveston on Saturdays. He looks out at the Gulf and says it's too bad that Florida and Mexico are in the way. He'd like to be able to stand here, on this single spot in America, and see both the Atlantic and the Pacific Oceans at the same time.

"It would be good for what ails you," he says, "to be able to see that far, see everything at once."

He puts his arm around Lance's mother, around her waist, and they watch the sun set. Lance thinks that from the shore the five of them must make a pretty picture. Anyone watching must think they're the perfect family, caught as shadows on the horizon, all of them facing west, together in their small rudderless ship.

Back in Houston Lance's father practices scales and learns all the words to "Bennie and the Jets." His voice is strong from singing a cappella at the monastery. Hazen Beatty stands in the front yard, listening with his eyes closed, a smile playing over his face. When Lance points this out to her father, he calls to Hazen to come inside. They talk about school, and Hazen says he's been writing stories during math class. He says the substitute teacher can't teach geometry, that she doesn't know a proof from a hole in the ground, that she thinks the isosceles triangle is a dangerous reef off the coast of North Carolina that swallows planes, boats, and people.

"We thought that was maybe where you went," Hazen Beatty says.

"May be," Larry di Fabbio says, "but I'm back now."

"That's good," Hazen Beatty says, "because it sure sucked to have you gone."

Lance believes it would be hard to say, at this moment, who loves Hazen Beatty more, her father or her.

Then suddenly it's September, and Lance's father is back at the high school in his usual white button-down shirt and khaki trousers, teaching integers, proofs, and quadratic equations to 125 students a day. Lance notices he's stopped talking about Jesus altogether. Before and after class his students, who think his long absence was due to some strange, contagious disease, cluster around him like flowers; they lean into his light. It's like he's a saint; Lance thinks she can smell it, like sweet peas, as if he's just come back from a holy war, a crusade, and if she stands close enough to him, a little of that holiness might fall on her too.

Lance thinks it's Hazen, though, who is most relieved to have her father back. She sees them together at school one afternoon, Hazen reading aloud to her father, a story he's just written, about a couple who love each other on pages one through three, but again on page thirteen, but don't seem destined to stay together for very long. She stands outside the classroom and listens to the whole thing, and when Hazen's voice stops, she moves away quickly down the hall because she doesn't want either of them to see that she is crying.

She goes to listen when her father tries out for the first annual Faculty Talent Show and lands two solos. He rents a tuxedo and stands on the stage in the gym on the Friday night after Thanksgiving and sings "What I Did for Love" and "If Ever I Should Leave You," which makes Lance's mother cry so hard she has to get up and leave. Lance finds her in the car with the radio on, tuned to a country-western station. She is singing along with Glen Campbell, loudly. Lance can hear her as soon as she comes out the back door of the gym, singing, "Galveston, oh, Galveston."

Lance holds her breath, thinking her father might backslide, might light out again if the going gets rough. He coaches the junior-varsity basketball team that winter, but she believes he doesn't even so much as nod in the direction of Jesus when the team is down 72–9 against Alamo High. She sees him smoking in the teachers' lounge, hears him telling jokes that begin, There was a German, an Irishman, and an Italian in a rowboat, the kind of joke everybody's father tells.

One morning on the way to school a dog runs across the street in front of the car, causing Lance's father to lock up the brakes. He pulls over and closes his eyes, then he says, Jesus fucking Christ. Lance expects the sky to open and a whirling black cloud with a human hand in it to descend and engulf them in swift and bloody destruction, but nothing happens. They pull back into traffic and the road closes up behind them, darkening to a single point, just as it has her entire life.

—

All this time, Lance still goes to the cemetery to look at her name on her dead brother's grave, but it isn't very often that she goes alone. She knows she's a little morbid, though in a sexy kind of way. She takes boys to the cemetery, not a lot of boys, probably five, if she's truthful about it. All these boys are nice, even sweet, and easy to figure out. They all have short, simple names, which Lance appreciates: Cole, Matt, Kyle, and Chard, who was really named Richard, but nobody called him that, so he could still get on Lance's list of uncomplicated one-syllable boys.

Lance rides to the cemetery in the boys' cars—most of them are old enough to drive or at least have fake licenses. They know what to do behind the wheel. Lance likes older boys, boys with the shadowy beginnings of soft hair on the chin and above the upper lip, so that, she tells herself, their faces look like an overcast sky. This is a conceit, she's learning in her English class, a metaphor that stretches the limits of credibility. She likes that, the limits of credibility.

Lance knows these boys are surprised when she tells them where they're going, but then they look out through the front windshield and smile to themselves, a thin, toothless smile that makes their lips spread out colorless, like the lips on a corpse, and Lance has to turn her face away and watch the scenery. It's how she imagines the faces of people look in Flatland, frozen and always a little scared.

She directs each of these boys through the two right-hand turns inside the cemetery gates and tells them where to stop. They get out of the car slowly and thoughtfully, as if they've been coming here for years and for the same reasons as everyone else.

"Look there," Lance says, pointing to her name and the dates on the marble stone.

"That's you," they always say, never a question, not once.

"Yes," Lance says. "Bet you never did it with a dead girl before."

These boys—Cole, Kyle, Matt, and Chard—can't speak. They shake their heads no, and then they step across the tiny plot to where Lance is standing on the other side. She closes her eyes and waits while their arms go around her waist, lightly and tentatively, as if they expect to find only air, not a girl's flesh. Then there's a moment of relief, Lance can almost hear their thoughts spinning like planets, like heavenly bodies: *thank goodness, thank goodness,* without having the least idea what goodness is.

They stand like that a minute, Lance's cheek against a sweaty T-shirt, then she turns her face up to get kissed. Sometimes, while the kissing is going on, she angles their bodies so she can open her eyes and look at her name and those two dates, November 1960–January 1961, when she wasn't even on the planet Earth, when she was maybe only an invisible needle in Flatland. She feels it all over again, like she isn't really here. In the dark it's all Cole, Matt, Kyle, or Chard, or only the heat between their bodies, or only a date and a time, only this day, June 14 or July 21 or August 3, 1976.

Somehow they get onto the ground, these boys and Lance di Fabbio, usually by first kneeling and then just tipping over, the way you see wounded and dying soldiers do in the movies. Lance lies on her side with Cole or Kyle, Matt or Chard, making sure he keeps his back to the gravestone. She believes if they see it again, her name and those dates, it will be too much for them, they'll have heart failure and die, and how would that look? Already she feels fear ballooning inside their hearts, making the beats sound hollow, like the glug of heavy liquid filling a container that somehow always stays empty. She holds them tighter now, as tightly as she can.

The fifth boy in the graveyard is Hazen Beatty, fifth and last because the city later puts a fence around River Oaks Cemetery, with a guardhouse and a locked gate. She and Hazen are out in their front yards, and he's wearing a red-and-white striped football shirt, and it's so dark that the wide white stripe in the middle of the shirt and the two across his biceps are all she can see of him. He calls to Lance to come over and take a look at the car he's just bought. He tells her he's been saving for three years, and now he's sixteen and owns a Plymouth Valiant that cost eight hundred dollars.

"Ever ridden in such a cheap car?" he says.

"Never," Lance tells him. "But it's a lifelong ambition."

She directs him to the cemetery, and to her brother's grave. It's much too dark to read the name on the stone, but Lance holds Hazen's hand and moves it over the letters.

"Lance di Fabbio," he says, as if he's meeting somebody after a long separation. "Your brother."

"I can't remember him," Lance says, "but sometimes I can feel him."

"Where are you?" Hazen says, holding his arms straight out in front of his chest, the palms turned up. "Come here."

Hazen kisses Lance and moves his hands slowly over her back. "Permit me," he says, and they laugh.

Permit me to feel and be felt by, Lance thinks the polite introductions in Flatland, of squares to triangles, triangles to hexagons, hexagons to needles. She opens her eyes to see the angles of Hazen Beatty's face caught against the horizon.

"I've wanted to do this for a long time," he says.

Later they stand by his car in the cemetery parking lot. Hazen starts to talk, then bows his head and falls silent.

"I've got to get out of this town soon," he says finally.

"Me too," Lance says back, and then they're quiet again.

"Don't look at me that way," Hazen says. "It's scary. Your eyes are so dark."

"I heard you read that love story to my father," Lance tells him, but she can't speak after that. She's afraid if the tears spill out of her eyes and run down her face, it will ruin something important. A breeze rises up out of the graves.

"It's just a story," Hazen says. "It doesn't mean anything." Lance doesn't believe this, and she knows Hazen doesn't either.

At home Lance's father is waiting up for her, her mother having long since gone to bed with her earplugs and face mask that says UNITED over her left eye and AIRLINES over her right. Her father is grading tests, or maybe it's homework, Lance can't tell. She sees only his face through the picture window as she walks up the driveway. He seems happy. Lance takes a look at her father now, a long, hard look. The light from the kitchen seems to shine through him in a strange way, straight through the milk-white of his skin. In this moment Lance sees that it isn't any kind of divine light, it's more like her father has become transparent. She thinks she can see right through him, straight to his heart, which is tilted to one side, looking like a man's crushed fist.

"Let me guess," she says, coming in the door behind him. "There's still hope for math students at Lamar High."

"Lance, Jesus Christ, where have you been all night?" It's as if he's just realized she's been gone.

"In Flatland," she tells him, because it's true.

II. True North

Enclosure in an otherwise open landscape attracts the protagonist is the first sentence Lance writes in her first notebook in her first class at college. This reminds her of her father and Flatland, the landscape of two dimensions, though she can't quite say why. When she received her letter of acceptance from Barnard College, her father warned her that New York was a dangerous place, its sharpest angles difficult to see, the potential for injury concealed everywhere. He folded open a copy of *The Wall Street Journal* to show her a bar graph of rising crime rates in the cities of America. New York was off the charts in every category, but he finally agreed a little danger was worth it.

"Danger is the soul of wit," her brother Peter said.

"I thought it was brevity," her brother Paul said.

"Nope," Peter said. "This is America, remember? It's definitely danger."

They all drive up to New York from Houston, three days on the road, but Lance sleeps most of the way. She wakes in Manhattan to the most amazing scene: kids and their parents unpacking car trunks all over the quadrangle, even out in the street, almost in the middle of Broadway. It seems to her that the sun is shining unmercifully, and everybody is driving silver cars and wearing white T-shirts and white shorts. There's a constant whirling of brown arms and legs, pastel-colored suitcases being lifted high into the air and set back down. It seems too that everyone is weirdly quiet. Parents and children talk to each other without opening their mouths, as if to speak would break some kind of spell.

In the middle of this bright white silence a funeral procession winds its way through the traffic on Broadway. She sees it like ink seeping into a channel, dye rising in a vein, the black limousines, three of them sneaking in and out of the parked cars, slowing and speeding up again to let a freshman or her mother or father cross first.

Up the street at Riverside Church bells are being rung by invisible sad hands, and voices are singing "Abide with Me" and "There Is a Balm in Gilead" loud enough to be heard blocks away. All afternoon the limousines stay parked just down the hill, but no one points to them or talks about their presence. When, unseen, the drivers get into their vehicles, circle the block, and come back to park right outside the Barnard gates, no one asks or is told who the dead man or woman or child is, or why the funeral seems to be taking an eternity. Lance never sees a hearse or a casket, and she wonders if it's only the limousines, only the bells, only the singing. She never sees a single mourner, only the chauffeurs lounging against the hoods of their limousines, leaning on the spit-shined bumpers, waiting for it all to end.

Lance thinks, you can make this out to be an omen or you can just let it alone, and she decides to let it alone. But only days later she thinks she might have made the wrong decision. She thinks she should have walked right up to the lounging chauffeurs, even taken them by the lapels of their shiny black suits, all three of them, resting so easily against their limousines, and asked them outright, who's dead here, and why, and why today? Instead, what she did was to turn to her father and ask him if they could go now, go on up to Cape Cod like they'd planned. They'd never been to the Cape and had decided to go now, since they were in the neighborhood, and classes didn't begin for another week. Lance wanted to leave her suitcases piled on the bed she'd staked a claim to. She wanted to get to the coast; she thought of it as the beginning of things, Plymouth Rock and the Pilgrims. She has this idea about starting college from the coast and moving toward the interior, getting educated that way, from the outside in.

—

During the first week of school, Lance gets two jobs, one cataloging rare books and manuscripts in Butler Library, and the other cleaning the rooms and bathrooms of her fellow students, a job that's politely called dorm crew. Every day she tells herself she should quit, she reminds herself how much she hates it, doing the literal shit work for other students, students no better than she is. But the truth is, Lance is fascinated by the personal possessions of her peers and their utter disregard for these possessions. She can't believe what slobs they are, what waste they indulge in. Fully half of the shoes Lance wears belong to people whose rooms she's cleaned. And they're good shoes too, Italian leather, Rockports sent down Federal Express from L. L. Bean, a pair of black satin spike heels kicked way back under a bed—in the heat of passion, Lance imagines—and never retrieved.

She's obliged to spend two hours a day on her dorm-crew route, but she works quickly, finishing all eight bathrooms in under an hour, and she spends the rest of the time in the most comfortable and well-appointed room on her shift. She sits in a leather armchair and reads for Natural Sciences 1 and English Romantic Poetry. She knows many of these rooms are occupied by what the college calls *legacies,* kids who sometimes have the same last names as a library or a playing field or a classroom building. She is jealous of all they have, the sweet ease of their lives. She finds in all their rooms stacks of round tins that once contained cookies sent from home. She enters these rooms and moves pencils, papers, and books around on their desks, not to harm or confuse, but to leave some breath of herself in the air.

In November Lance's mother comes up to visit her for Parents' Weekend. She is the last person off her flight at Newark Airport, and she walks down the jetway with the pilot. She tells Lance she'd asked him some questions and he'd invited her to tour the cockpit.

Over Columbus, Ohio, he had even let her fly the plane. He offers to buy Lance and her mother a drink in the airport lounge, but Lance says no, they have to catch a bus back to Manhattan.

"I hear you're at Barnard," the pilot says. "You must be pretty smart."

"No," Lance says. "I'm just lucky."

They ride the shuttle bus from Newark, and when the skyline of Manhattan rises out of the New Jersey meadowlands, Lance sees her mother's eyes fill with tears. She says she can hardly believe Lance lives there now, in the Big Apple, that it was exactly right what she told the pilot, she is lucky. Lance smiles, hands her mother a Kleenex, and asks about her father and brothers. Her mother says they're fine, and Lance can't tell anything from her voice. She takes her mother to her classes, to lectures on Gregor Mendel's peas and negative capability. They go to a student production of *Guys and Dolls,* and afterward eat filet mignon. They drink beer, which Lance is just learning to like.

"There are questions I could ask you, Mom," Lance says over dinner.

"There are answers I could give you," her mother says, "and some I can't." She pauses. "And some I won't."

On Saturday morning they rent a car and drive to Kennebunkport, Maine. They investigate the shops and the art galleries and walk on the beach for miles without seeing a single soul. They talk about how different the Atlantic coast is from the Gulf, how cold it is, how the wind will blow you deaf and blind. Later, in a bar in town, they meet two men, lovers who are planning to open an inn together. Lance's mother offers to go in with them and become their cook. She tells them she would do anything not to have to go back to Houston.

"What about all those cowboys?" one of the men says.

"No such thing," Lance's mother tells him. "Never seen a single one in eighteen years."

"Jack Beatty was kind of a cowboy," Lance says.

"The boys who drive the subways in New York get called cowboys," the other man says. "They must've all moved there from Texas."

"Jack Beatty is getting old," Lance's mother says, "old and forgetful. He forgets to come home some nights. That's what I hear."

"How come Dad went to live with the Trappists that time?" Lance asks.

"You know why," her mother says.

"Your husband's a monk?" one of the men says. "Honey, no wonder you don't want to go back home to Houston."

"It's not really like that," Lance's mother says. "It's not what you think. I drove him away once, but he came back." She smiles at the two men. "Now, why am I boring you with this?"

"People always come way up here and tell us their stories," the other man says. "We're good at keeping the little secrets. That's why we're opening an inn in Maine."

"Lance," her mother says, "I'm telling you. There isn't anything that you don't already know."

"Wow," one of the men says, "then you should probably just say the hell with college."

On the way back to New York Lance's mother tells her about Hazen Beatty. She says she's heard he's gone to California, to make weapons to sell to Third World countries. She's also heard he's joined the navy and taken up boxing promotion with his father. Lance is surprised by the way she hangs on her mother's every word. She'd lost touch with Hazen after he left Houston two years ago. They wrote letters for a while, and then nothing. She wonders if he ever comes to New York to see fights at Madison Square Garden. Her mother says she shouldn't worry about Hazen Beatty, that he'll always land on his feet. Lance thinks truer words were never spoken, at least not by her mother.

"Don't do what I did," Lance's mother tells her just before she steps onto the Newark shuttle. Lance feels her chest tighten. The lights in the Port Authority swim in her eyes.

"Which part?" she says, her voice rising and twisting in her throat.

"All of it, sweetheart," her mother says. "Or none of it. Whichever."

That's a lot of leeway, Lance thinks as she waves goodbye to her mother, that's a lot of rope to tie myself up good.

"I sound like a cowboy," she says out loud to the crowds in the Port Authority, and nobody notices. She thinks of her mother and father in Houston, facing each other across the landscape of a kitchen table, a hallway, the front seat of a moving vehicle. She wonders what it is that makes her want to travel so far from home and keep traveling. She wonders if she should have stayed in Houston and helped out. Captive in Houston.

I still think about them all the time, Lance tells herself, looking at the taxis lined up outside on Forty-second Street. I'm going to try to love it here, she thinks, looking around. Plenty of room to fuck up and still come out smelling like a rose.

—

Lance meets North Fallon in the spring of her sophomore year. He's her teacher in a class on Chaucer, which is his academic specialty. On the first day of class he tells his students he sometimes thinks he loves Chaucer more than life itself, but certainly more than Shakespeare, Pope, Shelley, and Amy Lowell. Lance can see that this endears him to almost everyone in the classroom in Schermerhorn Hall, but North Fallon's declaration of love makes its way particularly deep into her own heart. She looks at him more carefully, his gray-blond hair, blue eyes, and good tan. Then she stares out the window, and though she cannot see it, she thinks of all of New York City spread out below her like a promise. Privately she has always believed that just about everything in this world is worth loving more than life itself. She thinks, in fact, you'd be a hopeless idiot if you loved an abstract condition above and beyond people and places and even exotic food. Still, she knows not everyone would agree with her.

On the first day of class North Fallon says many things that Lance believes she'll never forget. He says history is mostly filled with non sequiturs and irrelevancies that only take shape later. He says the poet is a transparent mirror, and his audience is an unknown quantity, so there comes to be a need for a narrator, a go-between. It's like old-fashioned courtship, North Fallon says, running his eyes over the room. *Who can think of an example of what I'm talking about?* Lance's right hand rises as if it has a mind of its own.

"Matchmakers," she says.

"Exactly," North Fallon says. Lance thinks he takes a long look at her, as if he's making a mental note.

"In a dream vision," North Fallon continues, "the narrator and the poet are still essentially the same." He stops and looks down at his notes, then out at his students, concentrating on them one by one. "Dreams are like poems," he says. "Out of control, prophetic illusion, in which moral rules don't apply." He smiles. "You can see why they're so popular."

Lance thinks North Fallon will probably be a terrible teacher of the subject at hand. She thinks he might love Chaucer too much, but that he's probably good at teaching other things. He seems like someone born to give out information, which may or may not be useful. Like Dad, she thinks, born to tell people stuff and make them believe it's what they've always wanted to know.

After class Lance buys a sandwich and a Coke at Mama's Deli, and because it's surprisingly warm for the end of January, she walks down to Riverside Park to eat. She stares across the Hudson at New Jersey, which seems to shimmer under the winter sun. She thinks about North Fallon's class, about the middle of her second year in college. She thinks what she's learned so far could fit on the head of a pin. She remembers feeling this way back in October too, the air in New York like false, heavy breath. She's overcome again now by a sense of things falling out of themselves, out of windows, suddenly out of trees. Every sound she hears, every howling car alarm, all the fiendish dogs, the whole cackling city seems to be calling to her to remember what she's learned. But she only doubts all the more the books and papers, the flutter and babble of pages.

Exactly at one-thirty Lance looks toward Grant's Tomb and waits until she sees the black figure, the crow with a human face, take shape and grow larger as it rushes in her direction. She loves the sensation, waits for it almost every day, the black robe hurtling toward her, a young nun from St. Hilda's and St. Hugh's who jogs at midday, in full habit and a pair of blue-and-white Nikes. From two blocks away she looks like some creature that would fly out of an open grave on Halloween, a marauding spirit, Lance thinks, in language borrowed from Keats or Shelley. She's come to think of this nun as a vision of her dead brother, the little Lance di Fabbio for whom she's named, flying at her, trying to deliver some message, some urgent warning that Lance can't understand.

~

North Fallon's wife died a year ago, he tells Lance during his office hour. She's crossed Broadway to the Columbia University campus and walked up five floors in Philosophy Hall to see him. It's the third week of the semester, and Lance thinks she should make human contact with all her professors by then. North Fallon says he and his wife had both just turned forty. He says he is trying to reconcile the nature of poetry with the problem of grief. Then he's silent. He stares out his office window at the back of St. Paul's Chapel. Lance doesn't think she understands what he means.

"What do you mean?" she says.

"I mean sometimes I think what I do is bullshit," North Fallon tells her. "Have you ever been hunting?"

"Like for deer?" she says.

"Like for deer."

"I knew some people in Texas who did," she tells him, thinking about what Jack Beatty told her mother before he took her off on his motorcycle. "They said it was like a long dream."

"The killing becomes more important than the hunting," North Fallon says.

This is weird, Lance di Fabbio thinks. I only wanted to talk about the *Romance of the Rose*. She tries to get the discussion back on track. Guillaume de Lorris, Jean de Meun, Guillaume de Machant, Jean Froissart. These are all names she could say.

"I haven't slept for a year," North Fallon says.

I'm in over my head, as usual, Lance thinks. She feels a strange sympathy for North Fallon, and curiosity about him. She wonders why he's telling her this.

"To have such grief and not be dead," North Fallon says, shaking his head in absolute wonder. "I've discovered something, you know. I've discovered the world is made of sand, glass, metals, and hot air."

"There you go," Lance says. She excuses herself, explaining that she has to get to her Spanish class, where there's a big test waiting for her.

"Dos cervezas," North Fallon says and smiles. "That's all the Spanish I know."

The next week, North Fallon teaches Chaucer's *Parliament of Fowls*. He tells the class the poem is about how literature is a failure as a guide to life. The narrator is worried about being in love. Reading books got him into this predicament, and now he's terrified, and he wonders if books can save him.

"No way," Lance says without even raising her hand to be called on. She smiles, not at North Fallon, but out the window, at all of

New York City rising around her. She gets up and leaves the classroom and stays away for two weeks, missing all of *Troilus and Criseyde,* but she doesn't care. She walks a hundred blocks a day, from her apartment on 114th Street to the northern end of Greenwich Village, and then rides the subway back. She stops going to the rest of her classes too. Too much school will make me stupid, she thinks, knowing it's about the farthest she's ever been from an original thought. See, she tells herself. Jesus, it's happening already.

Toward the middle of the semester North Fallon starts to come into the library, with nothing in particular to look for, when Lance is working there. He talks vaguely of doing some research on his dead wife's family, the Sewalls of Massachusetts, but he never requests any books or manuscripts. He asks why she hasn't been in class lately, and she tells him she's taking a break.

"I've discovered this horrible thing," she says. "It's that I hate class. I like school, but I hate sitting in class listening to the teacher."

"Me too," North Fallon says. "That's why I *am* the teacher."

One day he comes in late in the afternoon, just as Lance is leaving, and he asks her to come home with him and have a drink. She says yes, without knowing why or thinking about the consequences. She's tired of thinking about consequences. She imagines a world in which there would be no consequences, a kind of moral Flatland. From a certain angle, everything you did would be inscrutable.

"When did you live in Texas?" North Fallon asks as they're crossing Broadway.

"All my life," Lance tells him, "Until I came to college."

"I've always wanted to go west," North Fallon says. "What was it like?"

"Flat," Lance says. "Flat, flat, flat. Like living at the bottom of a wide, shallow bowl."

"I can't even imagine," North Fallon says. "Was it hot?"

"Yes, but it's not the heat that gets you, it's the humidity."

"I've heard that. Do you miss it?"

"I miss my family," Lance says. "Sometimes I can't believe it, but it's true."

"What does your father do?"

"He teaches geometry."

North Fallon is quiet, and Lance wishes she could make this talk less like a tennis match and more like a conversation. She thinks about her mother and father and Peter and Paul, all four still at work. It's midafternoon in Houston.

"Geometry," North Fallon says. "That would explain your angular nature."

"My angular nature," Lance repeats, considering the words.

"You're all edge," North Fallon says, "all thin white line."

North Fallon's apartment is in a building on Riverside Drive and 114th Street, on the tenth floor, with a view of Riverside Park, the Hudson, and the whole breathtaking eastern flank of New Jersey. Lance cannot tell how many rooms there are in the apartment because all she sees are the kitchen, where North Fallon offers her a Rolling Rock, and the library. North Fallon has more books than Lance has ever seen in one room, shelved floor to ceiling in twelve bookcases of ten tiers each. Some of the titles are in languages she can't even recognize.

North Fallon points to a framed picture on one of the side tables next to the sofa.

"That's my wife," he says. In the picture Lance sees a tall woman with long dark hair. She is wearing a white halter dress and high-heeled sandals. The sun seems very bright, dazzling, all around her. She's walking, one foot out in front of the other, but she seems intent on the ground below her. Lance wants to see what North Fallon's wife looks like, but her face is hidden by the forward fall of her hair.

"She's walking on rice," North Fallon explains. "It's in the Philippines, on a plantation. The rice is drying in the sun."

"She looks like she's afraid she'll fall," Lance says.

"She's not. But it's an odd feeling for most people to walk on rice, like walking on tiny rollers. You're unsteady, if you're not used to it. You could be thrown off your feet at any moment. And you keep on thinking, *this is only rice,* but that just unsettles you all the more."

"I see," Lance says, though she knows in many very important ways she doesn't see at all. She wants North Fallon to keep talking, she wants the sound of his voice to cover the rushing sound in her ears, the noise of hurtling through space toward some unknown point on the horizon. She sips at her beer and listens quietly to the classical music North Fallon has on the stereo. She thinks it might be Mozart; she hopes so, because the only classical music she ever had any patience for is Mozart—actually only one piece: his Twenty-third Piano Concerto in D. North Fallon sits on the couch and turns to look out over the Hudson.

"I spend hours sitting here," he says, "counting strophes of sunlight, here in my tender prison of Beethoven."

"Oh, Beethoven," Lance says. She stares off past North Fallon's shoulders. The late afternoon glare on the Jersey hills looks like glass, or ice, it could be ice—even in April it's still cold enough. She wants to say to North Fallon, *Look, the sky's a mirror,* gray air reflecting gray earth, but all she can manage is a wild gesture with her empty glass. She wants to tell him she thinks of the horizon as a great hinge pressing everybody inside, making them all flat and insubstantial.

"It's like this every day," he says, meaning the landscape, the light across the Hudson. "Let me get you another beer. You look so sad, little Lance di Fabbio."

She is sad, and she thinks it's because this is the cruellest month, and because North Fallon's memories are so huge in this room, and also because looking down on Riverside Park she can see the sun setting tangled in a tree. She politely declines the beer and says goodbye to North Fallon, who shakes her hand solemnly, as if he's just granted her a diploma or, she thinks, some more hollow thing.

All spring Lance spends entire days in the library, twice a week, working on the children's collection. She's been cataloging editions of *Jack in the Beanstalk,* of which the library has quite a few. She loves the story in all its versions; the clever Jack, the mother who doesn't ask any questions, the giant's wife who understands the ways of the world, the young peasant girl who saves Jack and then marries him. She thinks of parts of this story as parts of a life she might have.

She's now moved on to the Charles Lutwidge Dodgson collection, pasting nameplates inside the front covers of all the library's *Alice* books. She wonders why he wanted to change his name to Lewis Carroll. She thinks she's being moved farther and farther back into the stacks, and that someday she'll just disappear. She feels half crazy, alone in that gloom where no weather ever comes, alone with books that leave pieces of themselves behind as she takes them from the shelves. The head librarian catches her reading a first edition of *The Wings of the Dove* and scolds her because it's too old to be read merely for pleasure. After that Lance spends her free time in Special Collections, paging through catalogs from auction houses, Christie's and Sotheby's. She finds herself craving emerald tiaras, baroque altarpieces, and marble statuary, huge riches that would take whole lifetimes to decompose. Her head aches from the dust she's living in. Every afternoon and far into each night the pain of it comes like a human voice singing one screamingly high note into her right ear.

"My temple is in ruins," she tells North Fallon a week later in the deep silence of his apartment. Then she says to herself, *what the hell,* and turns her face up to him to be kissed. It is a sweet, sad kiss, and Lance likes that, so she stays on for more, far into the night.

At dawn she gets up and walks down Broadway to Ninety-sixth Street. She thinks that in New York spring is more than just a season, it is a test. She thinks about how the days go, these pink mornings fading throughout the day to indecision and even the threat of more snow. The air has a tightness in it, the way she feels seeing racks of bright clothes on the sidewalks or the fragile necks of crocuses in their plastic pots. *More than a season,* she says out loud, and her voice sounds like the prayer of a whole city just getting up off its knees. Lance goes to the Cathedral of Saint John the Divine, where she sits down in the last row. Afterward she isn't sure how long she's stayed, she can't tell how far the sun's moved by the time she's said her last words, asking a careful blessing for herself, for North Fallon, for whatever it is they're about to do together.

Outside on Amsterdam Avenue she feels that familiar blindness, the sun painfully bright in her eyes as she leaves the darkness of the cathedral. Again she looks at the pots of crocuses and tulips, the racks of Indian cotton dresses, still not quite believing the crocuses' necks won't break in the wind, the seams of the colorful clothes won't split if she buys them, baring her heart as a pale, bloodless wound.

—

Lance does the proper thing and drops out of North Fallon's Chaucer class. She hates to miss *The Canterbury Tales,* which she suspects North Fallon will be pretty good at teaching, better than he was earlier in the semester. She thinks he seems calmer now, more organized in his thinking. She lies awake at night for what feels like hours, watching North Fallon's face while he's sleeping. There's always an eerie light in his apartment at night, light that illuminates and opalizes their bodies the way the moon would, but Lance knows it isn't the moon. On the night she decides that this luminous wash is reflected light from New Jersey, Fort Lee, Teaneck, and even Paramus, she laughs out loud, so loudly that North Fallon wakes up and turns toward her, reaching his left arm across her shoulders and pulling her close to him. She holds his hand with both of hers and thinks she never wants to be any farther away from him than she is right now.

"We can do a kind of independent study," he whispers, "so you won't feel you're missing anything." They lie still in the moonish glow. Neither of them makes the old joke about independent study and who'd be studying what or whom. Lance wishes North Fallon would say something, anything, to break the silence between them. In a few minutes she hears his breathing even out and feels the weight of his arm settle around her as he falls back into sleep. She feels a sudden stiffness in her heart, as if she's learned a terrible secret about him. But she knows it isn't just about him. She thinks people are always desperately alone, no matter how tightly they hold on to one another.

—

North Fallon says he is telling his Chaucer class some traditional fabliaux. His favorite is the Montaiglon-Raynand version of "The Snow Baby." A woman becomes pregnant and gives birth while her husband is away on business, and she explains the new baby by telling him this story: It being winter, and snow falling heavily, a little snow fell into my mouth, and I swallowed it. It was so sweet that from the little I swallowed I conceived this beautiful child. Later, the husband, who is not fooled, takes the child to market and sells him, then returns home to explain to his wife: The rays of the sun at noon fell full on our heads, and the boy, exposed to the great heat of the sun, all at once melted away.

"That's a scary story," Lance says.

"They all are, all the fabliaux," North Fallon says.

"Why do you think that is?"

"Your own laughter makes you nervous. You're shocked to be laughing at such horrifying events. You think these things could happen to you."

"Oh," Lance says, the sweet, coppery taste of New York snow suddenly on her tongue.

When he holds her at night, North Fallon says to Lance that it feels as if his skin is on fire, he feels burned wherever she touches him. He expects to look at his skin in the morning and see it charred, beginning to crumble around his bones, dusting them with a fine gray ash. Lance tells him not to worry because—she admits this is a leap of reason—she carries a picture of an iceberg in her wallet. She's carried it for years now, so long that she doesn't even remember where she got it, except that it's from a magazine, she can tell by the slick surface of the page it's printed on and the Chevrolet ad on the other side. The photograph, all in shades of aquamarine and gray, is of two icebergs shaped like ships, one in the foreground and another, much larger, one hundred yards behind it. Halfway between the two there's a sea gull or some other kind of water bird, banking down so that the tip of its right wing looks to be just skimming the surface of the water. Folded inside is the picture of Shalu the whale from Sea-Arama Marineworld in Galveston.

"Why do you carry a picture of Shalu the whale?" North Fallon asks, and Lance tells him about the trip to Galveston, the history of whaling in America, her feeling that the audience at Sea-Arama Marineworld and even Shalu himself had been sold a bill of goods. She doesn't mention her father and her mother, her father and the Trappists, or Jack Beatty. She thinks all that is a different story.

"An iceberg and Shalu the whale," North Fallon says, shaking his head in wonder.

"Well, what's in your wallet?" Lance says.

"Money," North Fallon tells her, "and my dead wife."

"You mean her picture," Lance says.

"Yes," he says, "from when we first met."

North Fallon tells Lance he once worked in a globe factory, at the Rand-McNally plant in Massachusetts. It was his first and last job before teaching, running the press that imprints thin sheets of metal with the mountain ranges of the world. All day long, globes swung on guy wires over his head, like a cross between an amusement-park ride and the heavens, the way God gets to see things, whole worlds moving around him, following the paths he's set.

It was where he met his wife, North Fallon says, his wife who was not a Sewall from Massachusetts but half-Japanese, half-Filipino from Quezon City. She was in charge of the oceans, she'd told him when they met in the plant cafeteria. She had a beautiful smile, and the tips of her fingers were always different shades of blue, teal, cobalt, and ultramarine from drawing ocean depths and shorelines. She'd told the executives at Rand-McNally that she could paint the oceans much more accurately if she could see them, and so in her first year of work, the company sent her to all the world's coasts: from New York to the Isles of Scilly, Rio de Janeiro to Cape Town, Cape St. Marie to Bangkok to the Great Barrier Reef to Tokyo and back to San Francisco. After they were married North Fallon accompanied her on this last leg of the trip, and they visited her Japanese relatives. One day he was taken by a translator to meet his wife's dead grandfather. They entered the family's temple and moved to a back room, which contained drawers like safe-deposit boxes and one huge urn, six feet tall. A gong was sounded, and the translator dug into the urn and presented North Fallon with his wife's father's ashes. North Fallon bowed and asked the ashes how they were doing. His translator later told him he'd done exactly the right thing by touching the ashes and speaking directly to them. These are the last words Lance hears before she falls asleep, and she dreams about ashes, clouds of them blowing into North Fallon's eyes.

"Let's go hunting," North Fallon says to Lance in the morning. "Let's get married and go hunting. I know a place in Pennsylvania."

"It's May," Lance says. "What could there be to hunt?"

"Birds, squirrels, that sort of thing. I want to show you this place. I think you'll love it."

For a week Lance walks around asking herself if she's in love with North Fallon. She finally decides she wouldn't know being in love if she tripped over it in the street. She thinks about her mother and father, measuring them against North Fallon and his wife who could walk on rice. She thinks about the boys in River Oaks Cemetery, about Hazen Beatty, and about his father. She stands in Riverside Park looking out at the Hudson, and she decides they're all different, there's no pattern, and then she turns north to wait for the young nun from St. Hilda's and St. Hugh's, whose flapping black robes she can already see in the distance.

When classes are over they fly to Houston so North Fallon can meet Lance's parents and her brothers. Everyone is very polite, and Lance is relieved, until her mother whispers in her ear, *At least now you'll get to travel.*

"True or magnetic?" Lance's father asks as they're sitting down to dinner.

"How's that?" North Fallon says.

"Is it true north or magnetic north you're named for?"

"I never thought about it," North Fallon says.

"Lord bless this food and tell us which kind of north," Lance's father says after they've all bowed their heads.

"Magnetic," Lance says.

"I would think so," Lance's father says, "since true north exists only on paper, on maps, in the second dimension."

"You know," Lance's mother says, "it's only on maps to show the fullness of the lie."

Lance marries North Fallon at Holy Trinity Church in Houston. The church is empty except for her family, and a few people praying quietly in the back. The side lamps send veils of light across the altar, a softening translucence, and Lance thinks North Fallon looks to be lit from inside. She tries to listen to the priest's words, but her mind wanders. She watches her parents: they are holding hands but staring off in different directions. Her father is counting something on the fingers of his free hand. She hears a cough in the back of the church and footsteps coming up the center aisle.

"Lance, remember me, Hazen Beatty?"

Lance turns around to look, and she doesn't know which is

more arresting, the sight of Hazen Beatty or the smile on her mother's face.

"Don't do it, Lance," Hazen calls as Peter and Paul lead him outside. "Have a fucking heart, Lance."

—

Back in New York Lance and North Fallon rent a car and drive to Newville, Pennsylvania, to his favorite corner of the public game lands. All the way south to Harrisburg on I-81 Lance can't shake the feeling that Hazen Beatty is in the car with them, that if she turns around, he'll be sitting behind her, asleep, his head fallen back and to the right so it rests against the window. She imagines he'll wake up in Lackawanna and ask where they are, and she'll tell him, and he'll drift off to sleep again. Instead, when they see the sign, North Fallon moves his hand on Lance's thigh and laughs and says there's no lackawanna between them. He doesn't sound like himself, she thinks. Maybe this is being a wife. Maybe this is how husbands talk.

The road into the game lands makes Lance feel as though she's under water. Oak, maple, and sycamore trees grow together, forming a canopy above them, the morning sunlight filtering through and dappling the windshield. She thinks she should hold her breath, that they need to get out of the car before it sinks into this element. They stop at the end of the road, where half of a stone bridge veers off over the creek. North Fallon opens the trunk and takes out his shotgun. They lean against the car's back bumper, with the shotgun resting between them. Lance thinks, suddenly, we must look like two people who've lost something.

"It's beautiful," she says.

"I knew you'd like it," North Fallon says, and there's a pause. "I will never be unfaithful to you," he says.

Lance looks at him hard, and her first thought is, *liar*.

"Why do you say that now?" she asks.

"It seems like a good place. Can you promise me that too?"

"Of course," Lance says. "I already did promise that, back in Houston, in front of my whole family."

"All right," North Fallon says. "Here's the other thing. What are your feelings about Salt Lake City, Utah?"

"Why?"

"There's a job there, at the university. I was thinking about it."

"About taking it?"

"Yes, about taking it. How would you feel about moving to Salt Lake City?"

"I've never thought about it."

"Maybe you could this afternoon while we're walking around."

North Fallon's interest, Lance discovers, is in small game: rabbits, squirrels, small birds. He likes hunting, he tells her, not for any of the reasons most men talk about, not for the exercise and fresh air or because it's the epic confrontation with nature.

"It's American," he says.

"It's older than that," Lance tells him.

"True," North Fallon says, "but all those thousands of years that people were hunting they were waiting for someplace like America to be invented, someplace captivating. Huge and free and empty."

North Fallon hits everything he shoots at, and as the day wears on Lance finds herself carrying two rabbits and three squirrels. The birds they don't collect, birds with tiny caves in their chests, blown open by shot. Lance looks down at them and feels unspeakably sad. She thinks of all these dead birds having families somewhere, children who won't know where their parents are or else will come upon their remains suddenly, in a clearing, and cry their alarming sadness into the wind to be mistaken by humans for song. She wonders what they're going to do with these animals. Eat them? Make their skins into something, purses or wallets, carry their feet for luck? Maybe, she thinks, what's American is doing things quickly and for no good reason.

They walk deeper into the heart of the game lands, following a path through pines and undergrowth down to the creek. Lance moves behind North Fallon, placing her feet exactly in his tracks. She tries not to make any sound at all, but when that proves impossible, she tries to make less noise than he makes, which is much easier. Ducks swim in a raggedy line, but North Fallon doesn't take a shot at them. She's struck by the shimmering teal of their wings, how metallic it looks, as if shot would only clatter off their sides and never harm them. Every second she expects North Fallon will stop hiking, turn and take her in his arms. She expects he'll clear a space for them among the fallen leaves, the drying grass, and lay her down there. Maybe even now he's looking for a place, a dark cave, a shelter in the high mast where a buck made a bed just hours before.

She imagines the eyes of deer watching them as they move down toward the base of Allegheny Mountain. In early daylight, not full sun like they're in now, deer belong to the hunter. He hangs in a tree, ten feet high, and they don't look up, it's said deer never look up. Lance thinks it must have something to do with their vision, their vision of an orderly world in which men stay on the ground, and so to see a man thrown off his feet, hunched over in a tree like the flightless bird, would make them act irrationally. It would make them sorry to see a man so alone, his eyes blinking into the morning light, searching through the fog ghosts for any other creature looking as lost as he feels. She believes if they could look up and see men in tree stands, deer would fall to the ground, fold their long white legs, and offer themselves up. They'd know then that the longing of hunters goes beyond their flesh, or any flesh and bones and blood, the longing of hunters is really every creature's desire to outrun itself, to be more than its flesh can hold, more than its heart and head can guide. If they could look up, deer would know that men need twenty hearts or twenty thousand beating to keep such a self alive. If deer could see this, Lance thinks, there would be no more hunting as we now know it.

But at night, she tells herself, deer are spirits no man, not even

North Fallon, can ever touch. He could shine a floodlight full in their eyes and think he's stunned them with what this world calls light. And for a moment they would stand still, frozen, then the black glass of their eyes would hurl a man back into the trees. What a man could see in the eyes of a deer at night would scare him more than anything he could imagine, and it might make even North Fallon turn off his lamp, bow his head, and drive away.

"Who was that in the back of the church in Houston?" North Fallon asks. Lance has been waiting for this question for weeks now.

"Someone I loved a long time ago," she says.

"I wanted to kill him," North Fallon says. "I might still do it."

"There's no reason for that," Lance says.

"I could, you know," he says. "It would be so easy. You might invite him out to visit you, or maybe he'd just come after you like a fool, and that'd be the end of him."

"Are you crazy?" Lance says.

"Yes," North Fallon tells her, "but not so that anyone would notice."

III. Texas

Looking out over the snaking sandstone of Hell's Backbone in southwest Utah, Hazen Beatty has to admit certain things to himself. He has to admit he's still in love with Lance di Fabbio. And he has to admit that the killing truly does become more important than the hunting. These are words he's read in a book somebody left in the cabin he's been staying in for the past five days while he fished and hunted around the cold gray waters of Barney Lake and Bear Creek and considered the question of what he's done with his life, which isn't a whole hell of a lot. He's hiked up to the scenic overlook on Highway 12 and stared east toward Impossible Peak and back west toward Box-Death Hollow, the ridges like a sagging, toothless jawline. Every day for five days he's watched the light change, the canyons deepen in shadow and then, an hour later, burst wide open as the sun tipped over off the high walls. He's tried to imagine how a settler might have moved through this landscape, where the red rock might sheer up right in front of your face, and everywhere you look there's more evidence of geological mayhem, canyons dug, rock face fallen open like a mouth in disbelief. All around you there's the silence that both precedes and follows cataclysm and conflagration, precedes and follows, only you don't know which.

Hazen Beatty has come here to fish and hunt deer illegally and see how long he can get away with it. He's come to escape the world of boxing promotion in Houston. He's tired of hawking glorified fistfights, he's stopped being able to see the beauty, grace, footwork, heart. He's tired of watching men's bodies ruined; he's gotten too good at spotting the single punch that permanently clouds the vision, the one that garbles the speech, the fall that's going to make a young man hobble slightly sideways for the rest of his natural life. His father told him that Cassius Clay could recite Keats. In the locker room he might say, "Thou still unravished bride of quietness," and Hazen Beatty would imagine himself there, picking a towel off the white fluffed pile and taking it over to Cassius Clay so that he could be close enough to hear the rest. "What mad pursuit? What struggle to escape?" When Cassius Clay said "Thou shalt remain, in midst of other woe," Hazen would imagine the words were for him, and only him, Hazen Beatty, son of all that was and was to come in America.

But Cassius Clay became Muhammad Ali, and Lance di Fabbio went off to college in New York City and married one of her teachers. Hazen went to the wedding, knee-walking drunk, and called out her name from the back of the church. That was a year ago, and it was the last he'd seen of her, but he'd followed her, tracked her like a comet, like the glittering, explosive thing she was. He knows she's living roughly two hundred miles north of where he stands right now, and he's working up the nerve to go see her.

And then he found this book somebody left in the cabin, a collection of poems and essays about hunting, and he'd randomly opened it up to a poem called "Rabbit Hunting." In the poem a couple is hunting rabbits, but the woman has something else on her mind—getting away from the man, it seems like at first, but then also wanting him to take more notice of her, listen to what she says, covet her, in general act the way he used to when they were younger. Hazen Beatty wishes he could hear this poem in Cassuis Clay's voice, or better, Lance di Fabbio's voice, which he doesn't remember as well as he'd like to, but he thinks it used to be low and steady, like a good, small motor, a sewing machine, maybe. He reads the poem again and wonders how it ever got into this book, it's so *sensitive*. He thinks the word half-ashamed. So *frightening*. In the five days he's been in the Bear Creek cabin, Hazen must have read the poem a hundred times, often out loud, standing by the window or in the doorway, looking up now and then to see the Henry Mountains, white-capped still in their great wisdom. This idea of people acting the way they used to when they were younger is making him crazy to get to Lance di Fabbio in Salt Lake City, 243 miles away. He invents scenes, imagines the whole world of seeing her again. He thinks maybe he'll get up to Salt Lake and find she really lives in Magna, or, he hopes, a town called Bountiful, and he'll ring the doorbell, shake her hand, go into the house, and lie down on the cool of her kitchen floor. She'll be fixing supper for her kid—he hasn't heard that she's had children, but he knows no report could be 100 percent reliable, and it's a child that's most likely to slip into a woman's life that way. Anyway, Lance di Fabbio would be making supper for her beautiful child, and Hazen would lie down on the linoleum and let the baby crawl over him like he was his own entire mountain range.

On the sixth day Hazen gets in his truck and drives back into Escalante to the Main Street Market. He turns in the cabin key to the manager, who is the uncle of a friend of a friend from Houston.

"Heading back south, then?" he says to Hazen.

"No, sir," Hazen says. "Up to Salt Lake for a few days."

"Won't get much rest up that way," he says and winks at Hazen. "Temptation," he says, pausing over the first syllable of the word like he's relishing its many tastes.

"Yes, sir," Hazen says. He buys a bag of Oreos and a liter of Pepsi.

"Everything shipshape at the cabin?" the old man says. "You seen any rangers?"

"Not a soul."

"How 'bout mule deer? You can tell by the look in his eye when a man seen a lot of mule deer. It's like a heavy dream and you don't come out of it easy."

"Quite a few mule deer up in the pass."

"Good. Now you have a safe trip up to Salt Lake, so you can maybe get a little white tail instead."

"It's not really like that," Hazen says.

"Oh, I know," the old man says. "You come down here to be purified, and sure enough, it worked."

"I believe it did," Hazen says. "I believe it did."

Hazen plans to follow the state highways through Fishlake National Forest up to Interstate 15 and straight into Salt Lake City. He wants to make the trip slowly so that it will take one entire span of daylight. He has a need to put half a state's worth of scenery between himself, his past, and his next meeting with Lance di Fabbio. He knows how the landscape will make him feel like a man rushing toward water, no matter how slowly he drives, the two sides of Fishlake National Forest hurtling down at him, sending their creeks—Otter, Peterson, Cottonwood, Willow, and Lost—down to Highway 24 as a kind of offering. This is the last of the snow, Hazen thinks, down from Sunset Peak to the west, from Mount Terrel to the east. All day long he watches these shoulders of mountains for some kind of signal. He thinks if he weren't supposed to go on north, he'd get a sign from them, a flash of gold along the rim of Mount Nebo, or even before that, in the Mussentuchit Badlands, the webbed dikes and sills, the buttes, bentonite hills, and volcanic outcroppings would shift and finally rise up, but none of this happens.

He works through his memories of Lance di Fabbio, casting them out like fishing line, seeing how far they'll play. The last one is always Lance in the parking lot of River Oaks Cemetery, standing next to his parked car, her hair rising up off her shoulders in the breeze, tears shining in her eyes. He does not remember what she said to him, or what he said to her. He thinks he'll get that part of the memory back when he sees her in Salt Lake. At the front door of her and her husband's house, she'll say what she said on that night all those years ago, and he'll say what he said, and they'll start over again from there.

—

Inside the Salt Lake city limits Hazen stops to find a phone book. He remembers Lance di Fabbio's husband's name was North Fallon, and sure enough, there he is, listed as residing in a house in the 400 block of Third Avenue. Hazen knows North Fallon teaches English at the university, and he's come to imagine Lance's husband is a Shakespearean, a real Renaissance man, and so the house will be filled with playbills, and videocassettes of all the plays, and maybe a larger-than-life-sized framed portrait of the Bard himself or Queen Elizabeth the First. He pictures this as he's getting out of his car and walking up the front steps. Lance is probably not allowed in her husband's study, he thinks as he rings the doorbell. He, North Fallon, Ph.D., M.Phil., M.A., B.A., B. fucking S., probably calls this part of his house the *foyer*.

And then there she is, standing in front of him, Lance di Fabbio, a year older than she was at her wedding. Hazen thinks he sees sparks shooting from her eyes.

"Hazen Beatty," she says. "Hazen Beatty."

"Hi, Lance," he says. "I was in the neighborhood."

She smiles at him, the beginnings of that lean, murderous smile he remembers, though now she drops her gaze halfway into it.

"Are you going to ask me in?" he says.

"Sorry," she tells him, her eyes going wide. "It's been a long time since anybody's come calling for me."

Inside the front door there's a long hallway leading into the kitchen. A staircase cuts off to the left, ten risers carpeted in crimson plush, before it makes a turn to the right and heads up out of sight. To his own right Hazen can see into the living room, where a dark green horsehair sofa rests on a white rug next to two uncomfortably modern looking chairs, silver rods with squares of black leather slung where the seat and arms should be. From over the fireplace a portrait of Queen Elizabeth the First stares back at Hazen with one eye half closed, a sneer on her impossibly small, mean-looking mouth.

"I'd like to offer you something," Lance says, "but all I've got is decaf tea and some malted-milk-ball eggs left over from Easter."

"Get the eggs, and we'll go someplace." Hazen wants to talk to Lance about the hunting rabbits poem, about her life, his life, but not in this holy tomb of a house.

They get in his car and drive downtown to the Blue Iguana, a Mexican restaurant Lance knows. They order food—chimichangas, quesadillas, tacos—but they can't eat very much of it, Lance because, Hazen thinks, she's nervous, worried about being seen in the company of a man who isn't her husband, and maybe alarmed by a certain lightness in her shoulders, a tingling on her scalp and in the bones of her face. Hazen can't eat because he's too busy watching his life change in the flutter of an eyelash, too busy marveling at the way he knew all along this would happen, that he'd get Lance di Fabbio back, but not without the veil of tears, the impossible journey, the long haul, the shot in the dark.

"How are you these days?" Hazen asks.

"Which days?" she says.

"Let's say the last two thousand, one hundred and fifty-five or so." Hazen counts the years this way because he knows Lance will love it. It will remind her of her father.

"My husband moved out to Texas a while back," she says. "Otherwise it's the same old same old."

"Left you, you mean?" Hazen can hardly keep the joy out of his voice.

"I guess you could call it that," Lance says. "He just got crazier and crazier, then he bought this property near Waco and went down there to wait for oil to be discovered on it."

"Are you happy he's gone?" Hazen says.

"I don't know what I am," she says. "I'm too tired. Some days

I never get out of bed. I just lie there and look at the ceiling and watch the light move over the furniture, and I swear my mind stays completely blank."

They move on to The Twilight, a bar down the street, and they drink boilermakers, the whiskey part of which Hazen has to buy at the front counter, as is the custom in Salt Lake City. He vows to steal the shot glasses for Lance, they say, IT'S TWILIGHT ALL DAY LONG, and he does. They head back to North Fallon's house, which Hazen now knows to be the house of a Chaucer scholar, driving first along the foothills above the university. Hazen sees Salt Lake laid out like a collar of diamonds, maybe more like a tangled necklace. He thinks he can't possibly be in Salt Lake City, Utah, that he and Lance di Fabbio stepped out of The Twilight and into Athens or Rio de Janeiro, or some other exotic city ringed by dark mountains.

Back at the house Lance shows Hazen the room that contains all her belongings, still in boxes because she's never unpacked in the entire year they've lived in Salt Lake. She shows him her gun, a Harrington-Richardson combination rifle and shotgun with its interchangeable barrel. Like John Wayne's, she says, even though it's a lie, John Wayne's gun was a Winchester. She's seen it at the National Cowboy Hall of Fame in Oklahoma City, and this part she tells to Hazen. Lance is so drunk she forgets how to load the bullets, and so drunk she points the gun directly at Hazen Beatty, who feels in that moment the surge of electricity men claim to love: the threat of death at the hands of a beautiful woman. They sit on the floor in the hallway right outside this room, on top of the air-conditioner vent. Hazen wants to touch her, but he won't let himself, not yet.

"You could maybe help me get out of my life," Lance says. "Do you know any lawyers? I think everybody in the whole world but me must know at least one lawyer."

"Lawyers are hard to know," Hazen says, to hide the fact that he's known hundreds of them in his promoter days.

"I used to be a smart girl," Lance tells him. "Remember? And then I was a smart woman for a little while, and then I went down the shitter."

"You look pretty good to me," Hazen says.

"You're sweet," Lance tells him and pauses. "I don't have any money. North sends me checks from Texas, but it's only enough to pay the bills and eat out at the Taco Bell."

"Money's no problem," Hazen says, wondering what crazy thing will come flying out of his mouth next.

"Are you rich?" Lance asks him. "North Fallon was a rich man, and I've come to the conclusion that it's why he went insane. Are you rich, Hazen? I need to know right now."

"Let's just say I'm full of potential," Hazen tells her.

They go back out to the car and drive to the Safeway, and Hazen buys ice cream for Lance. They sit in the car in Pioneer Trail State Park, under the invisible shadow of the Wasatch Front, with two plastic spoons and the ice cream carton. It's a flavor Lance has never had before, never even heard of—Cherry Garcia. She and Hazen try to decide what to do.

"You could just split," Hazen says, made bold by cream, nonfat milk, sugar, cherries, chocolate, lecithin, and guar gum. "*Sayonara, adios, au revoir, guten Nacht.*"

"Then I can't get the checks," Lance says.

"The checks. Right. I was forgetting the checks."

"We could go there, go talk to him. North, I mean. Go south."

"You're confusing me," Hazen says. "Go south to find North?"

"That's right," Lance says, smiling for the first time in years. "He's just a guy. You might scare him a little. Another man, I mean, with me. Two against one, sort of."

"Where is he?"

"West of Waco now. The town's called Flat."

"No shit."

"That's what he said."

"What did you ever see in him anyway? I tried to figure it out at your wedding, but I couldn't."

Hazen watches Lance stop to remember back. He thinks maybe he'll get it all now, the full story, complete with tears and gnashing of teeth, and he braces himself.

"He wasn't like anybody I'd ever known before," Lance says, closing her eyes and smiling a little. "He was smart, he'd been to a lot of places, read a lot of books. He used to know exactly what I meant when I said things. There's parts of it I can't explain, not now anyway. Maybe later."

"How do we get to Flat, Texas?" Hazen asks.

"I think we drive," Lance says. "I should tell you something, though. He once said he might kill you."

Hazen kisses her then, reaching across the space between them to pull her close. She kisses him back, softly at first, her lips barely touching his, then with more force, until neither of them can breathe. Hazen knows this kiss, and the lean, murderous smile, recognizes both from River Oaks Cemetery more than seven years ago in Houston, Texas. He thinks she said to him then, *I won't remember you, but I'll be able to feel you,* while the moon rose, making their bodies luminous, and all the dead bore witness.

—

Hazen tries to look into the vehicles he passes on I-70, traveling southeast out of Salt Lake City. They are all full, every last Taurus, Accord, Trooper, Wayfarer, and Blazer, full of wild tourist life. He thinks, nobody travels alone, not because they're afraid to, but because they don't have to. He sneaks looks at his old love, Lance di Fabbio, he thinks her entire name, riding beside him. He wonders if North Fallon became crazy all at once or by slow degrees over the course of several years.

"He never mistreated me," Lance says, like she's reading his mind, "not one time. He never hit me or made threats or anything like that."

"There's other kinds of mistreatment," Hazen says. He tells Lance he knows all about it from listening to boxers' wives and girlfriends. He understands all about verbal abuse and neglect. "I used to tell their wives to prosecute to the fullest extent of the law, even if it meant the son of a bitch went to jail and I lost the revenue."

"Tell me about your life," Lance says, turning in the front seat to face him. She leans back against the passenger-side door and rests her head on the window. She extends her legs over the seat so that her feet touch the car door on Hazen's side, her calves lying across his thighs.

"You're changing the subject," Hazen says.

"Yes," Lance tells him. "Go on. Talk."

Hazen tells Lance about his life since they were teenagers in Houston. He starts by telling her about his job at a government nuclear-weapons plant out in California. He says he quit the day an official told them that working with plutonium was no more dangerous than crossing the street.

"It was such a bald-faced lie that nobody in the auditorium moved or said anything for about a full minute," Hazen says, "and that's a hell of a long time for two hundred fifty people to keep still."

Lance thinks *it's bold-faced lie,* but she knows correcting people's speech is a leftover from her life with North Fallon, and so she doesn't mention it.

"It seemed like a bad idea to stay in a place where the people in charge have no clue that way."

Then, Hazen says, he joined the armed services, an elite branch of the navy known as the Seals, whose specialty is underwater missions of rescue and bombing. He tells her the Seals is the most demanding of the special forces, that the training alone was enough to kill you. Once he was awakened in the middle of the night, taken out of bed just in his skivvies, loaded into a helicopter, and dropped into the Pacific Ocean, off the coast of Coronado Island near San Diego. He had to get to shore by swimming alone in the dark, through schools of sharks, he believes, though he couldn't see them. He doesn't remember very much about the whole episode, but he thinks it might be the very night he started to talk in his sleep, which he now does every night, like clockwork.

"I know about those Seals," Lance says. "I've heard that if one member of the team can't go on, the others have to kill him and sink his body."

"I don't know if it's ever happened that way," Hazen says, "but we were told it was a possibility."

"I heard the Seals have letters already written to their next-of-kin," Lance says, "so if they're killed during a dangerous mission, they can keep sending letters home until the rest of the team has got to someplace safe."

" 'Dear Mom,' " Hazen says, quoting from one of his old letters, " 'send more of those oatmeal cookies. I just don't know where they go. Maybe my buddies are eating them. I just can't be sure anymore.' "

He tells her the Seals also get put through torture exercises, but he doesn't remember much about those either. Sometimes he'd pass out, but they never let anybody really get hurt. Hazen thinks that's pretty big of them.

After he was a Navy Seal, he worked for an animal channeler in Santa Fe, New Mexico, doing research. A regular channeler, he explains, is somebody who knows how to manipulate your joints, gauge body strength and muscle tensions, and then use that information to help you live a better life. An animal channeler does virtually the same thing. He'll make you lie down on his special table, like the kind of table you'd find in a massage parlor or a doctor's office, and he'll lift your right arm and ask you to lower it, pressing against his hand for resistance. From this muscle testing, he'll be able to tell you what's wrong with your pets. If they're sick.

"What did you do?" Lance says.

"I read up on the animals, not just pets, all the strange ones— alpaca, wallabees, whales. The Save the Whales people were trying to get animal channelers involved."

"Sounds like a scam," Lance says.

"Pretty much," Hazen tells her, "but business was terrible anyway. There were too many channelers in Santa Fe, and I was starving. Sometimes I ate stuff the restaurants would throw out in their Dumpsters. So I went back to Houston, and my father took me into the promoter business."

"I remember your Dad was on TV all the time," Lance says. "He talked a lot."

"Yes," Hazen says. "He loved that life, all the noise, the fights. He understood what people wanted, he could get them worked up to a fever pitch, the boxers and the media people. He'd come home late at night or even early in the morning, kiss my mother and wave the morning sports pages in her face and say, *I love this shit.*"

"I remember he bought a motorcycle," Lance says.

"Yes," Hazen says. "Once he took your mother for a ride. She wore my helmet, and the smell of her hair stayed in it for years."

"He loved my mother," Lance says.

"I think he did. Did she ever say anything about it?"

"Not exactly. She said there were questions she wouldn't answer. And she smiled when you crashed my wedding."

"She did?"

"She grinned like the damn Cheshire Cat." And Lance shows Hazen the smile.

It's exactly like yours, Hazen thinks, and then he feels his heart about to burst. He hears in his head a line about the sins of the fathers going visiting, and then it gets confused with something about a city on a hill.

"I guess we're like manifest destiny," he says.

"Don't give me that fancy talk, Hazen," Lance says. "You know I didn't finish college."

"Do you ever want to go home?" he says.

"To Houston? No. Do you?"

"I was just there," Hazen says. "I left on purpose."

They ride in silence for a while, passing the turnoff for Leadville. Hazen thinks what a heavy name for a town that's hanging so high in the air, about twelve thousand feet above sea level.

"Your dad used to ask me for tickets to the fights, and I'd meet him afterwards sometimes, and we'd go out for a beer. He'd ask me to tell him about the match, the way I saw it, like he was blind and listening to it on the radio. So I would, and I'd throw in details—what the guys were like in workouts, what they talked about right before and right after a fight. Your dad said I should write it all down, be a sportswriter. He gave me a book by a writer named Liebling, called *A Neutral Corner*."

"No such thing, a neutral corner," Lance says.

"Lance," Hazen says, "please be serious for a minute. I'm trying to tell you something here."

"I'm sorry," she says. "Go on. A neutral corner?"

"I guess that's it," Hazen says. "But between your dad and that book, well, it's something I want to look into. Being a sportswriter."

"So we have a plan?"

"The start of one, anyway."

Hazen has driven them almost to the Continental Divide, where water chooses its fate. They've been through the center of Colorado, the most beautiful state on earth, they tell each other, its alpine landscape astounding after the dusty, red ache of Utah. They can't believe the two states are right next to each other on the map. This fact, like seeing Lance di Fabbio after all these years, makes Hazen feel like he should doubt the truth of almost everything he knows. They drive past stands of quaking aspen, which become terrifying to him, the white bark ghostly in the late-afternoon sun.

Populus tremuloides, Lance reads from *Flowers and Trees of the Southwest Mountains,* the book he bought her at their last stop, and he says that name over and over to himself, *Populus tremuloides,* just to have something to hold on to. *From the willow family, sometimes confused with the birch,* she reads, and they watch the leaves shiver at the top of Monarch Pass, elevation 11,312 feet above sea level. They pull off the road here to look at a clutch of purple columbine in one of the aspen groves. They're standing at the easternmost point on the Continental Divide, and they think that must mean something. To the south the Sangre de Cristo mountains bleed slowly back into the earth.

They stop for supper at a diner called Rancho Deluxe, a few miles east, which advertises meals served in twenty minutes or your money back. On their placemats is a map of the United States with the Continental Divide slashing down through it in red ink. YOU ARE HERE, it says. Below that, a message reads, WELCOME TO RANCHO DELUXE ON THE CONTINENTAL DIVIDE. WE KNOW WHAT YOU'RE THINKING. YOU WESTERNERS ARE WONDERING, AM I REALLY GOING TO GET FED IN TWENTY MINUTES? YOU EASTERNERS ARE THINKING, HOW AM I GOING TO GET OUT OF THE PARKING LOT?

"I don't get it," Lance says.

"I think it's not a flattering portrait of America," Hazen tells her.

They drive south on Highway 287 for twelve hours, listening to Guy Clark and then Lyle Lovett. Lyle starts in on "She's No Lady, She's My Wife," and Lance laughs at the words, then says she wants a divorce more than anything else in the world.

"Listen," Hazen says when they've stopped at a 7 Eleven just south of Dallas. "Listen. The crickets are trying to break our hearts with their hammer-claw voices."

"I don't know exactly who you are anymore," Lance says, "but when you talk like that I think I could love you damn near forever."

Flat, Texas, is twenty-five miles southeast of Waco, as the crow flies—a phrase both Hazen and Lance love, and they confess this to each other. But to get there they have to drive through Crawford

Fields off I-35 until they hit Highway 84, travel west to Gatesville, then south on State Road 36 to Flat. All told, it takes two hours because Crawford's is rutted and clotted with herds of cattle.

In the center of Flat they stop at the Texaco station and ask directions to Poplar Street, where North Fallon lives. They wonder if they should call him first, then decide not to. It might give him time to act irrationally, Hazen says, and Lance says, like anybody would notice.

The house is a white saltbox with green shutters. There are peonies and pansies bordering the front walk, carnations and for-get-me-nots blooming in pots. The grass is cut and meticulously edged along the street. There are wind chimes crying softly on the porch. Two coffee cups sit on the porch railing. Hazen Beatty thinks he sees steam rising from them.

This is not at all what they were expecting, and so Hazen Beatty and Lance di Fabbio move from the car slowly, with the dreamy accuracy of sleepwalkers. They leave the car doors open and drift together toward North Fallon's front porch, his front door. Lance tells Hazen not to worry, that North Fallon probably won't even recognize him, and Hazen says he wasn't worried. They ring the doorbell.

North Fallon comes to the front door and stands inside the screen.

"Welcome," he says. "I was just examining the blisters on the feet of the dervish." He laughs then. "My wife," he explains, "she's a dancer, and a Catholic charismatic on Sundays."

"I'm your wife, North," Lance says.

"I've been meaning to talk to you about that," he says. "Please come in."

A young woman walks into the front room, and North Fallon introduces her as his wife, Alison.

"Her real name is Cora," he says, "but what the hell."

Alison, Hazen thinks, cannot be a day older than seventeen. She is a beautiful girl, blond and blue-eyed with long, muscular legs, broad shoulders, skin that shines where the bones are close to the surface—collarbones, cheekbones, finger bones, the knobs of her wristbones. Hazen can see how she's put together like a fine specimen of girlhood, how the various parts of her move under her cotton shift. She says hello and that she's heard a lot about Lance, says it all in perfectly grammatical English, without the trace of an accent, Texas or otherwise.

"This is called bigamy, Mr. Fallon," Hazen says.

"*Professor* Fallon," Alison corrects him.

"Let's not get all worked up, now," North Fallon says, turning to his second wife. "Lance, you may handle this any way you'd like."

"Except stay here," Alison says.

Thank God, Hazen thinks, she's got a will of her own. It makes him smile and reach for Lance's hand.

"Alimony," Hazen says.

"I don't recall having been married to you," North Fallon says and looks off past their shoulders. "She'll be all right, though. The big strike is going to come any day, I can just feel it. My heart throbs all the time now, like something's happening just under the surface of the earth. I'm bringing in geologists, seismologists, and psychologists from Baylor University. They say they can feel it too, the whole town set to blow wide open with crude."

"Are you ever coming back to Utah?" Lance says, and in her voice Hazen hears a caught tenderness that at first takes him by surprise. He understands it, though, how it is that lives can come together and make some kind of affection, which is kin to carbon, kin to fossils, seismic activity, and everything else that's constant in the earth.

"I don't think so," North Fallon says. "I like it here. I can predict the weather. Rain comes from the north, always. Light is every-where, in this house and outside, day and night, equally at all times and in all places. What is the origin of such light? I keep asking myself. Alison here, she helps me try to figure it out. I am her third husband, so she knows how to deal with the imponderables. At least she says I am her third husband. Of course, she may be lying."

"I'll tell you a little story," Alison says. "George Washington was really born right here in Flat, Texas. It's true about the cherry tree, but when little George said to his father, Daddy, I cannot tell a lie, his daddy said, All right, then, we're moving to Virginia. If you can't tell a lie, you have no business being in Texas."

"North," Lance says, but she can't go on.

"Lance di Fabbio," Alison says. "How did you get that name?"

"I had an older brother," Lance says, speaking only to North Fallon, "who died before I was born. That was his name, and when he died, I got it."

"You should have told me that sooner," North Fallon says. "It would have made all the difference."

Hazen looks at Lance and nods his head toward the front door, but she isn't paying any attention. He has this feeling that he's wandered off the planet Earth here, that these people are making sense to one another, but it's a language he has never learned.

"What about the house?" Lance says. "In Salt Lake."

"I'd like to keep the house," North Fallon says, "but you can live there as long as necessary."

"I don't know," Lance says, closing her eyes. "I don't know what necessary means."

"Alison wants the frequent-flyer miles," North Fallon says. "She wants to go to college up in Dallas and come home on weekends. She's thinking about S.M.U."

"Yes," Lance says. "She should go to college. She should go and learn everything she possibly can. Then she should forget it all and start over."

Hazen sees tears start to gather in Lance's eyes, and he has a strange and alarming thought: If one of those tears spills over and runs down her cheek, some thrall will be upon her and she'll stay here forever, no matter what Alison says, waiting with North Fallon for oil to be discovered in the town of Flat, Texas.

He takes Lance by the arm and pulls her out the front door, down the porch steps, and back across the lawn to his car. She doesn't resist, but he feels she isn't walking of her own volition either. At the car, he takes her in his arms and holds her, her back against the driver's-side door. He doesn't want her to be able to see the house. He looks in her eyes and sees they're dry.

"What was it in there?" Hazen says.

"For just a second," Lance tells him, "it was like being in the room with my father, right before he went away that time. I can't explain it."

"That's okay," Hazen says. He doesn't want Lance to explain. Right now, all he wants to do is hold her, and then get her the hell out of this town. He thinks a woman is both a magnet and a needle—women attract things that can hurt them, and then they won't let go.

Lance and Hazen get in the car and drive away. They leave Flat, Texas the way they came in, through the middle of town, past the herds of impassive cattle, over the rutted fields. Hazen leans forward and stares into the sun and then down at the shimmering pools it makes in the road ahead. For the rest of the afternoon he watches Lance without speaking. He knows she's thinking about the pieces of a life they've just seen. They spread the map out on the seat between them, tracing the roads they'll follow. *Here,* they say when the tips of their fingers touch, *here.* Together they drive into the great bowl of Central Texas, heading west.

From any point, Hazen thinks, we look like shadows, just hard, luminous edges, a trick of light and perspective, maybe, a mirage dazzling and shimmering like tears in a woman's eye. This is because all around us there's only flat land, only perfect horizon, and so we'll never disappear.

IV. West

Lance di Fabbio and Hazen Beatty set out to drive as far west as they can go, angling up from Central Texas so that they'll cut across the San Francisco Bay at a forty-five-degree angle.

"Here?" Hazen Beatty says.

"No," Lance di Fabbio tells him. "Keep going."

He's asked her this every hundred miles or so, and she likes it that the question comes always out of curiosity, never weariness, never irritation. Hazen just wants to know, and Lance believes she'll be able to say yes soon. Right now she just wants to drive, facing forward so that the highway feels as if it's running straight through her body like an arrow. She wants only to move and be nowhere at the same time.

"North or south?" he says at the corner of Van Ness and Pine in downtown San Francisco.

"I hate even to say the word," she says back, "I hate it like hell, but I think it has to be north from here."

South is out of the question. Lance refuses to travel along the San Andreas Fault going south, and she refuses to go anywhere near Los Angeles. Only yesterday did she learn that the name doesn't mean Lost Angels, but she can't quite recover from twenty years of thinking this way. In Los Angeles, she thinks, you can see your whole life in a handful of the dust that blows in from the freeway, down from the Hollywood Hills. People in southern California walk around without histories, their whole life stories waiting to be made up in a flash and told to breathless audiences. Lance wants the story of her life to just happen to her, without comment, like everybody else's does.

She's been thinking almost constantly about North Fallon and Alison in Flat, Texas, moving back and forth through the half hour she and Hazen were in their house. *Alison seems so sane.* Lance hears the sentence over and over in her head, until it becomes one long hiss of soft consonants. She remembers loving North Fallon, and then there was his long absence. She felt in those months like a house left empty with all the windows open—not good, but probably safe enough. She missed him less and less. And then there he was in the flesh, breaking her heart all over again. She thinks, strangely, that the heat has something to do with it. She wants to be cold, to wear long pants and sweaters, to freeze North Fallon out.

So at San Jose, she said north, and just south of Berkeley she said north again, and north at Van Ness Avenue, and then *no, no, no, don't stop,* all the way up the California coast.

Hazen convinces Lance to stop for a time in Redwood National Park, to see the world's tallest tree. He says they have to slow down some, give the truck a rest, start to act like tourists instead of fugitives from justice. Lance wants to know how they keep tabs on these tall trees.

"Other trees must be getting bigger all the time," she says. "How could you ever be sure you were still the tallest?"

"Hope," Hazen tells her, "faith, self-confidence. Anyways, it's just a tree."

"I know," Lance says. "I was just being empathetic."

They register and request hiking permits at the park visitors' center, then drive up Bald Hills Road to the Tall Trees Grove entrance gate. After that a gravel road winds for seven miles down to the start of the trail. Lance reads all the Park Service literature while Hazen tries to drive gently, to keep the gravel from eating away at the tires. On some of the sharper turns the vehicle skids sideways, and Hazen says *whoa*. They smile at each other, and Lance keeps on reading, telling Hazen they'll be descending a hill-slope forest to an alluvial grove where the world's tallest tree was discovered in 1963. It rises 367.8 feet into the foggy air. Lance tries to remember if she's ever visited the world's tallest or largest anything, and she decides that until today she's lived her entire life without measuring it on any such scale. She thinks again of the years she lived in New York and the year with North Fallon in Salt Lake City. She tries to remember what she did during the day. She wishes she had children riding in the backseat right now, two of them or even three, who would be some evidence of having lived in or at least somewhere nearby the world these past few years.

"I've never seen a redwood," she says out loud to Hazen Beatty, the thought choking her, stalling in her throat to become a sob. "Can you believe I've never seen a goddamn redwood?"

"Well," Hazen says, "here we are, darling, making up for lost time. By the end of this trip, you'll be so sick of redwoods and pink rhododendron and fog and all these stories about how redwoods burn down to a shell and keep on living that you'll freaking beg me to take you back to the desert. I'll have to keep you from setting forest fires to burn them all down."

The car skids right, nearly to the edge of the gravel and the eight-hundred-foot drop onto the alluvial flat.

"Fire is good for them," Lance reads. "It helps the Douglas fir get established."

They park the car and start down to the Tall Trees Grove. The path drops 650 feet at a severe angle, and Lance thinks she should start to run and let gravity carry her to the bottom. She knows Hazen would just watch her go. She knows he would smile at the vision of her turned into some kind of voiceless forest banshee, legs kicking out behind her, arms flung wide for balance and drag, like the dropped flaps on an airplane. She wouldn't stop until she got to the bottom, and then she'd sit in the shade of the tallest tree in the world, waiting for Hazen Beatty to show up. She thinks maybe that's what she's been doing for the last seven years of her life.

Instead, she takes hold of his hand and opens the Park Service brochure to read about forest diversity, fire, the ancient streambed, the Trinidad Trail, osprey, goosepens, the mother tree, river crossings, maples and bays, shallow roots, spike tops, Bert Robinson's brine vats for salting salmon and steelhead trout, Native American cultures, the elephant tree, and widow makers. She reads off these headings to Hazen, who says it sounds like part of a poem. These are the attractions tourists are supposed to stop and contemplate, but Lance doesn't want to stop. She doesn't want to be told what to see.

All around them sunlight filters down through the redwoods in watery shafts. The undergrowth of fern and redwood sorrel and thimbleberry trembles in breezes that come out of nowhere. How can the wind even get in here? Lance thinks. It's like a whole secret world. It's too bad people are allowed in, she thinks. Even us.

"Lance," Hazen Beatty says, "where are we going?"

"Hazen. To see the tallest tree. You know that."

"Yes. No. I mean in the grand scheme of things. Where are we driving to, when we get back in the car this afternoon?"

Lance stops walking and turns to face her old love Hazen Beatty, pulling at the front of his shirt. "Let's just get there, and then we'll really talk about it."

"Get *where*, though? That's all I'm asking. Just so I have some idea about mileage, gas, oil, engine wear and tear, that kind of thing."

"Into Oregon. The first coast town we come to. We'll stop there and make big plans."

The trail winds down below Lance and Hazen in a funnel of redwoods and licorice fern, blooming rhododendron, and these, Lance thinks, are only what we recognize. She feels herself and Hazen falling toward the shallow bed where Redwood Creek, Tom MacDonald Creek, and Bridge Creek mix their muddy waters.

Clouds are drifting in over the rim of trees above them, heading west to east across the expanse of of the park. Lance imagines being caught down here in a rainstorm, maybe the second great flood, watching as the creeks overrun their banks, as water rises around them to fill the park, raising the creek level to its ancient height and depth, thousands of years ago when it first began to cut its way through the earth, the earth that looked absolutely nothing like it does now. She thinks it would be a fine way to go, to lie underwater forever at the base of the world's tallest tree, then she decides no, she'd fight like hell. She'd hold on to Hazen, and they'd rise with the flood level, roll down the Klamath River, and catch themselves on the lip of California just before they washed into the Pacific Ocean.

In Brookings, Oregon, Lance tells Hazen this is the place.

"It's a pretty good town," she says. "On the water, got a post office, a Rexall, a supermarket, and a native industry."

"Which is what?"

"Easter lilies. Look." Lance points to a neatly furrowed field. The plants in the rows are low, none over a foot tall, and from the road the foliage looks tightly curled. She tells Hazen he might at first mistake it for lettuce, until he noticed a few white bell-shaped flowers. It's late June, and so Lance wonders what's to become of these flowers, nearly a year too early for Easter. Part of the reason she wants to stay is to see whether the lilies could bloom for that long.

She's read in the AAA guide that this particular swath of western Oregon has a curiously temperate climate. The farmers here, she tells Hazen, could grow bananas if they wanted to. She feels it happen; as they drive across the border between Smith River, California, and Harbor, Oregon, Lance feels the air change in the branches of her lungs, on her skin too; it comes like an embrace, kind and gentle, a touch from someone you haven't thought about for years. Lance thinks that if she were a flower, she would most certainly bloom here, and for a long time.

"All right," Hazen says. "But how about we take a look around before we buy beachfront property?"

"Absolutely," Lance says.

It's early afternoon, so they pull into the campground at Harris Beach to get a good spot for the night. The ranger turns from talking to a sheriff and another couple to assign Lance and Hazen a campsite. They can see that the ranger is furious, white-faced with anger. While she takes care of the paperwork for Lance and Hazen, she's still listening to the conversation going on behind her. Before Hazen can pay her, she turns away.

"Listen," the ranger says to the other couple, "forget this invasion-of-privacy crap. Here's the bottom line. When you took the job, you signed a statement about drugs and alcohol. I don't give a shit what you do in private, but we're talking minors here."

"Are you going to press charges?" the sheriff asks.

"No, I'm not, but it's because I never want to see them again. You're out, folks. Now."

The sheriff asks the couple if they're ready to go, and the man jerks his thumb over his left shoulder toward a Winnebago. Lawn chairs and rubber floats are strapped to the sides and back, and there's a speedboat on a trailer behind. The sheriff then recites what sounds to Lance like a formal restraining order, barring the couple from the Oregon state parks for one year. Their faces stay perfectly empty, even when they look at the park ranger again.

"Be gone," she says, sounding like she's casting a spell. She turns back to Hazen and Lance, talking more to herself than to them as she shuffles their vehicle permit and beach pass.

"Sorry you had to see that. They were selling dope to the kids here. Goddamn park hosts."

"Very hospitable," Hazen says.

"Shoot," the ranger answers him, "*hospitable* would be *giving* it away." She looks up and smiles. "It just burns me up. All we ask is that they turn on the film projector on Wednesday nights. They get to stay for free, just for doing that. We've had trouble this summer. I swear, people used to be nicer."

"Maybe they'll get that way again," Lance says. "Maybe it goes in cycles."

"I hope you're right," the park ranger says. "All I know is I'm tired of selfish people. You're in C25. It's a nice one. Okay? There's a movie tonight, on baby animals, I think, if we can find somebody to take care of it."

Hazen and Lance park in their campsite and walk down to Harris Beach. Fog is just beginning to drift in from the north, weaving itself around a bend in the beach like a white scarf trailing behind the woman wearing it, unraveling from around her neck. To the south of the public beach there's a tidepool bordered by a wall of rock that rises sixty feet into the air. The tides have eroded the middle of it, forming a cleft, and surf crashes in and out of it. Lance wants to have her picture taken with that blue glimpse of the Pacific in the background. She thinks it's weirdly symbolic, like being photographed in front of a tree so that it seems to be growing out of your head. They hike south along the beach, parallel to Brookings's stately homes, all glass and wind-softened wood, all facing the ocean at different angles.

"Someday maybe we could live in one of those," Lance says.

"With the lottery, anything is possible," Hazen says. "Or is there a lottery in Oregon? It seems like too clean a state for that sort of thing."

"My mother would love it up here," Lance says. "I should write her a postcard. Her and Dad. I should tell them what's been going on."

"Your mother. Lance, are you going to turn out like your mother, do you think?"

"Hazen, I've already turned out. This is how I've turned out. I'm a done deal, Hazen Beatty. Actually, the person I could still turn out like is my father. He was a late bloomer."

"I think we're about as far from Flatland as we can get," Hazen says, looking up past the cliffs and all the glass houses of Brookings, up to the coastal hills rolling greenly away to the northeast. "I think you're safe here."

"Really?" Lance says. "And where is *here?*"

"Voilà," Hazen Beatty says, opening his arms wide, toward Lance and also toward the Pacific Ocean.

They climb to a high rock, where they can sit and look out at the ocean and the gathering afternoon fog. They sit away from the trail, but not so far that they can't see anyone coming up behind them.

"Can we do this, Hazen?" Lance says. "Just stop someplace and make it up as we go along? I mean, is there anything we forgot to bring?"

"People do it all the time, pack up and go. They drag their entire families with them. We can find jobs. Don't worry."

Lance looks up the coast of Oregon as it winds north. She believes this is something North Fallon never said to her—*Don't worry*. She suddenly feels very young, five or six maybe, an age she doesn't remember, when her mother and father took care of her without expecting anything in return.

"Okay, then," she says. "Voilà."

"You bet your ass, voilà," Hazen says. "Damn straight, voilà."

Lance and Hazen walk back up to site C25 and spread their foam mattresses and sleeping bags out in the bed of the pickup truck. They lie down with their heads facing outward, looking into the oleander and blackberry bushes that separate them from the road beyond the campground. They open beers and settle down to read the local paper. Hazen goes for the want ads and the real estate section. Lance studies the front pages—the world and national news—and then her horoscope, which tells her she'll meet the man of her dreams at a party. She sneaks a look at Hazen and feels a kind of clutch and stirring deep in her gut.

"Welcome to the party, Hazen," she says, and he looks back at her, trying to get her meaning, then smiles, shakes his head, and goes back to the paper.

Lance thinks camping will probably be good for her. She's never realized it until now, mostly because she never camped with North Fallon, whose idea of hell was a tent and a communal shower. She sees how camping makes her slow way down, how you can't possibly be a good camper and be in a hurry. She wants to turn to Hazen now and tell him something important and final, but she doesn't want to rush this either. She reaches over his back for her pack, drawing her fingers lightly across his shoulder blades as she goes. She pulls out a bag of sunflower seeds and makes a pile of them in front of her. A blue jay lands on the tailgate to watch. The sun makes its eyes into silver beads, like buckshot. A veteran, Lance thinks, pretending to watch other stuff but keeping his attention on the goods. Expectant—no, *hoping*. Expectations are different from hopes. Hopes, we've got, me and this blue jay, but expectations, none. Maybe, Lance thinks, I'm learning not to expect anything of anyone, except your basic common courtesy. She thinks it's a good lesson.

"Jesus," she says out loud, "I'm happy."

⸺

Lance di Fabbio and Hazen Beatty take a furnished apartment in south Brookings and look for jobs. Lance finds one right away, waitressing in the Flying Gull Restaurant and Lounge. Hazen has a harder time of it. Lance tells him it's okay, to take his time, but she can see he's anxious. He gets too quiet. Every day for three weeks she watches him go through the want ads, make phone calls, or go to interviews and come home with nothing. Then he sits in the bar at the Flying Gull, talking to the bartender and the pianist.

Later at night he tells her he feels like he's led her down the primrose path.

"Whatever that is," he says. "It sounds right, though."

"I never have known what that means either," Lance says, "but if we're on it, it's not so bad."

Lance works the dinner shift at the Flying Gull, where the clientele is mostly families staying at the adjacent Best Western or truckers on the long run up Highway 101 to Washington State, maybe Canada. She serves food efficiently and without a lot of chatter and collects huge tips. As has been the case all her life, children are naturally drawn to Lance; even children who have done nothing but whine all the way up from Crescent City become attentive and sweet in her presence; they coo and laugh, eat up all their supper, and fall gently asleep as she moves back and forth, to and from their tables. Their parents are stunned and delighted, and they leave extraordinary sums of money under a water glass or tucked beside a plate. Lance thinks someday one of these parents might just leave the child, and she imagines herself becoming a mother that way.

After the supper crowd thins out, Lance spends most of her time in the lounge, taking drink orders and helping out behind the bar or listening to the pianist, if it's a Thursday, Friday, or Saturday night. His name is Bobby Diamante; he's nineteen and trying to make it out of Brookings, maybe up to Portland for the Mount Hood Festival of Jazz this summer, and then to Boston, to study at the New England Conservatory of Music. Bobby tells Lance he has a day job writing feature articles for the Brookings paper, but it's easy, he says, because nothing much ever happens. Mostly he does reviews, of books and recordings, movies. He likes to help Brookings keep up with the rest of the world. But when Bobby Diamante plays the piano, Lance thinks he loses all consciousness of the world around him. It's only him and the music, one indistinguishable from the other. Lance finds this comforting, like having Hazen stroke her hair at night when they're just falling asleep.

When she leans against the bar in the Flying Gull and closes her eyes, or walks between the tables and the booths carrying a tray of drinks, it's as if she's floating and the music is washing over her like a tidal bath.

When she comes off her shift at two-thirty in the morning, Lance finds she can't make herself go directly home to the apartment in south Brookings. She needs to clear her head, and so she takes to walking on Harris Beach in the dark, hiking north until she can't go any farther. Tonight she sits down in the sand and stares out into the ocean, which is lit strangely and unevenly by lights from the bluff above her. She thinks how, in some ways, the world is even flatter here than it was in Texas. She can see why somebody like Bobby Diamante, somebody who had spent his whole life here, would want to get out. Bobby Diamante reminds her a little of Hazen, when she knew him back in Houston, all those years ago, when he'd just bought his first car, that Plymouth Valiant. He has the same jangling in his bones, that look on his face like he's already left town.

"Hazen Beatty," she says out loud to the Pacific Ocean, over to the Philippines and Japan, where North Fallon's father-in-law, that dust devil, swirls in his ceremonial urn.

"Lance," Hazen calls from forty yards down the beach, "is that you?"

Lance calls back Hazen's name again, stands up and turns to face south, listening to the *schush* of his steps in the sand. Then she walks back to meet him.

"Are you okay?" he asks her.

"I'm fine," she says. "I was a little too jazzed to come home just yet."

"That Bobby Diamante," Hazen says. "Do you have a crush on Bobby Diamante, Lance?" She can tell that he's smiling.

"No, not a crush. But sometimes I think I want to adopt him. He reminds me of you when you were about that age."

"Me?"

"Yeah, you."

"How?"

"I don't know, lost in the distance somehow, like you weren't completely there."

"You like that?"

"I guess I do." Or, she thinks, it's just the truth of how people are—never fully paying attention, always a small part of them off somewhere else.

"When did you figure out North Fallon was crazy?" Hazen asks out of the blue.

"What?"

"I mean, speaking of lost in the distance," Hazen says, and he hears Lance sigh.

"I guess it was pretty soon after we got to Utah. In fact, I can tell you the day and the hour. We rented a place at Lake Powell that first summer, and it was pretty nice, right on the lake—a good place, I thought at the time, to start out a marriage—comfortable, a little secluded but not too much. North had a speedboat, a Baja, and he went out in it a lot. He'd be gone for most of the day and then come back for supper. I read and made jam and all that sort of summer-wife stuff. It wasn't bad. I kind of liked being alone.

"One day he left in the morning, and left a turkey for me to smoke. There was a smoker at the house, but the one time we'd fired it up before, I got it too hot and cracked the top, and so I wouldn't use it. North told me not to, in fact. So I waited, and he showed up at six in the evening and asked where the dinner was and what was I doing just sitting around all day. I reminded him about the smoker, but it was too late, he said, and he picked up the turkey and threw it off the porch into Lake Powell. 'Fuck the turkey,' he said and just hurled that sucker into a watery grave. Then he went upstairs and packed his stuff and drove back to Salt Lake without me. He was back the next day, all apologies, but you don't forget something like that."

"Jesus, Lance, is that true?"

"Cross my heart and hope to die."

They sit quietly, and then Lance feels Hazen's weight on her side as he falls asleep. She feels herself drifting off too, and she lets it happen. She dreams she's in a boat—a Boston whaler, like her father always wanted. She's drifting, not out but in, closer and closer to shore, where people she doesn't recognize are waiting for her. They know her, though, and they're calling her name. She waves to them, thinking they'll become familiar to her as soon as she gets to dry land.

When she wakes, the air is hazy with fog, but it's light enough so that shapes are visible, the barest outlines of the landscape where it rises and falls. Lance stands up and tries to pull Hazen to his feet. She tells him she's getting chilled, that they need to get home. As they start back around Cape Ferrelo she tells him about her dream. He listens quietly, and then he starts to talk about Floyd Patterson, the boxer. Lance thinks he might still be half asleep.

"My dad told me once," Hazen says, "that Floyd Patterson said that a dream was just an empty space waiting for somewhere to fill in."

He says this in a tone of voice Lance has never heard him use before, full of sadness. He takes hold of her hand and gives it a hard squeeze. She can feel her own bones close to cracking.

"I would have fucking killed him in Texas if I'd known," he says.

"I know," Lance says, "I know, Hazen."

Ahead of them, around the south corner of the Cape, black rocks loom up suddenly where Lance has never seen them before. There's a strange vibration in the air, a soft clicking and crying. Lance and Hazen stop walking, and each drops the other's hand, as if being separate might help them listen. They ask what they're hearing in whispers that get drowned out by the echoing voices of a thousand children lost in a thousand dark tunnels.

Up above them on the bluff Lance can see three pairs of headlights muffled by fog, and then, slightly below, two lantern beams moving down toward the beach. They walk toward these lights, and when they're about a hundred yards from the beams, there's a deafening report, like gunfire, and the whole beach shakes. Lance feels as if her legs are going out from under her.

"Earthquake," Hazen says, trying to hold her around the waist.

"No, no," Lance tells him. "I think it's a whale." It's knowledge that feels as if it's come to her from a long way off, maybe out of her dream about drifting toward shore.

Lance and Hazen keep moving ahead in the jangling darkness, and then they see that it's not one whale, but more like ten, all stranded on or near the beach. Down the ridge of headland, a few at a time, people are starting to edge in to get a closer look, and there's a thin line of light made by cars slowing down in the roadway at the top of the cliff. Lance thinks anyone who doesn't know better might wonder if dawn wasn't coming in from the wrong direction, moving north to south.

"You're not from Greenpeace, are you?" a woman's voice asks from behind one of the flashlights.

"No," Hazen says.

"I'm supposed to clear this beach," the voice says. The woman shines the light back under her own face as she speaks, to show them it's the park ranger from the Harris Beach campgrounds, the one who gave the boot to the drug-dealing park hosts.

"What's going on?" Lance says.

"Whales got stranded. We got to see what we can do for them. Can't have a lot of people getting in the way now, but you can stay here if you want. Since I know you're nice people."

Hazen asks what's going to happen to the whales, and the ranger says she doesn't know, but a couple of them aren't in very good shape.

"They die from internal bleeding," Lance says, not at all sure how she knows this fact. "Out of the water, in gravity, their own weight crushes them to death."

"Greenpeace tells us to keep them wet and talk to them to calm them down," the ranger says, as if to answer her.

"I don't think I'd know what to tell them," Hazen says.

"Me neither," the ranger says back.

Lance and Hazen stand looking at the whales as full dawn begins to break over them. They're gray whales, Lance can see this now, she can tell from the uneven crust of barnacles on their skin. She thinks they look like giant kosher pickles, and then she feels ashamed, like she's made a joke out of something serious and sad.

"Let's go home," Hazen says. "I feel like we're gawking at a car wreck."

Later in the day Lance wakes to find Hazen gone and the story of the stranded whales on the noon news shows from Crescent City and Portland. There are haunting predawn photographs and then live film footage of the huge, dark bodies. They remind Lance of other pictures she's seen, by photographers who claim to have caught the Loch Ness monster rising from the depths. The evening papers are full of information about gray whales: how they migrate from the arctic and down the California coast to breed, that they were once thought to be extinct but are now strictly protected, that they are the most primitive of the mysticetes and therefore have the longest necks. Like right whales, gray whales have no dorsal fin, only a series of low bumps on the back near the tail. Known to whalers as "devil fish" for their fierceness and aggression, harpooned gray whales have been known to charge frantically, capsizing boats and drowning sailors. The bond between a mother and her calf is very strong, and much of the viciousness of the species arises from this bond. Then Lance reads this sentence: "They could hardly be blamed." The article is signed "Bobby Diamante, with Hazen Beatty." Lance feel as if it's her own name there on the page. She dials Bobby Diamante's number.

"Hey, star reporter," she says when he answers the phone. "Seems like everybody I know works for the paper."

"Yeah," Bobby Diamante says. "What a surprise. He knew all about whales. It was stunning."

Lance asks Bobby Diamante if he knows where Hazen is, but

he doesn't. Then she asks if he's going back down to see the whales today, and he tells her he was practically out the door. They meet above Harris Beach and then drive north to the Cape. When they get there Bobby shows the sheriff a letter from the editor of the paper, and he lets them cross through the barricades. They make their way down through the sand, over a path that's been dug clean in the past twenty-four hours by reporters, photographers, volunteers, and tourists. A quarter mile below, Lance can see a crowd of probably fifty people standing in the shallows. Fifteen or so are farther out, chest deep, talking to the whales and pouring water over their backs. Lance and Bobby can hear their voices, like mothers reassuring frightened children, saying *there, there.* Lance thinks she even hears singing. The words *Momma's going to buy you a mockingbird* carry up from the beach, and tears fill her eyes. She slides a little in the sand, and Bobby Diamante takes her arm, exactly as Hazen might have done, might do, she thinks, will do. They walk across the beach toward the water, and Bobby tells Lance that Hazen said this is the most dangerous time for the whales. They're waiting patiently, as gray whales mostly will, for the tide to come back in and carry them, but there's still not water deep enough for them to swim, and so they can't raise their blowholes from the water. Then they drown.

When they get closer, Lance and Bobby see that two of the eleven whales are still mostly onshore, and motionless. A woman in camouflage pants and a red parka is taking a blood sample from the fluke of the larger whale. "Forty feet," Bobby says quietly. Lance can't believe how huge the whales are, towering over them, the biggest living things she's ever seen. Bobby turns to the woman. "Can I ask you a few questions? I'm from the local paper."

"Shoot," the woman says. Lance thinks she's swearing as much as giving Bobby the go-ahead.

"Are these two dead?" he asks.

"Yes," the woman tells him, and then turns away. It's clear she's tired of being bothered by people from the press.

"How did this happen?"

"Which part?" she says, her voice flat.

"All of it, I guess. Baleen whales hardly ever strand, isn't that right?"

The woman turns her head quickly to look at Bobby. She's impressed that he would know such a thing, and so she gives him her full attention.

"That's true," she says. "We think they got too interested in the kelp beds. Gray whales love to play in kelp, and we think maybe this bunch played too long. But honestly, it's always one of the biggest mysteries for us."

Lance walks away from Bobby and the woman, over to the second whale. She approaches it from the front, thinking about how she would treat a horse, that the animal should see her coming. The open eye that looks out into the Pacific is glazed and crusted with sand. Lance moves her hand in front of this eye, half expecting the whale to blink and rouse itself, but nothing happens. The eye stays fixed, staring into Lance's eyes, and she reaches out to pat the whale. Its skin feels rough and dry, not sleek as she expected it would.

"You crushed your heart," she whispers to the whale.

Bobby Diamante joins her and together they wade out waist-deep to where Greenpeace volunteers are tending the whales, keeping them wet and walking them slowly into deeper water.

"How's it going?" Bobby calls to the nearest volunteer, a young man wearing an Oregon State baseball cap.

"Pretty good," he says, giving them a thumbs-up. "I think old Moby here is going to make it back."

"Moby?" Lance says, wading in closer.

"Yeah," the young man says. "Maybe it will make her feel big and strong. You know. Like she can do whatever she wants to."

In another hour, Lance hears Bobby say, the tide will be at high, and the volunteers will have helped the whales move into water deep enough for them to swim back out to sea and continue their migration south to Baja, California. In the newspaper article, Bobby and Hazen called Baja the site of the whales' *nuptial lagoons.* This sounds to Lance like a place all marriages need to go, especially early on, and she shakes her head and shuts her eyes tight. She wonders how often this old heartache is suddenly going to come upon her. She thinks that if only she and North Fallon had gone to the nuptial lagoons instead of hunting in south-central Pennsylvania or boating on Lake Powell, they might have had a fighting chance. She looks back at Bobby Diamante, who has gone on to talk to another volunteer, and again she has that flash of Hazen at nineteen, and it eases the clutch in her heart. That's how Hazen stood, she thinks, that's how he talked to people, he looked them in the eye, and he bothered to know something about them before he started in on the conversation. She loves this about Hazen just as she admires it in Bobby Diamante. They don't waste people's time, they don't chatter, their aim is true.

"I'm all done here," he says to Lance. "You want to stay for a while? I'll warn you, though: It's not going to be pretty. The lady scientist told me these two have to be disposed of."

"How?"

"You sure you want to know?"

"Bobby, look at me. I'm a big girl."

He tells her it's like this. He says you can't bury them because their organs will liquefy and soak the beach. So what you have to do is dismember them, burn them, and bury the remains that way. He tells her it's pretty gruesome. And that one of them is carrying a fetus.

"When will all that start?"

"When the others get out into deep water."

"So they won't be able to watch."

"Something like that."

Hazen is home when Lance gets back to their apartment, sitting at the kitchen table with the newspaper spread out in front of him. She rests her hands on his shoulders and lays her cheek on the top of his head. He says it looks like he has a job at the paper, and Lance whispers congratulations. She reaches her hands down inside the front of Hazen's shirt, running the palms over the muscles of his chest, out the sleeves, over his shoulders and biceps and back. She tells him his heart is beating, and he says that's a good sign.

They leave the apartment and walk north into Brookings, down Main Street, past Woolworth's, the Blueberry Café, and souvenir shops. The town is crowded with tourists and truckers, some who were passing through Brookings anyway and some who came to see the whales. Hazen and Lance turn east, thinking they might walk all the way out to Mount Emily, the site, they've heard, of the only aerial attack on the U.S. by a Japanese war plane during World War II. It turns out to be a longer trip than they thought, so they stop to rest outside the Brookings Memorial Park. Above them to the east they can see the peak of Mount Emily, the blue sky beyond it deepening into evening. Below, the Pacific Ocean is making its way to shore through fingers of fog.

"My dad always said, 'Call when you find work,' " Hazen says.

"We should both call," Lance says. "It's probably time."

"I wonder what they're all doing right now. Your mom and dad, my mom and dad."

"Probably things we don't want to see," Lance says, and she thinks, they're probably taking each other apart in ways we're only beginning to understand.

They stand together looking out over the memorials and the azalea bushes blooming along the southern fence, and Lance wonders if Hazen is doing what she's doing: remembering River Oaks Cemetery in Houston, an evening like this, maybe a little warmer, maybe not as bright. They hike to the crest of the hill, where there's a full view of the coastline and the ocean as far north as Pistol River.

"I guess we're here for awhile?" Hazen says.

"Looks that way," Lance tells him. "So let's see who else is here."

They make their way downhill through the rows of memorials. Lance is looking for names she likes, ghost names, the patron saints of Brookings, the names that will watch over them now.

"Find one you like," she says to Hazen.

"And do what with it?"

"Just remember it." Lance starts to read. "Selma Kirby. Maria Jackson. Elmo Tallent. J. F. Kimball. Elijah Bristow. Annie O'Brien. And over here, sheltered from the storm, Samuel Boardman. Maybe the guy the state park is named for. But it's hard to tell in this condition."

"Nobody here with your name?" Hazen says.

"Not here. Not so far, anyway," Lance says. "Who were you named for, Hazen?"

"A town in Nevada. My dad says the best names come from the state of Nevada, right off the road map. Beatty too. It's down near Las Vegas. My great great-grandfather changed his name to Beatty when he stopped there on his way west. At least that's the story."

"Why Nevada?" Lance asks.

"Because nobody would ever think to look for you there."

That's right, Lance thinks, because when you get to California, you've arrived at the edge, it's a big event, cause for celebration, even at Bakersfield or Sacramento, places far from the coast. But you can rest first in Nevada, she thinks, bide your time, change your name, maybe gamble yourself a fortune.

That night Hazen comes to the Flying Gull at the end of Lance's shift. It's a Thursday night, so Bobby Diamante is there too, just closing out a set of songs from *A Chorus Line*. He doesn't usually sing as he plays, but tonight he says he can't help himself. Lance goes to stand behind Hazen's bar stool, and she puts her arms around his chest. She presses her cheek against his broad back and moves her lips along with the words, which she remembers her father learning, late at night, all these years ago. She knows she is the world's biggest sap, but she doesn't care. In the days to come, she thinks, it might be something she'll pride herself on, a trait she'll want to pass along to her children. She thinks all this with shattering clarity, there between the dark of the Flying Gull and the soft flannel of Hazen's shirt.

At closing time Lance tells Hazen and Bobby that she wants to go back out to check on the whales, to see that they got away safely. Bobby smiles and says he was thinking the same thing. He pats his breast pocket where he's carrying his press pass, and he looks at Hazen.

"Me too," Hazen says. "You drive."

Lance rides up front between Bobby and Hazen. She extends her right arm over the top of the seat so that her arm rests lightly across Hazen's shoulders, and he leans back against the seat. It's like the pressure of a hug, and that's the way they've learned to travel since leaving Salt Lake City three weeks ago.

Bobby shows his press pass to the park ranger on duty, who says there's not much to see, just the two dead whales and one straggler, an undergrown yearling, who will be out with the next tide. He tells them that almost everybody's gone home. They can see that the beach is still lit by a spotlight attached to a Park Service pickup truck.

Lance walks ahead of Hazen and Bobby down to the shallow water. She recognizes the one volunteer as the keeper of Moby she met earlier in the day.

"You must be beat," she says to him. "Tell me what to do and I'll take over for a while."

"You'll freeze," he says. "I'm wearing a wetsuit."

"I'm okay," Lance tells him, walking out deeper into the water.

"Just walk her, then. Like this." He shows Lance where to place her hands on the whale's back. "From here to about even with that last bouy. Go a little deeper every time you make one circuit. Talk to her, tell her your whole life story if you have to, but just keep talking."

Hazen and Bobby are in the water now, standing beside Lance. "Can we help?" Hazen asks.

"The three of you can switch off," the volunteer says, "so nobody gets hypothermia. That's how we've been doing it."

He points to a woman standing between the two whale carcasses, backlit by light from the Park Service truck.

Lance di Fabbio, Hazen Beatty, and Bobby Diamante walk the young whale between the buoys. They move her to waist-deep water, slowly, touching her lightly near the middle of her back. Farther out, Lance imagines, the mother is waiting for her young to be restored to her, waiting to continue her trip to the nuptial lagoons. Lance wonders what this young whale is seeing now, with one of her eyes turned east and the other turned west. She wonders how the world looks when vision gets flattened out that way, if it isn't a kind of reprieve to be able to see out in opposite directions but only one at a time. She touches Hazen's hand over the whale's silky back, and in that moment the animal tenses, gathers herself, and darts forward toward open sea. At the same time a cloud of steam shoots out of her blowhole, warming Lance's face and blowing back her hair. She lets go of the whale and finds she's holding on to Hazen Beatty's hand, and they're all three, Lance, Hazen and Bobby, calling *go, go,* their voices choked with tears. The man and woman on the beach hear them and start to move the spotlight out so that they can all see the young whale breach once, rising like an island. Her fluke crashes on the surface of the water, and then there are only waves rolling out of the darkness, and the three shadows cast toward the horizon, rippling, Lance thinks, like waving ghosts or strange sea birds, fluttering slowly awake, dazzled by all that coastline stretched out in front of them, surprised by how much of it there is, more than they ever dreamed.

About the Author

LIZA WIELAND was raised in Georgia. A graduate of Harvard College and Columbia University, she currently teaches literature and writing at California State University, Fresno.

About the Type

This book was set on the monotype in Garamond, a typeface designed by the French printer Jean Jannon. It is styled after Garamond's original models. The face is dignified and is light but without fragile lines. The italic is modeled after a font of Granjon, which was probably cut in the middle of the sixteenth century.